THE AROLLAY CHRONICLES

THE AROLLAY CHRONICLES

The Journey

A Novel

James F. Gavin

iUniverse, Inc.

New York Lincoln Shanghai

THE AROLLAY CHRONICLES
The Journey

iUniverse books may be ordered through booksellers or by contacting:

iUniverse
2021 Pine Lake Road, Suite 100
Lincoln, NE 68512
www.iuniverse.com
1-800-Authors (1-800-288-4677)

This is a work of fiction. All of the characters, names, incidents, organizations, and dialogue in this novel are either the products of the author's imagination or are used fictitiously.

ISBN: 978-0-595-43878-5 (pbk)
ISBN: 978-0-595-88201-4 (ebk)

Printed in the United States of America

For my family and friends who inspired me my whole life. To Mr. Twinam, Mr. Rodriguez, Mr. Taggart, Mrs. Cambria, and Mrs. Nissley; you guys helped me find my true potential when I thought it never existed. To Coach Murray—for helping me know that even when it feels like bad things keep happening and you just want to quit … to suck it up and keep going anyway. To Mrs. Stendardo, for showing me that writing is fun and for showing me what a book really looks like. To my roommate Tony for putting up with my incessant talk about this book and dragging you into it. And last, but most certainly, not least, to my college English professor, Prof. Meyer, for critiquing my book 'Like a Balrog on Dwarves'.

Thanks.

Do note that any similarities in physical characteristics that a character(s) might have with someone in the real world is by complete coincidence. If any one takes offense to this, you have my sincerest apologies.

Names, Places, and Pronunciation

Aria—Sounds like Ar-ya. A hawk with an attitude. She is assigned to protect James by the Lady of the Gray Wood. By using the Mind Speech, she can communicate with James.

Trae'len—Sounds like TrA-uh-len. Means Strong Hero in the Words. A horse with a one track mind. Can also use the Mind Speech with James.

Arollay—Sounds like Air-O-lay. A land of magic and mystery. James is brought here and is thrown into a series of events that will forever change the fate of this land.

Se'Cruz—Sounds like Seh-Crew; the Z is silent. A blacksmith who resides in the village of Yattion in Intaru. He is the Speaker of the Council and father to Miranda.

Intaru—Sounds like it looks. The Fire Kingdom; located south from Gattar. A warm climate year round that allows for crops to be kept safe even in winter seasons.

Gattar—Sounds like Guh-tair. The Ice Kingdom; located north from Intaru. A cool climate year round, but summer does get pretty hot.

Dannil Gashain—Sounds like Guh-shain. A carver and decently rich man in Yattion. He had a son who died in the war and a wife who died shortly after.

Alamar Telanre (Janury)—Al-uh-mar Tell-AUN-ray (JAHN-yur-ee). An outlaw in Intaru, and a powerful Fire Wielder with many secrets and a vast amount of knowledge he likes to keep hidden. His is very skilled with close ranged melee fighting and specializes with both short and long knives which he uses to quickly over take his opponents.

Proga Telanre—PRO-guh Tell-AUN-ray. A Fire Wielder who betrayed his brother, the Emperor, to the kingdom of Gattar, though no one knows why. Proga was found out and killed, and his family was killed, except for his son, who fled with his caretaker.

Shai'lun—Sounds like Shay-Lûn. A creature made out of the power by combining it with shadow. They cannot be harmed by physical weapons or power, but according to the legends, there was a way to use the power to defeat them.

Spirit Totem—A human able to communicate with the dead. They are able to bond to the dead and give control to them through their power. As strong as this might make them, there is a serious risk involved since the living world cannot touch the dead without dying itself.

The Spirits—Desrik Scythlen, sounds liked it looks. Marlao Blood, Mar-l-ow (kind of like the 'ow' you say when you get hurt) Bl-ahd. Tiana Paine, Tee-ah-na Pain. Kinran Death, Kin-Ran DE-aht. These spirits are the only ones capable of communicating with James Richards and Alamar Telanre.

Haenya—Sounds like HAIN-yuh. Alamar's horse, female, unknown breed. Haenya means Dark Heroine in the Words.

Elite—The twenty one most powerful and skilled warriors in Intaru. They are the Emperor's main squadron of fighters and do his personal biddings and follow no one else. The leader is known as Lord Commander, though no one knows his real name besides the Emperor.

Bonding with an Animal—The Land gave the creatures minds and great intelligence along with the abilities to use its power for themselves. Thus, creatures began to realize that by Bonding their minds with that of a human they could communicate with them and grant them great wisdom. The Land knew this could be bad and would upset the balance in many ways, so it made a law that only specific humans, those of pure hearts or those chosen by the Land's human form, the Lady of Nature, could speak with the animals.

Æ and AE—This is a sound used by the people of Arollay in an odd way. It sounds like both an A and an E blended into one sound. I.E.—Hælen would be pronounced: HAY-eh-len. Yet with words like Haenya the 'a' and 'e' are separated making it sound like HAY-nee-uh.

<u>Names with'in the middle</u>—Some people may think this is just a fancy way of writing a word, but it is not! The apostrophe acts like a comma in a sentence; a pause, only swifter. For instance the word Malan'dur would sound like Malan—dur not Malandur.

CHAPTER 1

▼

GREETINGS

Chaos shall drive to shift the scale,
Bringing destruction through fire and hail.
Heir to the legacy, he shall use
The power of his ancestor, he shall abuse.

Salvation comes from the un-empowered land,
Power never seen flows from his hand.
The past shall aid him,
The dead shall aid him,
Chaos plots his doom.

Life and Power, two paths he is to take.
Strength and Death are his destiny,
Death and Life follow in his wake.
His powers revealed by the Lady of the Tree.

Chaos shall draw him here,
Fire and destruction draw him near.
He who lived at world's start
Shall be revived by his art

The Land is torn, its people slaved
The powers are vanquished—none are saved.

The one who comes from the un-empowered land
Shall destroy us all by his hand.

*   *   *   *

THE sun was hanging low in the sky, barely touching the tree tops that ran all along the ground for miles to see, as a group of men marched towards their destinies. There were no birds, or crickets, squirrels, or any other animals out there. It was only the men, and yet they felt as if they were truly not alone. The sky was a mix of reds, oranges, purples, and blues, with clouds dotting it here and there. The ground was a rich green with the only brown tightly encircling the trees.

The horses pulled the carts along behind the men, looking longingly at the grass. The armor on the men shown in the fading light making them seem as angels rather than the bringer's of destruction. Swords and lances, arrows and bows, weapons of varying size, shape, and use were strewn about then men hanging from hips or backs or even being carried in their hands, waiting to be used. They stared forward, never looking to the sides, or behind them; no one would dare challenge them.

Cold gray eyes filled each face with dark circles underneath them from lack of sleep. Even though they never stopped, each face was clean shaven to allow all to see the fury etched on their faces as if made of stone and carved by a master hand. The only thing that could be different between them was the color of their hair, varying from the darkest black to the lightest yellow. Each head had the same close cut hair, however, because long hair got in the way during battle and nothing was allowed to get in their way.

In rows of seven men, shoulder to shoulder, they marched through the land, passing empty farms, houses, smiths, even entire towns. There was no one around but them. Thousands of men, and yet only one leader. Only one person they looked up to and revered above all else. The General, leader of the Majki tribe, and the uncrowned king of the land where they lived; he was the only hope they had left in this world, and no one ever disobeyed him.

The General sat a top his own horse, a black stallion that had carried his father in his last battle, and the most powerful weapon the General had. They were both wearing armor like the others, yet theirs was not glowing with the fading sun light, it glowed with the power and spirits of all who wore it before them. The Ancient Armor, able to fit only one man: the rightful heir to the Majki.

It was then that the General held up a hand signaling the troops to stop. As they did, he continued onward, slowly making his way through the barrier of trees that had surrounded them for countless days. They all held their breath as the General, their leader, vanished behind the trees. Moments passed as they waited, no one moved, no one breathed … The sudden cry rang through the silence of the forests, the soldiers unsheathing their swords, knocking arrows, and hefting spears and pikes as they rushed to the aid of their General.

The first to breach the forest barrier gasped as …

"James! The bus is here!"

Blue eyes shining behind small rectangular glasses blinked several times as they stared into a pair of green eyes. At first it was like looking into the forest where the General and his men had been only moments before. Giving his head a shake, he marked his page and closed the thick book before placing it under his arm.

James Richards stood up from the bench he had been sitting on and picked up his back pack off the ground. Slinging the strap over his shoulder he followed Darrel onto the bus. The tall skinny kid had his Crazy Game system in hand, and from the music coming from it, he was paused in the middle of some big battle. Like handling a newborn he set the Crazy Game in his pants pocket and started off towards the back of the bus.

Making sure he still had his book, and that his backpack wouldn't hit anyone, James followed Darrel to the back where two empty seats sat waiting. Dozens of familiar faces passed as he marched farther into the prison transport. Some of them looked up and waved with a mock salute, he returned them with a nod and continued on. By the time he made it to the back, Darrel was already sitting in his seat and had his Crazy Game out. His fingers moved with incredible speed and accuracy over the buttons as the cheap music continued.

James took the seat across the narrow path that led from the front to the back of the bus and gave a nod to the kid sitting beside Darrel. He waved back after brushing his hair to the side. His light blue eyes stared down at the miniature screen that Darrel was holding and flashed. Chris wasn't one who really liked video games; he was more of an athlete himself, though you wouldn't tell by the looks of him.

Chris Tamponi: age 18, blonde hair, blue eyes, normal complexion, and the slightly flabby leftovers of muscles that hadn't been worked in months. The school had prized their athletic programs so much that they had their own trophy case built in honor of the athletes who brought them so much 'fame'. Yet only last year, when the results of the Presidential Academic Exams came back, they were shocked to find that their prized athletes' scores were the worst in the entire country. The following week the school had cut most of the funding to the athletic programs and put the extra cash into buying better computers, books, study areas, and even more teachers.

People complained that their kids needed the athletic department, but when they saw the horrid grades that their children had acquired, they stopped the rioting. As for the really athletic students, they all transferred out of Sylvan University and went to other schools that weren't so picky. Chris, however, was forced to stay at the prison by his parents when they found he had scored the fifth lowest score of them all. Now he spent most of his time studying, reading the texts books, or doing five minute workouts in the remaining training room. Confining his scowl from Darrel he pulled out a notebook and began reading it. Darrel, however, continued playing his action packed game like there was no tomorrow.

Darrel Black: age 18 ½, black hair, green eyes, slightly tanned complexion (though where he got it from no one knew) and the knowledge of just about every RPG [1]game available. Some people thought him a bit of a nerd, some even went so far as to say he was a freak, but James saw him as a hidden genius. The fact that he could retain all that knowledge about the games was astounding to him. He could tell you where to turn and what treasure to open in just about any game in seconds. He'd even helped James once when he had been stuck in his own game a few months back.

James wasn't as avid a player as Darrel, but he played some games when he got a chance. He was more into his books, but not the same ones as Chris. He loved reading science fiction, fantasy, adventure, even so far as to read a few mysteries. Books were wonderful things to him. They were like a portal to another world that only a few people could really go to. When he read, he felt the breeze that whipped through the crowd standing at the gallows, waiting for the board to be kicked from beneath the doomed. The heat of battle would course through his veins making it hard to realize that it was only a book at times.

While he wasn't considered a nerd or a freak or anything like that, people did tease him about his affinity for books. But that was to be expected in a world such as this. In this world people would taunt some one for the smallest thing; be it a pimple on their nose or the fact that they just got dumped by their girlfriend for someone else. Things happened in this world that sickened him to the core. And the only escape he could find was to go to another world through the pages of his books.

---

1. RPG—Role-playing Game

James Richards: age 18 ½ dark brown-black hair, blue eyes, fair complexion (nothing special), the know-how of books that people didn't really know existed sometimes, a little tall for his age at 6'5" and a skinny 195 pounds. Yes it was a typical life. Typical unless you considered the things he'd had to go through to get where he was. James' parents were rarely, if ever home because of work, and it had been that way for a long time. He'd gotten used to it, but it was still stupid how he would sometimes forget their faces.

The city bus strolled along the streets, stopping at the occasional traffic light and stop sign. Other cars passed them in their hurry to get where they needed to go. Some went so far as to honk and shout angrily at the bus. Yet the driver didn't pay any attention to them; so the students did. Whenever someone shouted something, one of the people in the middle of the bus, sometimes even the back, would stick their head slightly out the window and either shout something back or give them the "birdie".

Shaking his head at the immaturity, or downright stupidity of the students he reopened his book to where he had left off.

It was then that the General held up a hand signaling the troops to stop. As they did, he continued onward, slowly making his way through the barrier of trees that had surrounded them for countless days. They all held their breath as the General, their leader, vanished behind the trees. Moments passed as they waited, no one moved, no one breathed … The sudden cry rang through the silence of the forests, the soldiers unsheathing their swords, knocking arrows, and hefting spears and pikes rushed to the aid of their General.

The first to breach the forest barrier gasped as he saw the thousands of lights below. Thousands of camp fires sat in unorganized rows hundreds of feet below them. Several of the troops brought out their looking glasses and almost shouted with …

"Hey James …"

Gritting his teeth, he turned to Darrel who had set his game down and was looking across the isle at him.

"Yeah—what is it?"

"Do you think you could help me study for the psych test tomorrow? Chris is being stupid and won't tell me a thing." He made a fist at the thought but continued on. "C'mon, man. I really need your help here."

With a sigh, he marked his page again and placed his book in his backpack. Taking hold of his thick psych book he opened it to the chapter they were studying and began quizzing Darrel.

"What are the eight parts of the brain that we have been studying this quarter?"

"I thought you were quizzing me on Psych. C'mon, gimme a real question."

"That is a real question, moron." Chris said. Darrel shot Chris a death glare, but the other seemed not to have noticed. "Part of psychology is the study of the brain and how it influences the human body. The eight parts of the brain we are studying now are only a few of the ones that take care of the entire body."

"… and your point is …?" Darrel asked.

"The eight parts of the brain that we are studying are: the Cerebellum, Cerebrum, Medulla, Amygdala, Cerebral Frontal Cortex or CFC for short, Brain stem, Thalamus, and the Hypothalamus."

"Correct, as always." James turned to Darrel. "Now you try it."

"Um … er … Hyper thalamus, Brain stem, CPC …"

"CFC …" James corrected. "What is it short for?"

"Um … Cerebral … Forward … um … Oh I give up!"

Darrel slumped back into his seat with a grimace that made it look like he was close to tears. He seemingly ignored his game and just stared forward. James heard him mumbling under his breath. It sounded like part of his game … again … Wait a second …!

"Hey Darrel, could I see the booklet for Demon Basher 4?" Both Chris and Darrel looked at him. "I just wanna see something, that's all. Well can I?"

Darrel continued looking at him for a moment before reaching into his backpack and pulled out a small booklet. The cover had a very large man with even larger guns in both hands, blasting away at about seven or eight different creatures in varying states of grotesqueness. He had a similar game like it at home, Demon Basher 2, but it did have some major differences. James began flipping through the booklet, scanning each page as he flew through it. When he was done, he closed the book and set it on his lap.

"Okay, Darrel." He said finally. "One more time, shall we?"

"What? Oh, give it a rest James. There's no way I'm going to be able to …"

"If you shoot the level 16 demon, Carithtos, in the stomach 7 times before finally bashing it in the head with the butt of your gun, what happens?"

…

"Easy. Carithtos would fall back into a state of unconsciousness because you cracked its skull. That's the secret glitch I found in the game. When Carithtos is knocked unconscious, you have to take your battle knife and ..."

"Okay, okay. I don't need to know that part. Now," He opened the psych book to the chapter again and turned it to Darrel. "This is the picture of a human brain, with all eight parts that we're studying noted and highlighted. Please look for a moment at the front of the brain and what it does for the body."

"James, why-?"

"Just do it. Humor me."

"... Whoa!" Several people looked back as Darrel shouted. "If the front of the brain is busted open like that, then ..."

The two of them kept talking like this for the remainder of the bus ride. James would ask Darrel what would happen if blah-blah-blah, then Darrel would reply with some odd answer; following suit James would then show Darrel a part of the brain and Darrel would recognize it in some fashion. By the time they got to school Darrel was beaming. He was naming all eight parts and what it was they did in accordance with what body function.

Everyone was piling off the bus as James slipped his psych book back into his backpack. As he stepped down from the bus to the ground, Chris turned to him almost laughing.

"How did you know that he would be able to remember all that? Or even learn all that in a matter of minutes?"

"Easy." He replied with a shrug. "What was the first thing we learned this year in Psych? Memory. Darrel has a remarkable memory if you look at it the right way. Do you think that you could remember how to go through seventeen levels of the hardest maze I've ever seen without getting lost once after only your second try? Basically, all I did was make his mind compare that know-how with the stuff he needed to know. Simple."

Chris bust into a fit of laughter as the two of them made their way through the crowd and into the prison people called school. The hallways were packed tight with students left and right talking and digging through lockers and making quite a racket. As they passed by a group of students wearing the old football jerseys, one of them shouted something at no one, but the comment itself made a few people laugh and others turn away in disgust. James and Chris were with the latter.

Turning down into A hall Chris said goodbye as he found his locker. James and Darrel continued on through A hall and passed D and H hall to finally end up in J hall where their lockers lay in wait. Spinning the dial through its combination James grabbed his math book and stuffed it into his backpack in between his psych book and the smaller reading book. Darrel said goodbye as he made his way to the communications room where the announcements were made each day. His job was to start things off with the pledge and the random news.

Turning from his locker James walked head first into someone and they both fell to the floor. James got quickly to his feet and offered a hand to the person he'd trampled. A familiar blonde haired, brown eyed face stared up at him. It was Chrissie Malloy. Chrissie wasn't really a friend of his, but she didn't hate him either; but she had a major problem with men. Chrissie was naturally beautiful, all in all … hot was the better word for it. She was only 18 but she looked at least to be a mature twenty one.

And with most beautiful women in this world they were treated as such, but sometimes not in the most polite of ways. People gave 'cat calls', as his mother once called them, as she walked down the hallways. She ignored them and just walked on, but the words still hit home.

She reached up and took his hand and he pulled her up with an apology. She responded with a quiet and quick 'thanks', hefted her books closer to herself and vanished into the maze of people. James watched her go with pity and sadness; it wasn't right that she'd have to fear people …

Making his way once again through the labyrinth of students James found his homeroom in the middle of H hall. Chris had beaten him to the room already because he was sitting in his designated seat at the front reading from the same notebook. Mrs. Politee was sitting at her desk with her nose in a book almost as big as his psych text. She was probably the one person in the whole school who read more than he did, and that was saying something.

James' seat was at the back of the room completely opposite of Chris. Whipping out his book again he continued where he left off …

The first to breach the forest barrier gasped as he saw the thousands of lights below. Thousands of camp fires sat in unorganized rows hundreds of feet below them. Several of the troops brought out their looking glasses and almost shouted in horror at the sight. Over ten thousand men were sitting around those fires, all wearing black armor. Some of the people with better scopes saw the white crossed swords crest on their chest plates and helms.

The General folded the scope and placed it back into his pack. Turning to his troops he unsheathed his sword. The gleaming metal seemed duller than usual.

"Men, down there beneath us is our goal—The Black Army of Numenberg." Several of the men had bowed their heads at the news. "Yet despite their size we have destiny on our side. We have the promise of the Lady of the Wood that we shall all return safely to our loved ones. But for those of you who do not wish to fight, you have my full pardon and may leave without losing any honor in my eyes." None moved. "Then, my comrades, we march to battle!"

Thousands of battle cries rang as thousands of swords and bows and spears were drawn. And with unimaginable fury the General led the charge down into the camp of the Black Army. Like a roaring river they poured from the forest and into the open plain …

"GOOD MORNING SYLVAN UNIVERSITY!"

The entire class jumped in its seats as Darrel's voice boomed from the speakers. They could hear yelling from the communications room as Darrel tried to quiet down. People were shouting to turn the volume down on the speakers in the background. James closed his book and set it back in his backpack as Darrel continued with the volume turned down.

"Sorry 'bout that. Today there will be a meeting of the Jap-anime club at 4 o'clock. Also Thursday and Friday there will be a blood drive in the main lounge for all those who wish to give blood. Anyone willing to help with the Acting club's scene setting can come to the campus theatre today and tomorrow between noon and five …"

James listened half heartedly as Darrel went on and on. He wished he could continue reading but he couldn't focus on the pages with the announcements going on. He was about to lay down for a quick three minute nap when a sharp blast of pain erupted from his chest. Quick as light, his hand was clutching at the center of his chest where the pain flowed forth like magma from a volcano. It was worse than before; he couldn't breathe, he started seeing spots in front of his eyes.

"Mr. Richards are you alright?"

His head snapped up as the pain vanished. Mrs. Politee was looking at him over the rim of her book—as was the rest of the class. His eyes scanned the room and stopped on Chris who had set his notebook down and had turned completely in his seat to stare at him.

"Yes I'm fine, just a cramp."

The rest of the class turned away, some snickering, but Chris continued to stare at him until the bell rang to start the day. Everyone got out of their seats and made for the door to the already crowded hallway. James rushed to the door and was out into the maelstrom of students before Chris could stop him.

The halls of Sylvan were old; so old that the ceiling tiles were brown with age. The lockers were ancient and starting to rust in places despite the new paint. The floor tiles were an ugly mix of brown and yellow to add to the grotesqueness. Ducking into a gap between two rows of lockers James waited for the crowd to settle down. His hand wandered to where the pain had been, but it was completely gone now. It hadn't been the first time the pain had surged. It had been happening for a week now, but he was sure it wouldn't last much longer.

"You really should go to the nurse or the doctor, ya know."

Chris appeared out of the crowd like a specter through a solid wall. James didn't look at him. Chris knew about the pain and continuously bugged him to get it checked out. But a certain incident a few years past kept him far from the nurse or the doctor …

"I don't need it checked; it's just a cramp, that's all."

"Oh shut up, Richards." Chris said with a tone of voice that sounded too much like their teachers'. "You know as well as I that this is no cramp. You've had it for eight days now and each time it gets worse. I admit I'm getting worried."

"Hey guys, whatcha doin' here?" Darrel said as he popped into the gap beside them. "Your class is down in B hall, and you-know-who here hates to be late." He added nudging Chris.

"James had the pain again."

The smile faded from his other friend's face along with the childish gleam in his eyes.

"In the middle of homeroom?" He asked. Chris nodded. "James this is bad. It usually doesn't start until eleven. If it is getting more frequent then you should …"

"I want you to go to the nurse's office." Chris said, interrupting Darrel.

"No, Chris!" People looked at them as they continued down the hall. "I told you it is nothing. I don't get sick and I don't need to go to the nurse's office! I don't …"

"You don't know what this is! What if it is something serious? What if this is some kind of disease? You need to get it checked out, and I mean now!"

"Enough Chris, alright? How many times do you have to say the same thing over and over? It gets really annoying ya know that?"

"I will keep telling you until you listen, you moron!"

Chris turned back to the crowd and continued towards class. James soon followed. They walked in silence, not that they could hear each other in the noise anyway. He bumped into a ton of shoulders and they bumped into him in return, but no one bothered to apologize, it was impossible to cross the hallways without knocking into everyone on the way. Finally he saw the door he was look-ing for.

Room B213, AKA the Psych ward. James and Chris made their way across the raging current and in through the doorway to hell. The brown and yellow tiles clashing with the multiple colors of the chair backs and the shirts and pants of all the students in them made his head spin. Chris grunted and pushed him into the viper's den.

The head snake himself was sitting in the teacher's chair smiling at them with a closed mouth. Deep green eyes watched them as they made their way to the chairs at the back of the classroom and sat down. Mr. Wicker was wearing his trademark plaid button-up shirt of red, green, and brown with his even browner pants that revealed bony ankles and long plaid socks. People said that he should not be allowed to teach kids because of the way he dressed, and the way his eyes seemed to be able to watch them all at once without moving or blinking.

As they sat down the bell rang and the torture commenced. Mr. Wicker had them take out their texts and notebooks and started to write on the chalk board. When he turned back to them a badly drawn picture of a human brain was in the middle of the board with eight lines poking out of it pointing to the eight parts of the brain they were studying. Wicker droned on in his slimy, oily, and ever-so-boring voice about the eight parts they studied. Pointing to each part with his meter stick as he mentioned each one he watched them all try to write everything down as he spoke.

James chanced a glance at the clock after a while. *Only half an hour left to go* he thought, *not bad … not bad.*

"Mr. Richards!"

James jumped in his seat and looked up at Wicker's cold hard face. He wore his thin lipped smile again and that meant only one thing …

"Please come up to the board, without your notebook, and properly name the parts of the brain that are marked on the board and a brief description of what they do."

With a hole in his stomach James got up and walked through the desk rows up to the front of the room. Taking the small piece of chalk from Wicker with a sigh he began to write the answers: Hypothalamus, Thalamus, Cerebellum, Cere-brum, Medulla, Amygdala, Occipital Lobes, and the Septum. When he was done he wrote a quick and brief description of what they did. Finally setting the chalk down and turning to Wicker, smiled, and waved his arm to the chalkboard.

"There you are Mr. Wicker. The eight parts of the brain and a brief descrip-tion of what they do. Is there anything else?"

Mr. Wicker's eyebrows creased in at the smart remark, but kept silent. He shook his head and motioned for him to take his seat. With a smile James retreated back to the confines of his desk and sat down with a grunt. He may have been dozing off at that particular moment, but he had been paying attention earlier. Wicker always chose him to repeat what he had just taught. He thought it must be a grudge or something.

As he started to pick up his pen again the sharp pain in his lower chest came back again. This time it hurt not only his chest but this time he felt it creep down his arm. He heard himself gasp as he grabbed the spot tightly with both hands. Doubling over onto the desk his head hit the hard wood hard making Wicker look over at him. He thought he heard the professor calling him, but he couldn't be sure. There was a ringing in his ears that wouldn't go away making all other sounds seem far off, almost distant. The room seemed to spin as he tried to breathe, whirling and swirling around his head. Something hard hit him on the back of his head and everything went black …

CHAPTER 2

▼

FAREWELLS

"WELL, I must say this is very strange ... very strange indeed"

"Well don't just stand there looking impressed! Help him!"

"I am! I am!" the first voice said again with a note of impatience. "Please, leave me to my work. Security?"

"HEY! Get your hands off me, you bastard! I said LET ME ..."

A door closed in the background and the shouting dimmed to nothing. James tried to move, tried to speak. He wanted that voice to stay. It was a familiar voice but he couldn't remember exactly who it belonged to. There was a stinging pain in his chest, but it didn't feel as bad as it had back at school. *Wait! Back ... at ... school?* Where was he then? Trying to open his eyes he felt a hand on his forehead and a woman's voice above him. She was talking to herself again, but he heard every word.

But there was something else. Something really weird. Even though his eyes were closed and he couldn't move, he could some how see, maybe sense was a better term, but he could feel everything about him.

"What an unlucky kid ... I wonder what this pain is his friends claim he has? Or even yet, what it's from. Hmm, very interesting." She pried his left eye open and peered into it.

Deep brown eyes stared into his own, never blinking, just boring into him ... A small brown mole was sitting on her face just beneath her left eye, above the hospital mask ... it shouted at him making a wave of nausea rush over him, causing his breath to catch. The sudden movement caused the nurse to start and stand up right. Taking a pen from her chest pocket she began to write on a note pad produced from somewhere. He heard the door open again and a deep voice spoke to the nurse.

"What is it?"

"He's beginning to wake up, doctor, or at least he moved for the first time since he was brought here."

"Hmm, okay." He said quietly. "Take him to radiology and have that chest of his checked for tumors, bacteria, or anything else that you can think of that might cause something like this. Afterwards you may take him back here, open the curtains and let that friend of his come in to see him. And make sure that the kid wears a mask at all times. I'm not a hundred percent sure this is not contagious."

"What do you mean by that? Have there been others?"

"Yes. He may have been the first, but six others have come here with the same symptoms; chest pain, trouble breathing, right down to passing out in the middle of class." The nurse made a sound that said she thought it might all be a scam. "But according to the teachers that came with each patient, they all seemed to pass out at the exact same time."

"That can't be true!" The nurse said with exasperation spilling off her words. "There is no way that seven kids in different parts of the city all had the same thing take them and wind up here all within minutes of each other. There is just no possible way!"

"Judy, I understand what you're saying but please take him to get the scan now, please? When he is done bring him back here. At that time you may let his friend in as well as his family."

"Very well, doctor." She said moving around behind him. James felt his bed begin to move and tried to moan that it made his chest hurt, but he didn't make a sound. "Unfortunately, his family has not arrived yet. But I will tell his friends that they may see him after he is done being scanned."

"So, this is where you are hiding ... I have finally ... found you ..."

What was that? Or who was that?

The bed pushed against the door and went out into the hallway. Immediately he heard the familiar voice calling to him getting closer, but the nurse's stern voice stopped it with a sharp snap. She told him to come back later and though it protested the voice finally went away with a quick 'later'. The bed lurched back into motion and James found himself turning left, then right, then right again. There was a quick bump followed by a bell that sounded somewhere above him.

Gravity seemed to push at his back for a moment ... he was in an elevator, going down, down, down ...

When the bell toned next he was moving again another right and a left before he finally stopped. He tried opening his eyes again, but still nothing. The nurse was moving about again, the heels of her shoes clicking lightly on the floor. Something squeaked above him. *The CAT scan* he thought with a shudder. He hated the nurses at school because they were just mean to every kid who came to them with a problem. He went there only once when he had been a freshman, the experience still brought shivers up his spine.

"Now, Mr. Richards," The nurse said in a sweet honey filled voice. "I'm going to scan your chest for whatever might be causing your pain. This won't hurt at all and it will be over before you know it."

That's what the school nurses had said when they laid him down on the bed to give blood. The needle had gone in his arm and the blood started flowing. When the bag was full, they pulled the needle out and started to apply a bandage to the place. But the blood just kept on coming. It wouldn't stop; they had to place gauze on the spot to let it soak up the blood. He had been scared then, and all they did was tell him to hold the gauze there and not to move until it stopped.

James finally snapped out of his thoughts. The bed was moving again, right, then left and into the elevator. Up, up, up, ding, and out he went over the bump and finally stopping back in the first room. The nurse was humming something as she opened a window and pulled open a curtain.

"I'll go get your friends so they can come and see you." The door opened in the back. "Though I don't see the reason ..."

Her heels clicked as she walked away and opened the door. As soon as they were open three pairs of feet were heard running across the floor and stopping next to him. He wanted to open his eyes above all else, just so he could see their faces, but his eyelids didn't want to work. He felt a hand brush against his face and then grasp his left hand. He worked the muscles in his hand and squeezed. One of the people gasped and held onto it all the more harder.

"James ... can you hear me?"

He knew that voice! But, it couldn't be! Why would she be here?

"Chrissie, I don't think he can. The doctor said he was still unconscious."

"No, Darrel!" She said quietly, but hard enough to crack ice. "I felt it. He gripped my hands just now. No ... he is conscious."

They spoke over him, like he wasn't really there, but he knew that wasn't true. If only I could move or speak ... do something!

"There! I saw him!" Chrissie said holding onto his hand even tighter. "He moved just now. His head turned just a little bit! James? Can you hear me?"

They saw! I moved … okay, let's try something else … James focused every ounce of energy he had to open his eyes … even a little. He felt them begin to twitch a little, not really opening, but moving almost as if he were in REM sleep. *Just a little more … come on now … OPEN!* As the thought passed through his mind his eyes burst wide open, burning in the sudden brightness of the hospital room. He closed them again to shield them from the light, but opened them again slower, trying to focus on the faces.

Chrissie's long blonde hair was hovering over him as she stared down at him, eyes shining with tears she wanted to hold back. Darrel and Chris were beaming down at him also holding back some tears, but not as effectively as Chrissie. Darrel vanished and he saw him running out the door shouting for the doctor. *Moron,* he thought, *the doctor is gonna think I'm dieing what with the racket he's making.*

He turned his head over to Chrissie who smiled even wider and hooked both sides of her hair behind her ears. Working the muscles on his face he smiled up at her then arched an eyebrow. She laughed and wiped the tears with the back of her hand.

"When I heard you had collapsed in class I was worried." He continued to stare. "You're as stupid as you look sometimes, you know that? James, you were probably the only one in that entire school who didn't look at me like I was some prize they wanted in bed or whatever. Whenever you looked at me, I saw something in your eyes that was different from everyone else's. I know it sounds like something from one of your books, but it is true.

"All my life I have been stared at because of my body, because people saw me as beautiful, not who I am. Their eyes were cold to look at, even scary at times. But your eyes … they were never cold, yet at the same time never warm. I know you don't care for me that way, and to tell you the truth I'm kinda glad. I-I don't think I could like someone that way right now, even if I wanted to. Now do you understand?"

He shook his head, but smiled anyway. He understood … girls were confusing, that's what. Just then the doctor came bursting into the room. He looked rabid. Grabbing Chrissie by the arm he moved her out of the way, not too roughly, but enough so as to make her move. He turned to her and almost shouted. She didn't have a mask on—none of them did. She simply stood her ground and looked the doctor square in the face, crossed her arms and scowled right back at him.

Throwing his hands over his head the doctor turned back to James and started peering into his eyes, examining his face at every angle. He pressed down on his stomach and asked James if he felt any pain. James simply shook his head each time; even when he came to the part where the pain had basically crippled him earlier. Standing up and writing in his own notebook, the doctor looked completely perplexed.

"I don't get it." He said biting on the end of his pen. "I just don't get it. It makes no sense."

"What doesn't make sense?" Darrel said appearing behind him.

"Well, he doesn't seem to be experiencing any pain anymore, at least not that I can tell. What's more," he flipped through the notebook, "his scans don't show any sign of tumors, infection, muscle problems, or anything at all. According to those, he's perfectly healthy."

"And that's a problem how?" Chris asked arching an eyebrow.

"If he is this healthy, then what caused the pain? Why did he pass out like that? It just makes no sense. Not to mention those others …"

"You mean the people … who collapsed at the same time … that I did …?" James asked feeling slightly winded as though he'd been running.

Everyone jumped as he spoke. He edged himself higher up on the bed with his elbows. It caused a small stab of pain in his chest, but he ignored it and finally sat up in the bed. The light blue 'gown' he was wearing hung loosely on his shoulders as he sat there twisting his neck left and right trying to work a kink out of it. Again the doctor inspected his face and tried the pressure on his stomach again, but the same results followed. When he was done he handed James his glasses.

"That is correct, Mr. Richards." He said standing back up.

"Please … I hate that name. Just James. Mr. Richards is my dad's title, not mine."

The doctor looked at him questioningly, but went on anyway.

"All seven of you arrived here at this very hospital within minutes of each other. I haven't had a moments rest all day. You all came here unconscious and not moving at all. We had you all scanned and examined. Your vitals were normal, surprisingly, but none of you were moving an inch. None of the machines said that any of you were in danger, but the people who brought you said that while in class you were doubled over in pain and almost crying."

James looked to Darrel and Chris who both nodded with grim faces. He didn't remember much of anything that happened beyond the fact that he had been in pain and then blacking out. Chrissie was on the verge of tears again, but she held them back. James cracked his neck finally and made to get out of bed.

The doctor and Chrissie both made to stop him but he told them to let him go. The doctor protested, but he finally backed away, ready to grab him if he started to fall.

Swinging his legs over the side of the bed he let his feet touch the cold floor. Setting the gown straight so as to cover himself, he started to stand up completely. Once he was standing straight up he felt something tug on his arm. When he looked down at it, all the blood seemed to drain from his face. Darrel grabbed the doctor by the arm and told him to take the IV out of his arm.

"What? Why?"

"A few years ago when he went to give blood at our school, they stuck a needle in his arm and when they were done they took it out." Chris said quickly. "But when it came out he didn't stop bleeding for almost five minutes. He has been terrified of needles and hospitals ever since. If you don't take that thing out, he'll pass out again!"

By now James' face was completely white and his eyes seemed dilated, but the doctor quickly got a cotton ball and some clear liquid. Wetting the cotton ball he pulled off the tape holding the IV in and slowly took the needle out. Dabbing the place with the cotton ball he told James to hold it there for a moment while he got a bandage. When it was all over, the color in James' face was back to normal, but he still seemed a little breathless.

"Th-thanks." He said as he applied the bandage.

Chrissie was at his side the entire time, holding onto his arm for support both mental and physical. He asked her to let him go for a moment so he could stretch and walk around, so she did. Setting both hands on his back, James bent backwards as far as he could go sending a series of cracks running up his spine. Darrel grimaced and gagged. Righting himself he started off towards the other end of the room, weaving in and out of the racks of medicine and machines.

The hospital beds were harder than they appeared, and he felt like a stiff board from sleeping in one. Turning back around he made is way across the room again and stopped next to the bed.

"Are ... there any 'connections' between me and the other six?"

"W-what? Oh, uh ..." The doctor looked through the notebook flipping through several pages. "No, not really. Well ..."

"What is it?"

"I doubt it is a 'connection', but none of your parents have arrived here yet." A frown creased his face. "Despite the fact that we called their home phones, cell phones, and work phones, none of them have made it here yet. My guess is traffic, but still ..."

"Don't expect my family to come here." James said with every ounce of malice he could muster.

A quick jab of pain rushed through him, making his knees buckle, but he caught himself on the bed and made it look like he just sat down. It went quickly, so he didn't make a scene. He wondered if the others had woken up yet, or if they were still in that half awake state. Hearing everything, but not being able to see or move. This was too weird for his taste, despite all the books he had read where people had strange things happen to them all the time, he couldn't see it happening to him. Nothing ever happened in real life.

"DOCTOR!"

Everyone in the room jumped as the nurse came bursting through the door red in the face. The doctor grabbed her by the arms to stop her from running past him.

"Doctor … the other patients … they're awake! They all just suddenly opened their eyes and are walking around like nothing happened at all! And …"

She stopped as she looked at James seeing him up for the first time and almost fainted by the looks of it. She caught herself with a shake of her head and straightened again. Taking a few more breaths she went on. Apparently they said they felt like they were half asleep and kept mentioning hearing everything that people were saying but couldn't seem to do anything to respond. Chris asked if that was how he had been while they were working on him and he said he had been.

"It was weird." His hands hung at his side, resisting the urge to move and try to describe what it was like. "Even though my eyes were closed, somehow I could see everything around me. I could hear everything around me. People saying things like, 'Now we're going to do this' and 'we're going to do that'. Not to mention the fact that it was un-godly hot the entire time. And who was it that said, 'I have finally found you. So this is where you have been hiding'? I thought that was a little odd."

"No one ever said something like that. What did the voice sound like?"

"Hang on a sec." Darrel said stepping forward. "If you're so sure that no one said anything like that, then why do you want to know what the voice sounded like?"

"Yeah, that's right." Chrissie said crossing her arms again. "Maybe while you were out tending to the other patients, someone came in here and …"

"Wait …" Everyone turned to James as he stood up. "Even though my eyes were closed the entire time I could tell if there were people near by. I don't know how I was able to just yet, but when I heard that voice the only one in the room was the nurse and there's no way she could sound like that. The voice was, well … it was deep and rough and well … sounded nothing short of evil. My stomach seemed to get a hole in the bottom as it spoke to me …"

"Odd words from someone your age." The doctor said with a laugh.

"I've told him a hundred times not to read so many books." Darrel said walking around the doctor. "He always says something like that because of them."

The nurse was leaning up close to the doctor whispering in his ear. He nodded a few times and never lost the grim look he had on his face. When she was done he told her something the rest of them couldn't hear and she left the room at a quick walk. The doctor turned to them and said he had to go and check on the other kids.

"I'll be back to do one last test in a little bit. James I want you to stay in bed and the rest of you let him rest, okay? You may stay here and even put the curtains back around you; in fact I suggest you do that now anyway. When I come back I will wake you and tell you about the final examination. Deal?"

They nodded in agreement as James started to get back in the bed. He adjusted the top part so it left him in a half lying half sitting position and tried to rest. Chrissie pulled the curtains around them and sat down on a chair at the front of the bed. Darrel and Chris took their chairs and sat on the other side of him. Darrel had his Crazy Game out and the little beeps and crashes told him he was playing Demon Basher 4 again. Chris took a notebook out of his backpack and started reading it.

"That reminds me." James said as he watched Chris. "What about the math exam today? What did Meaner say?"

"He said that we will take the test tomorrow, but it will be a different one from the one they took today. So I am going over my notes again to refresh my memory." He glanced over at Darrel who had his nose about an inch away from the screen and rolled his eyes. "Some people should do the same. They could really use the grades."

Darrel glared at Chris who simply shrugged and went back to his notes. James laughed. Those two would never change, and he was glad. Darrel's lack of interest in school rivaled Chris' lack of interest in video games and the two of them raged back and forth like wolves fighting over food or something. Chrissie was smiling as well, not the usual smile she would wear to make people think she was in a good mood, but an actual smile. *I don't think I'm ready for something like that myself* he thought. Women were too much of a mystery to him for him to commit to one right then.

The next day, as James put on his own clothes that his Chris' parents had gotten him from home, he was in a bad mood. *They never came. Not once! WORK!*
WORK! WORK! That's all they ever did! He hated his parents so much he wanted
to scream, but he kept his anger in check any way. He was excused from school
today because the doctor didn't want him doing too much just yet. The final test
was just to see if the pain would come back again over night, but it hadn't, so he
was allowed to go home.

Chris' mom and dad were going to take him home since their workplace was
the closest and were waiting for him to get dressed so they could go. He tried to
hurry, but not because they needed to get to their own jobs and Chris to school,
but because the longer he stayed in a hospital the more he dreaded it. He knew it
was stupid to be afraid of the doctors like some little five year old, but the memory of all that blood leaking from his arm was enough to make him want to cry.

When he was fully dressed he walked out of the dressing room and into the
hall. Chris was waiting for him and together they walked through the labyrinth of
the hospital. The two automated doors swung open to allow them out of the
nightmare house and into the dull, overcast day of the real world. The blue
Dodge Caravan pulled up in front of them and they climbed into the bucket
seats. Mr. and Mrs. Tamponi turned and smiled to him and asked if he was better. He smiled back politely and said he felt fine.

Mrs. Tamponi was wearing a dull blue skirt with a black belt and golden
buckle around her waist. Underneath the coat was a white shirt that had what
looked like a little arrangement of flowers embedded on it. Her oval glasses hung
low on her long pointed nose and brought her hazel eyes into focus. Her long
blonde hair shown on top of her head in a tight bun was being held up by what
looked to be a scrunchy.

Mr. Tamponi had his gray coat on over a black button shirt with another gray
tie around his neck. A golden wrist watch sparkled in the dim sunlight, but not as
much as the wedding ring on his finger did. His thick black hair was the opposite
of his wife's, absorbing all the light that tried to shine on it. James looked over at
Chris' light brown hair and wondered where on earth it came from. When they
had their buckles on Mr. Tamponi shifted gears and drove away from the hospital.

Traffic was light this early in the morning, so Mr. Tamponi zoomed along the
roads weaving in and out of the few cars that were out already. Before he knew it,
the car was pulling to a stop outside his house and he was waving goodbye to
them as they drove away. Pulling the key from under the rug in the front of his

house he unlocked the door and walked in. Kicking off his shoes and tossing them in a corner he looked at the living room.

Off white carpets hugged the walls from one side to the other, never showing the hard wood floor beneath them. He liked the hard wood floor, but his mother didn't and had the carpets put there instead. He didn't see why she did; she was never home to enjoy them anyway. The tan colored couch sat against the heater and faced the widescreen TV that sat on the dark wooden table in a corner. His school picture hung a little off to the right from the TV, in a gold frame. His mother's picture was just beneath his only a little to the left followed by his father's picture a little more to the left.

James turned and walked into the kitchen with its cold tiled floor and clean white walls and opened the fridge. Milk, carrots, day old spaghetti, meatloaf, and some microwave dinners. Nothing looked good enough to eat for breakfast. He hadn't exactly eaten a lot of food at the hospital. The food there was okay, but not really to his liking. Mac-n-cheese wasn't his favorite and the chicken there tasted like rubber. With a shrug he grabbed a banana from a basket on top of the fridge and ate it.

As he threw the peel into the already full garbage can a vaguely familiar sound met his ears. A rare sound to hear at this time of day, at least. A car door slammed shut and he could hear the sound of high heels on the driveway. James dashed to the living room and stopped as his mother walked through the door.

Her short hair was as dark as his and hung just below the circular earrings she wore everyday. She had a small nose like him and a few freckles on her face here and there. She stood up from taking off her shoes and smiled at him. She set down her briefcase, crossed the floor and gave him a hug. He couldn't believe it, she was actually home, and actually spending it giving him a hug. He couldn't remember the last one he'd gotten. She pulled herself away and looked at him and smiled again.

"Well, you look well." She said. "Are you feeling better? I got the message the doctor left and came home as soon as I could. Michael wanted to come, he really tried, but he was stuck in work and couldn't get away."

Figures, dad's always 'stuck at work'. It was okay, he guessed, at least mom was home. Maybe she would actually stick around until he had to go back to school tomorrow. They could sit and have dinner, and then maybe breakfast before he left. What would they do in between meals? She was good at chess and checkers, maybe she could teach him how to play or maybe …

"I have some more news, some really great news, James." He looked down at her, he forgot how much taller he was over her. "I have a new assignment!" His stomach burned, his hands started shaking in anger. "It's down in Virginia. Mr. Killington wants me to go down there and see if I can't smack around the guys down there into joining our organization! Just think, if they do join, we will be the largest organization in the business! I might even get promoted, which means I can ... James? James, where are you going?"

He couldn't believe it! She was home not two minutes and already she was talking about work! He had been in the hospital most of yesterday and all last night, and she didn't even seem to care! Slamming both his feet into his shoes he almost pushed the door off its hinges as he stormed out the door and down the street. He didn't hear his mother calling after him as he ran through the neighborhood and into the more active part of the city.

Fists clenched tightly at his side and a grimace etched on his face so sharp that three people backed out of his way as he walked passed them. It sounded as if they started talking about him when they thought him out of ear shot, but still he ignored them. He thought if he tried to say something a little harsh he would explode and say more than he thought appropriate and that could only end with him getting hurt.

The tall buildings loomed over him as the day went on and he continued through the town. Tall as they might try and be, they couldn't stop the sun from peeking over their roofs and beaming on him. His neck soon felt like it was burned and his shirt was starting to stick to his back, not to mention the fact that his head was sweating profusely and his stomach was dead empty.

There was a McKing's down the street from where he was, and they served breakfasts this early. He checked his pockets and sighed with relief to see his wallet was there. He knew he had at least ten bucks in there and that would be more than enough to tide him over until his mother was gone from the house. After getting his bearings straight he headed off south towards the McKing's.

Wonder what I'll get ... whatever is fine.

Cars flew by taking their drivers to wherever they needed to go. Several honked their horns as they passed making him jump as they drove away laughing. Others simply yelled at each other through the windows. By the time he got to the McKing's his mood hadn't improved at all.

"Welcome to McKing's. May I take your order?"

"I will have ..." James scanned the menu for a moment, "I will have the Bacon-egg-and-Cheese bagel ... and a chocolate milk."

"Will that be all? That will be three dollars and thirteen cents." James handed her a five and she gave him back his change along with a receipt. "It will be ready in a minute. May I help whose next?"

James walked down the line of registers to the end and waited for his food. When someone called his number he came forward, gave them the receipt and took his food to a seat in the back. The Play Arena had only one little kid in it that was being watched by a very nervous mom as he slid down the slide into the plastic-ball pen. The kid was laughing but the mom was calling to him asking him to come out now so they could go.

It was good for fast food. A little grease dripped on his chin but he wiped it on the back of his hand then on his shorts. The only real good thing was the milk, thick and chocolaty tasting all the more like an actual chocolate shake. When he was done he threw the wrapper and cup away and headed towards the door. He glanced at a clock in the wall; 9:27. It was almost time for his second class at school, he thought, Chris would have his nose in his notebook scanning over his notes one last time before the test while Darrel would be trying to think of some way to cheat while cramming anything and everything he could into that thick head of his.

He would have to take the test tomorrow, and it would be different from the other two of course. *Guess it's about time I started studying myself.* So with his mood not any better when he came in, he left. Not wanting to have to endure the cars again, he decided to take a side route through some back streets to get to the library. It may be a little longer, but it was definitely better than being honked at constantly. Turning down an alley between the Kalh's and Price Cutter a block away from the McKing's he started walking a little faster.

He didn't like this part of town that much. People smoked pot all the time, not to mention the fact that there were rumors of a drug seller and a gang base. The walls of the two stores gave way to a long back road with fences lining both sides and dirt and weeds popping up all over the place. Houses of all shapes and colors and sizes peeked over the fences, silent from the lack of people around at this hour. Taking a deep breath he started down the road.

About halfway down the road it happened. The pain in his chest just burst forth, flowing through his entire body this time. *I shall have you ... this time. You shall ... not escape me again!* He immediately fell to the ground in a fit of convulsions, twitching in pain. His head hit the ground making stars appear before his eyes and the world started spinning again. Every muscle in his body seemed to be on fire, burning and burning! He tried to cry out, call for help, but his voice was caught in his throat, choking him.

Then it was gone.

The burning, spinning, and pain just stopped and he was left there on the ground in a ball gasping for breath. His hands were still twitching as he lay there staring at the ground. Steadying his hands he pushed himself off the ground and on to his knees then was on his feet, leaning up against one of the fences. Taking a few wobbly steps he started off towards what he thought was the direction of the hospital.

I must be crazy to go there, but this is serious. Damn it …

There was another small gap between two houses that led back to the main street and that to the hospital which was only a few minutes drive from his school. The two houses were about three feet apart from each other allowing him to squeeze through rather easily. Just as he was about to enter out into the streets, something caught onto his foot. He looked back thinking to see some street bum or druggy trying to mug him or something, but instead he saw it was … the ground?!

Right where his foot was sat a pool of, what was it, water? No, water wasn't gray colored, and this didn't feel wet through his shoes. He tried to tug his foot loose from whatever it was, but as he did it latched on tighter while getting a better grip on his ankle. James started to panic, whatever it was it was starting to pull at him now, not just hold him. He felt his body being pulled lower towards the ground while the puddle thing got bigger very quickly.

He felt the puddle leech up his leg, sending a shiver up his spine and making him go limp. His entire body was like jell-o on a hot day and the puddle was soaking him up like a sponge. He tried to call out for help, surely someone out in the streets would hear him and come to help, but his voice was gone. A sick feeling swept over him and the pain came back two fold from the last attack.

Suddenly it felt like a branding iron was pressed against his forearm. He tried to cry out, but his voice was still caught in his throat. His insides burned and twisted as the puddle continued swallowing him whole, into the dark depths. His torso was almost completely swallowed now and it continued to sink deeper and deeper.

NOW COME TO ME!

The last thing he saw before he was completely swallowed was a bird flying over the streets and out of view …

Over head the bell rang to end the second class of the day and the scraping of chairs could be heard throughout the school. Chrissie closed her books and stuffed them into her backpack before clutching it to her chest and walking out the door and into the tempest of the hallway. People bumped into each other making them bump into more people forever in a never ending cycle.

Stepping into the current she was immediately forced to walk down the B-wing and past the D-wing and finally making her way to the K-wing and her locker. She never really looked at the floor or the lockers, their colors were too ugly. Spinning the dial on her lock she opened the door and set her backpack down on the ground. Kneeling on the floor she dug out her history book and set it into the bottom part of the locker-ladder she had bought a while back to better organize her locker.

Shifting the books on the first shelf she grabbed the thick psychology book and set it in the main pocket of the backpack. Closing the zipper she swung it over her shoulder without thinking. Standing up she turned back to the maelstrom, took a deep breath, and dove in. For a few more minutes she was pushed and bumped into, as she tried to steer her way to the classroom over in the A-wing.

But as she came up to it the crowd wouldn't let her through. She tried to cross the raging currents, but they were too strong and she was forced back into the B-wing. When she saw a break in the waves she dashed into it only to be forced into a space between a locker and a classroom. She almost fell on the two people already there, but caught herself before she more than bumped into their shoulders. She looked up at the two people and gasped.

"Chris, Darrel, what are you two doing here? I thought your next classes were in K-wing."

"Well they are." Chris said with a frown. "But the stupid crowd is too thick for us to get there now, so we're waiting for it to thin down some before trying to get to class before the bell."

"What about you? Aren't you somewhere in A-wing?" Darrel asked.

"Same here." She said looking over her shoulder at the crowd.

"So what were you saying?" Chris said turning back to Darrel. "You got a weird feeling in the back of you're head?"

"Yeah … it was so weird. One minute I'm taking Meaner's test, and the next minute I have the strongest urge to get up and leave and look for James."

"What do you mean 'look for'?" Chrissie's brow furrowed and she clutched her backpack straps tighter. "He's at home, right?"

"Well that's where my parents and I dropped him off. But whatever, this feeling you said you got, it was probably just your brain starting to work for the first time since … God knows when."

"Funny guy." Chris ducked as the paper ball flew passed his head and bounced off the wall. "This is serious, Chris. I don't know why or how I know, but I am positive that something has happened."

"Alright, alright … look why don't we go over to his house after school? Will that make you happy?" Darrel nodded. "Good, now let's get to class before … RIIIIIIINGGGG!!!!!

"Damn it, Darrel! Now we're late for class! MOVE IT!"

Chrissie watched as the two of them rushed off; well Chris rushed, and Darrel was being pulled along. When she was alone, she looked down the hallway. There were a few people left who reluctantly strode into their classrooms. What if Darrel was right? What if James was in trouble? Maybe the pain had come back again and he had collapsed somewhere. His parents, according to him and his friends, were never really home so that would make him all alone while he was in pain.

"Miss Malloy, what are you doing just standing there?"

Chrissie jumped and turned to see Mr. Wicker peeking out of his classroom door. She hated that man … she really hated that man. He was probably checking to see if he could get some kid in trouble for lagging behind … *OOPS! That's me!* Turning on her heel she walked as fast as she could without making a scene and into her classroom …

Is this what death is like? I wonder if this place is like the Hell that Moira had to go through to save her husband from the clutches of the devil. Maybe if I run into the guy I can ask him.

He laughed. What was he doing? Here he was, floating around in some dark place that had no end to it and he was thinking about the *Adventures of Moira Naomi*. He must be mad.

But, what else is there to do? I can't think of any way out of this. In the books, the hero has some partner come and rescue them from the dark places. But I'm no hero and I have no partners.

"Come to me, my tool …"

What the …? Where did that come from and what was it?

"Come to me and help me …"

Help … you …?

"Together we can bring an end to it all …"

An end? To what? Why bring an end …?

"An end to all … all the living … all the mortal …"

But … I don't want …

"Wh-what's this? I-I am losing my hold … No! He must cross the border at least …!"

I don't want to end it all …

"Damn it, I have no more power …"

The voice was shouting in rage as it faded into the distance. Above him or below—the darkness had no real direction to it—a small orange light started flickering. All around him the space seemed to heat up as the light grew stronger. Soon it stopped flickering and the light was shining in a constant beam. Not knowing why he reached for the light, not with his arms, with his mind.

Taking hold of the light he started pulling himself out of the darkness. Now the light started shimmering in the distance and the area around him started to change, he could feel the tightness of the dark start to lift. The space started changing, becoming ... becoming what? Where had he felt this odd feeling before? He knew that he had somewhere back home. The light continued to shimmer ...

Shimmer? That's it!

Water. He was in water, a pool of water somewhere ...

The city ...

Right, he had been in the city on his way to the library so he could study for the math test tomorrow.

With that thought running through his head he felt his arms and legs start swimming towards the light and hopefully the surface. His clothes were soaked through and weighing him down, but he didn't care; the sudden realization that he couldn't breathe pushed him harder than anything else could have. The light was getting brighter, closer, the more he swam but his lungs were burning from lack of air. He had to get to the surface ...

With a splash and a gasp James breeched the surface of the water.

CHAPTER 3

▼

LOST AND FOUND

HIGH above, a hawk circled the sky; silently watching as something came bursting from the lake center. Ripples broke out in every direction as the figure of a human appeared. Now that was an odd thing, even for the hawk. Turning in a tight circle it flew down and landed on the branch of a thick birch and watched the human. It splashed around for a moment before stopping dead still. Could it know it was being watched? The hawk turned its head and peered down closer with a golden eye.

James looked around him with eyes wide as plates. He was surrounded by tall trees, not buildings, ranging from what looked like birch, pine, and maple, not Kahl's, Price Cutter, and houses. The lake water was freezing despite the fact that it was almost summer back home. He shivered, but not from the cold. Back home? If he wasn't in the city, surrounded by buildings and streets and people, then where was he, surrounded by trees and water?

Nothing made any sense. Where was he? How did he get here? And how could he get back home? He looked up into the trees and saw a hawk staring at him with a large golden eye. *I am not your prey you dumb bird.* Again he shivered and realized he was still in the middle of the lake. Spotting the closest patch of land he made for it. He wasn't the best swimmer, but he managed enough to get to land.

Only when he reached solid ground did he realize his glasses were missing. He could see pretty well without them but things had a blurry outlining, and he got major headaches when he wasn't wearing them. Turning back to the lake he cursed his luck. They were probably at the bottom, and who knew how deep it went. Taking a deep breath he dove back into lake and started for the bottom. The water was pitch black when he reached the sandy dirt floor and even though he ran his hand over the surface for them he couldn't find them. When he couldn't hold his breath any longer he pushed off towards the surface.

Again he broke the surface of the water and made for the patch of land. Leaning against one of the maples he looked up into the thick branches over head. They were slightly blurred and the light wasn't great but from what he could tell it was midday. The sun was high over head trying its best to penetrate the barrier of branches.

"This is just my luck!" he shouted. "First I wind up—wherever this place is, then I lose my glasses, AND I'm soaking wet! Can this get any worse?"

With enough rage boiling in his veins James stalked off into the forest. Above a hawk screeched and took flight and the trees rustled in the wind, but he ignored them all. His shoes squished with the water and his shirt and shorts weighed him down, but he ignored them too. He was so focused on finding his way out of this forest and back home he surprised himself.

So focused that his foot caught on an uplifted tree root and he fell flat on his face with a shout. James lay there in the dirt with his mind spinning his head throbbing. But instead of getting up and dusting himself off, he cried. He was scared. That was what he was, scared of being lost and alone in some place that he didn't know. Scared that he might not be able to make it home or see his friends again.

"Why do you cry?"

James' head shot up and his eyes cringed at the bright light above him. But despite the light he found himself unable to look away, for standing in the light was the most beautiful woman he had ever seen. Her long golden hair fell just short of the ground. Bright green eyes, eyes he could have stared into for eternity, stared back at him with the softest look behind them that made his rage and sadness evaporate instantly. A long golden dress covered her from top to bottom, but it looked faded, like if he looked closer he could see through it. Then he realized he was still on the ground.

Without thinking he got up and knelt before the woman and his right fist on the ground and left arm crossing his upright knee. With his head bowed low he said the only thing he could think of.

"My Lady."

She had such a sense of power around her that it was all he could do no to fall on his stomach and beg her to command him. Instead she smiled and knelt down next him and placed a hand under his chin and lifted his face. Her touch was like silk, no—softer than silk, and those eyes were so beautiful. The Lady smiled and reached behind her and when she brought her hand back she held something in it.

"I think these are yours."

"My glasses!" Taking them from her outstretched hand he set them in place and looked back at the woman in thanks.

With his vision fully restored she was even more beautiful than ever and the aura of authority over her became even stronger. The Lady took hold of his shoulders and helped him to his feet.

"Lady, where is this place?"

The words spilled out before he could stop them and he held his breath afraid she would be upset at his manner. Again she laughed, even softer than before, it made his insides squirm. Holding a hand before him she began walking into the forest.

"You are in Arollay, James Richards."

Again he couldn't keep himself from speaking.

"Arollay? Where's that? And how do you know my name?"

"Dear boy, I am the Lady of the Gray Wood. Anything that happens in my forest is known to me. And you are someone special, someone important by the looks of it."

The two of them walked into a break in the forest where a small flower patch lay bathing in the clouded sun light. The flowers were bright red and yellow with blue and pink mixed in here and there. The Lady walked to the edges of the flower bed and stared at it. James could only wait for her to continue. He still didn't know where this Arollay place was or how he got here. And what did she mean he was an important person?

"You sure have a lot of questions and not so much patience." The Lady said without looking at him. "You wish to know where you are, yes?" He nodded. "You are in a world apart from your own, one across a barrier that separates our worlds from each other. This world is Arollay, a land of many things magical and mysterious. Your world is known to you as Earth, a land of technology and civilization that is thousands of years more advanced than this."

James felt his stomach turn, and managed to hold his food down with great effort. Another world? How can that be possible? It didn't make any sense. How could he be in another world?

"How ... how can this be?" He sat down hard in shock. "Why me? Why did it have to be me?"

"A question many people ask everyday when something bad happens to them. I do not know why it was you who was brought here, but I may have an idea as to the reasoning behind it." She glided over to him and knelt down. "Show me your right arm."

His arm? He didn't know what anything had to do with his arm, but he did as she asked. Taking his arm in her left hand, she placed her right over the back of his hand. It was then that he saw something different about it. Along his hand and forearm the skin was lighter, almost like a scar—that burning feeling when he was bring dragged into the darkness, it must have been more than just a feeling. She began whispering something and a soft green halo appeared around her hand. The light was very warm and comforting, like a massage. Setting her first two fingers on his hand she dragged them down his hand and forearm and stopped halfway. A twinge of heat ran down his arm after her fingers and stopped where they did.

Just when he thought things were normal, as normal as they could get right now, something more outrageous, more shocking than anything thus far happened. As if someone with a black marker were writing on his arm, line after line began appearing on his skin. They snaked their way around each other, connecting, crossing, until finally they stopped in the three most bizarre rune-like symbols he'd ever seen. The first, on the back of his palm, was a single line pointing towards his fingers with two parallel U-shaped lines breaking it at its center. The second, on top of his wrist, was two lines crossing like an X with a circle at the epicenter.

The third rune, just below his wrist, was a circle with a small v at the center and a horizontal line crossing above it without touching the circle. He stared at the three marks one after the other, over and over. His fingers ran over his arm but it didn't feel any different. The Lady only nodded and stood.

"It is as I thought." She turned back to the flower bed and crossed her arms behind her back. "The Words, Ygramier ... I never thought to see them again; yet here they are, marking this youth." She turned away from him and began pacing slowly around the garden. James strained to hear her. "Odd as it is ... explains how he got here ... where did the first come from ... what can this mean? Why does the Law hide this from me? Something is amiss in Arollay."

She spoke like he wasn't there. He sat there staring at his arm and the three runes. What was so strange about these runes? Sure, he'd never seen anything like them before, and it wasn't every day that things were drawn by an invisible force on someone's skin. The Words ... what're they?

"The Words are a series of phrases that are used by the creatures of the land and me." James looked up. *How does she read my mind like that?* "These words are not used for conversation like we speak, but instead they are used as mediums, or channels, for certain abilities and powers. Each word has power within it, and each word can be used with another. But like I said, these words are not fluent enough to be called a language, and thus are not used as such."

"So you know what these markings mean, right?"

"Yes." She turned to him with an empty face; it was unnerving. "The first one, on your hand, is the rune for Tuhugara or death. The second, on your wrist, is the rune for Amahyl or strength. And the third, on your arm, is the rune for Eliferen or life. These were the three Words that the Land forbade any creature to speak because of the destructive powers they all carry.

"Knowing how dangerous they were, they never spoke of the words to humans or anything that was not aligned with them in the ways of life."

"But, why are they inscribed on my arm?"

Her face was softer now, and the glow from her eyes was back too. "I do not know why they have appeared on your arm; that is the mystery. But do not fear James Richards. You are not capable of using the Words because you do not know the *true* meaning of the words. While you may know their translations, without their meanings, their essences, they are as harmless as the words we use now."

That was a relief. He didn't want to have to worry about dying from explaining what the words were to someone by accident. The people back home would think they were just tattoos, odd ones at that. He shivered at that thought; back home ... how was he to get back? Could she help? Surely she could. Someone of her abilities could do anything.

"I cannot send you home."

His breathing stopped, his eyes widened slowly, his heart slowed. She couldn't send him home?

"But why?! Why can't you? You ... you said that you were not human, so that must mean that you have powers no one else does! Surely you can send me back through the lake ...!"

"James, my powers are indeed great," she said slowly. "Far greater than any mortal's in fact; but the kind of power used to bring you here is much greater and more dangerous than mine." She looked at him with those green eyes. "Even if I knew the power, I do not think I would use it, for that would endanger the world even more."

He couldn't believe he was hearing this. She couldn't, no … *wouldn't*, help him! His breath caught in his throat as he stepped backwards into a tree. He was stuck here, in another world; in Arollay. He could never get home …

"That is not entirely true, James." He looked up from his thoughts. "There might be a way to get you back home."

"There is!? Tell me please!"

The Lady held up her hand and he settled down. She looked at him with a very serious look and walked closer to him. Laying a hand on his shoulder she looked into his eyes.

"The only way I can think of to get you back to your own world is to find the one who brought you here. They are the only one I know of who has the power to do so. But," James held back his question and closed his mouth. "But I don't know who that person is, where they are, or anything about them. So I am unable to help you."

Figures, he thought.

But maybe, maybe this wasn't entirely a bad thing. He was in another world, yes, but the Lady had said it was a world of magic, and he'd loved books about that kind of world the most. And he had felt in need of some type of vacation away from his ordinary life. Sure, this was a bit extreme, but still … He wondered if his mother would be looking for him by now.

He turned from the Lady and began walking in a wide circle around the flower bed looking at the tall trees, the brush underneath them, and the wildlife that was starting to wander around. Everything was so peaceful and pure; nothing could defile a place like this. If a forest was this wonderful, what did the rest of Arollay look like? He wanted to see it now, even if it meant he wouldn't get home right away. What were the towns and cities like? According to his books they were usually only a quarter, if that, of the cities back home.

People in this kind of world wouldn't have jobs like his parents. They would be farmers, merchants, bakers, tanners, blacksmiths, potters, even peddlers. Instead of cars there would be horses and wagons, maybe even some carriages for the wealthy. What kind of animals lived in Arollay? Were they anything like the ones in his world, or were they so bizarre that his first sighting of them would blow his mind? The more he thought about the possibilities, the more he wanted to get out of these woods and see them!

Then he realized his mouth was hanging open and his eyes were round as plates. Shaking his head he started back toward the Lady. His shoes squished from the water that was still in them. Wait … his clothes! If Arollay was nowhere near as advanced as his, like the Lady had said, then they wouldn't have polyester shirts and khaki shorts or sneakers. He'd stick out like a sore thumb!

"Ah, yes, what to do about that." The Lady walked over to him and circled him, looking at his wet clothes. "We definitely cannot have you running about in those; people would notice. Maybe I can … yes, yes, that shouldn't be a problem."

She walked behind him and turned the collar of his t-shirt over and read the tag. *How does she know what it says? Do they use the same letters as we do? I hope so! I don't want to have to relearn my ABC's!*

"Yes we use the same characters in writing as you do, though ours has some minor differences." She paced around him twice, taking in his middle width, and overall height. "Well, I'm sure I can get close enough." Stepping over to a tree, she placed a hand on the trunk and the halo of green light enveloped her hand again. "Ytre, comolyn ihr tuum amahyl."[1]

James listened to the words she spoke; he only recognized the last. As the words reverberated through the empty grove the wind picked up and the sound of birds taking flight broke the silence that had been. Yet he saw that the same hawk that he had first seen and had followed them, stayed perched on a branch of a tall maple across from the Lady. *Dumb bird.* The trunk of the tree began to shimmer like water. The green light around the Lady reached into the tree making it shimmer more and more. Then it stopped; quicker than he could blink, the trunk was solid again. Hanging on a stub of a branch that hadn't been there before was a set of clothes.

He recognized them from something he saw on the cover a book. *Wow, I read a lot more than I thought I did. Feels kinda sad.* There was a white long sleeved shirt at the forefront. Its long arms looked cuffed, but didn't have any buttons. It was a baggy like shirt that was about equal in length to the t-shirt he was wearing now. Behind it was a half-sleeve tunic; probably made out of cotton by the feel of it. It was as brown as the tree bark it had come from with a hint of dark green, and had black strings from the center of the chest up to the neck that looped through silver rings. There were belt loops through it and a black, seemingly leather, belt with a silver buckle.

---

1. Tree, lend us your strength

Behind the tunic was a pair of pants, brown like the tunic, and long enough to fit him from waist to the bottom of his foot. There was a string at the waist for resizing, but no pockets. Then he saw what was laying underneath all the clothes on the ground; a pair of boots. They were black like the belt and were big enough to go half way up his calves and had laces running all the way up the front. They were the coolest things he'd ever seen.

"These will help you blend in while you are here." The Lady smiled at the look on his face. "I wish I could do more to help you."

"My Lady, you have done more for me than most people in my life thus far." *Wow, I think I'm already starting to talk differently. Oh boy ...* "I thank you from the bottom of my heart."

"Do not thank me, please." She dropped her gaze. "I cannot bring you back to your world, I am not ..."

"My Lady," she looked up as he took her hand, "Right now that does not matter. What has happened cannot be undone except by the one who did it, like you said. I will look for this man and make him send me back home. Until then, I will live my life here, in Arollay. Please, do not be sad over something that you have no control over."

She smiled and turned back to him with her face aglow. "You are a kind person, James Richards."

The Lady turned her back while James changed into the new clothes. The shirt was the first and fit more comfortably than any shirt he'd worn before. It was parted down the middle with white laces looping through which he tied half-way and left them loose. The tunic was loose, like a windbreaker, but so much warmer. He hadn't realized the change in weather at first; it was much cooler in Arollay than his world for some reason. Keeping the belt untied, he went to work on the pants. They went on nicely and did indeed go all the way down to the bottoms of his feet.

The black leather was already broken in and seemed to mold around his foot like a second skin. Before tying the laces, he tucked the pant legs in so that they slightly bulged at the boot tops. He looked like the stable boy on the cover of *Eric's Magic Tale ... Wow; I gotta stop comparing things to my books ... yeesh!*

The Lady turned when he was done and smiled saying he looked very nice. She said she had one more thing for him so he could keep his old clothes. Placing a hand on the ground and whispering a few more of the Words, she produced a dark brown pack! It was big enough to hold his old clothes and shoes and even a little more. There was a single strap that fit across his chest and was wide enough that it wouldn't cut into his shoulder if he wore it for a long time. He didn't know what else to say ... so he said, "Thank you."

"Now come with me James, it is time you rest and since you have had a hard day I shall let you stay in my wood for the night." Taking the lead she started into the forest again with James close behind. "I have a place where travelers may rest whenever they stumble into my domain and now it shall be yours to use."

The two of them walked on in silence the rest of the way. The Lady stared straight ahead the whole time and James kept himself buried in thought. Everything was happening so fast. But he accepted them now with little question. He was in another world, with no way to leave, but somehow he wasn't as upset about it as he had been at first. Maybe this wouldn't be so bad.

Above, he heard a bird take flight and looked up to see the same hawk that had been watching him when he had first appeared in the lake. It was a dark brown color with a little black here and there. It kept staring at him with one big golden eye making him wish he could disappear. A thought came to him.

"Lady, you said this was a magic place, right?" She nodded without looking at him. "If that's so, does that mean I can use magic too?"

She stopped for a second before continuing into the forest, a little quicker it seemed. He had to lengthen his stride to keep up with her now. Her golden dress hovered just above the ground as she glided through the woods, the brush and dirt never seeming to get in her way or ever touch her. His boots crunched under every twig and chunk of moss he stepped on, and his pant legs brushed against each other with every step.

"Your world has no magic in it, this I know." She never once looked at him while she spoke, she only walked on. "However, you are now part of this world and in Arollay, all that are born are empowered with one of two types of power. Being from another world I do not know if you have this same power." She paused for a moment as if in thought. "Yet, if you are capable of using one of the powers then that might explain one reason why you were brought here. Whoever it was could have planned on using your strength for their intentions. But, I cannot say for sure."

"Two types of power?" he asked. Use his strength? He did have the rune of Power on his arm so it was a possibility that he was strong. But how strong was he really? And what would they use him for?

"Arollay's people are split by their powers." She said as they walked by a family of deer. "The people on this continent, Intaru, are capable of wielding fire. Fire magic is pretty much self explanatory. An Intaruan can make fire from the air or a spark of some kind, and use it to destroy anything that normal flames can burn.

Yet, where a normal fire would take some time to burn down a tree such as these, an Intaruan could incinerate one instantly with a simple fireball.

"The people on the continent to the north of here, Gattar, are gifted with the power to manipulate ice. Ice magic is a bit more complicated and more difficult to use than fire. From what I learned by watching mankind, Gattarians gather the water around them and change it into a form of ice: snow, icicles, or even very, very, cold water. Yet that isn't all they can do. Gattarians, if trained in the art, are capable of using their powers to heal. I don't know how they do this though, so I cannot say anymore on the matter."

"When you say 'split by their powers' you mean by the fact that fire can melt ice which in turn becomes water and therefore douses fire? Or is there more to it than that?"

"Yes, there is more to it than the simple differences of fire and ice. The people of Arollay are split by their powers ... because they are at war."

War? Not here too ... I thought I would have left that ... bah, who am I kidding? War is universal.

"This war was started almost one thousand years ago when the Emperor of Intaru was almost assassinated by a Gattarian. He declared war on Gattar, yet the ice nation didn't stand by and watch as they were invaded. They sent their own troops to battle the Intaruans. Each side was equally matched and still is to this day. Battles occasionally erupt between them, but every time neither side can manage to gain ground."

This was too much. One thousand years worth of fighting ... people dying in futile attempts to get revenge for a crime a millennium old! People were stupid when it came to government ... it had to be contagious. There was no way that the people in Arollay were as thick headed as ... never mind. He would just stay away from the army of whatever nation he was on and make sure that he was not recruited into their war. He wasn't about to die like that!

The woods began to get thicker as they walked. The trees got higher and higher until he couldn't even touch the lowest branch by a few feet. The trees began to vary more as well. There were pine and spruce mixed in with the maple and oak, birch and cedar. He thought that some of the trees couldn't live in this kind of environment at first. Didn't one type need more water and different weather to grow than another? He was almost sure of it, but didn't know which ones were in which category. Then he remembered the Lady's power and dropped any doubts. She would, of course, have many different types of trees in her part of the land. It wouldn't matter what they were, she could keep them alive even in the desert.

Finally she stopped at an extremely thick maple with very low branches. It stuck out from all the tall branched trees around it, but it was beautiful none the less. The Lady waved her hand and the branches parted, revealing a hollow at the base of the trunk. It was big enough for him to walk through standing straight up and wide enough for two of him to go through at once. Inside was a dug-in fire pit ringed with round stones and dry dirt. Up against the side of the hollow, far from the fire pit, was a bed of leaves and moss long enough for a grown man to lie on comfortably.

"This is called a Traveler's Tree." The Lady said leading him inside. It was spacious. "There are many of these trees in my domains across Arollay and many people use them when needed. They have housed countless humans over the centuries and now this one shall be yours to use for the time being. When I am able to find a safe place for you to live in the outside world, then I will let you know."

She turned to him and gave him a serious look. "Beware, James Richards. Not every creature in these woods knows that you are under my protection, yet out of fear of humans, they stay away from these trees. So long as you stay here, no animal shall bring you harm. Now ..." Before she could finish, the hawk that had followed them screeched loudly from outside. The Lady turned to the hollow's entrance for a moment and seemed to stare out into space. "I must leave you."

"Wh-what?" Leave him? Here? Now? "Is something the matter? Is there anyway that I can help?"

"No, this is something that must ... never mind." She turned back to him and placed both hand on the sides of his head. A pulse of warmth ran through his limbs; it felt like being dipped into a hot bath after a cold day. "Ju uhr Kalyn, uhr bwer tuum limh ov ytr Kamrian."[2]

The words seeped into his mind and, like a vine to a fence, wound themselves around his memory. When the words were forever imprinted into his mind, the Lady took her hands away and walked to the hollow's entrance. She stopped for a moment and turned back to him. He stood there, unaware of anything around him but the same phrase repeating over and over in his head.

"I leave you now, James Richards." She said. He couldn't hear her, but she had to say it anyway. "Arollay's future rests on your hands. Only you can save it or destroy it. What I have given you is all I can for the time, until we meet again. I leave you with one final blessing; the strongest I can give. Otre ytr espirs kamri loum tuu, ae ytr Iaed jullin tuum neara. Farewell." And she was gone.

---

2. By my Power, I open your mind to the Watcher

James stood there, staring with a blank look on his face for a minute after the Lady left. When he finally snapped out of the trance, his first thought was where he was; then he looked around and remembered. Taking a seat next to the fire pit he stared at the ground. Everything around him was quiet, for once, and he liked it. There wasn't a sound to be heard from the animals, the trees, or other people … it was so calming.

But what was going to happen to him when he left the forest? He would go out and find a village or town like he planned, of course, but he had no money except for the few dollars that were in his wallet in his pants. He knew that Arollay's currency would be nothing like his own and that left him in a large pickle. Everything, no matter what world you were in, cost money; which meant he would have to find work somewhere first. But what could he do?

He wasn't very strong, so working at a smithy was most likely out of the question. He did know how to cook, *and I'm pretty good at it too,* he thought with a little arrogance. So maybe he could find an inn or tavern and work there; that way he could make some money and hopefully get a room at the same time. But what else could he do? His hand writing wasn't bad, but not great, so a scribe or whatever they were called was out. *I can't sing to save my life so barding is a no go, I can clean, so again tavern work, can only play a little piano but I doubt they have those here … man I guess an inn is my best bet.*

His thoughts were interrupted by the growling in his stomach. There were two large lumps that looked like leaves lying next to the bed. Wondering what the Lady had left him with, knowing full well that it wasn't going to be a peanut butter sandwich, he opened the first one. It held a small pile of large cats-eye marble sized red berries. Taking one he popped it in his mouth only to spit it back out. *Good lord, that's sweet!* Setting the berries down he opened the other wrapping and was glad to see some fruit he thought he recognized; an apple like fruit, one that looked like half a pear, and some strawberries. *Of course the mother nature of this world wouldn't provide meat from her creatures … oh well, it's better than nothing I suppose.*

When the fruit was gone and the berries wrapped up and put into his pack, he sat back against the side of the tree and let his mind wander a bit. Another world … another life. What were his friends doing now? By the looks of the sun it was probably somewhere around noon or one, so they were either at lunch or just getting to history. *HA! I don't need to go to history class anymore! Yahoo!* He stared for a moment. He hadn't used that phrase in a *long* time. *I guess being in another world where the speech isn't as advanced, I am starting to think more and more about the slang we use. Once I get in contact with people I'll have to be careful of what I say. Anything strange like 'yahoo' or something and people will wonder.*

What would he tell people he met? They would want to know where he came from and he didn't know any cities' names or those of some small villages. He couldn't say he was from another world; they'd hang him for being mad or something. What did the people in his books do in situations like this? He couldn't think of one he'd read recently that had someone being sent to another world like this, but …

"Got it." He smiled triumphantly. "If anyone asks where I'm from, I can act like I have amnesia! That's perfect, really. That way I can be ignorant of things for real and people will not think that I'm just plain stupid. They'll think I can't remember things and teach me. Guess I should start working on a story then. Let's see …"

A few hours passed by with nothing of interest happening. He had completed the tale he would tell people, and was satisfied it would fool anyone enough so they wouldn't be able to question him too hardly. He was just about to lie down for a nap when he got the urge to 'go'. Ducking under the hollow's entrance he stepped up next to a tree sitting next to the traveler's tree.

He was just finishing when he got the funny feeling like he was being watched. He looked around but there wasn't anyone around; then he looked up into the trees.

There, perched on the branch of a maple across from the traveler's tree and only a few paces away from his current spot, was the same hawk that had watched him when he popped out of the lake. It had also followed him when the Lady had taken him to the grove. What was it following him for? Could the Lady be using it to watch him?

Ducking back into the hollow he lay on the bed of leaves and tried to go to sleep. After lying there for a minute he sat up, untied the belt around his tunic and took it off. Setting it on the ground next to him and unlacing the top of his shirt he went to work taking off his boots. He didn't need to completely unlace the boots, just loosen them a bit before he could slip them off. Sleep felt closer with the uncomfortable things off and when he rested his head on the soft pile of leaves, it rushed through him faster than thought.

There is trouble … you must wake up …! Blurry pictures formed inside his mind, overtaking the dream. He felt fear, but was it from him or *for* him? Sleep still controlled his mind, but more and more the feeling of fear grew until it overpowered it. His eyes opened and he sat up from the bed of leaves. It was dark outside; moonbeams broke through the branches in places outside the hollow of the traveler's tree. He rubbed the sleep from his eyes and pulled his boots on, tightening the laces quickly.

Grabbing the tunic and stuffing it over his head without bothering to tie the belt he crept up to the entrance and peered around. The forest was pitch black after a few yards, but the occasional moonbeam brought more of it into focus. There was complete silence all around, even more so then from earlier that day. He was about to dismiss the feeling as his imagination playing games on him when he heard something a little ways behind the traveler's tree.

He leaned a little farther out of the hollow so he could look. There, only a handful of yards behind the tree, were a group of men. From the shadows he could make out, there seemed to be only six of them, but there could be more outside his vision. One of them passed into a moonbeam, throwing his features into view. He had a full beard covering the lower half of his face and a mop of stringy dark hair sticking out in all directions. His clothes looked somewhat like James' but more broken in.

He had a black vest instead of a tunic that was draped over his shoulders. There was a dark colored shirt underneath it, but with the poor light, he couldn't tell the color. Yet it was the glint of steel coming from his hand that caught his attention the most. Sure enough, there in his left hand was a short sword. He'd seen a picture of one before on the internet and knew it wasn't the best weapon around, but in the right hands …

The man looked over towards James' direction. Ducking back into the hollow he pressed himself up against the wall and hoped beyond hope that he hadn't been …

"Hey, I saw someone over there!"

DAMN IT! What do I do? Think, think!! But he couldn't come up with anything. If he tried to run, they would chase him down, if he stayed … if he stayed they might kill him, or maybe they would only take him prisoner. There was a slight chance, a *very* slight chance that they weren't bad people and would be able to take him to some village or …

"You, I know you're in there!" The man said in a deep gruff voice. "Come out slowly on all fours. If you don't I will burn the entire tree from the inside out!"

Definitely not good guys! Quick as a flash he was crawling on all fours out of the traveler's tree. The man who had found him used the flat of the sword to lift his face to him. The others came out from the shadows and looked at James as well. They wore similar clothes to his first capture.

"Who the flaming hell is this?" One man said to his right.

"The hell should I know?" The one with the sword said. "Probably some kid from the village that came to rescue his girl." The others laughed. "What's your name boy?"

"James. James Richards."

"What the flaming hell kind of name is that?" someone said behind him.

"An odd one." The man with the sword replied again. "So, boy did you come from the village? Are you one of the village dogs come for revenge? Did you come for the girl?"

Village? Girl? He suddenly had a terrible thought. *Oh no! These guys must be bandits or something. They must have raided a town close by and had some girl prisoner.* He gulped.

"Well, why won't you answer me, boy?" James flinched as he pressed the sword harder to his neck. "I won't ask you again; are you from the village?"

Okay, okay … should I play along or go with the amnesia … "I am from … the village, yes."

The men behind him laughed darkly as the one with the sword to his neck squatted down so they were face to face. His eyes were brown, very brown, and he had a dark complexion underneath the beard. The worst part was—his breath smelled like month old milk!

"A brave fool you are, coming after us alone like this." The others laughed again. "Or *did* you come alone? Did anyone come with you?!"

"N-no, they—they stayed at the village." He was trying to think up a story, something he could say, but it was harder than he thought and the fact that he was surrounded by six men, all armed, didn't help matters. "I-I wanted to get her back, but the others … they were too scared."

"Now why would they be scared of us?" Someone behind him asked with a laugh. "We didn't hurt them *that* badly."

"Shut your trap, Yasa." The man to his right said sternly. "Gronl, just kill the kid and let's go. Meran doesn't like to be kept waiting."

James' breath caught in his throat and he closed his eyes. This was it!

"Aw, but think of the price he could fetch on the market." *Market? Oh crap! Slavers!* "He's a decently tall boy with a little muscle to him. He'd make a fine worker. We could even play with his numbers a bit and make him worth even more! Meran would agree with me. I say we take him with us."

I have to get away from these people! I don't want to be a slave! Maybe he could out run them. He was kind of fast, not track-star material, but still fast. If he could push past one of the men to his right then he could make a break for it through the woods. He looked to his right at the men standing there and saw that the one closest to him only had a small knife in his hands and wasn't that much bigger than he was.

The man with the sword stood up to speak with the one who wanted to just kill him. With the sword gone, all he had to do was go … NOW! Quick as he could, he shot off the ground and literally ran over the man with the knife. Behind him he heard the men shout curses and threats as they gave chase. His legs flew across the ground faster than he thought they could go, leaping over the tree roots and brush.

He ran passed a spruce when a flash of urgency rushed through his mind. He almost tripped from shock, but he righted himself and kept running. The urgency then turned to anger making him pulse with adrenaline! What was happening to … Just like in his dream, a picture popped into his mind, overtaking all thought. It was blurry, as if he was looking at it without his glasses, but he could still make it out somehow. He saw a small bird, a morning finch, bank in mid air as a flacon dove passed it.

Without thinking why, he leapt to the ground and covered his head with his arms. As he skid across the dirt a blazing light flew through the air right where his head would have been a second before. It blazed like fire and rammed into a tree a few feet away igniting it and burning it to a cinder instantly. It *was* fire! The men shouted behind him as they got closer; so he got up and ran faster!

What the hell was that!? He thought as he ran through the brush. *Wait! The Lady said the people of this land can use magic or something like it. These people must be fire people! Why is my luck trying to kill me?!*

Trees rushed by as he blew through the woods at speeds that would shame any track runner! His life was on the line, he was Superman now! Dodging around another spruce he saw a light a little ways ahead. It looked like a small fire. Maybe they were people who were really pursuing the bandits! Behind him, the bandits shouted from far off. He was faster than he looked, that or they were slow for grown men.

The trees gave way to a clearing where the fire was burning in a small stone pit. James stumbled through the brush with hopes to see people, but instead saw no one. Before he could start running again, the night erupted in a blaze of fire encircling him and cutting off his only chance of escape. The fire domed over closing out the night sky.

Then six figures materialized on all sides from the fire dome, laughing and holding swords and axes and knives. They started closing in on him, smiling evilly, hefting their weapons. With nowhere to go James could only watch as they raised their weapons …

The moon was still shining through the branches in the small clearing when James woke. His left eye was swollen shut and his head was pounding. Not to mention the fact it felt like he had a bruised rib or four. Those men were relentless! They didn't stop beating him until he was locked safely behind the bars of his cage. He felt blood trickling down his left arm, soaking through the shirt. He could hear them laughing and shouting as they drank and sat around a burning fire.

Everything was fuzzy to look at because he had thrown his glasses off before they started beating him. The only problem with that plan was that now he couldn't see five feet out of the light from the fire. He tried sitting up slowly and, with sharp pain from his ribs nearly crippling him, managed to get into a sitting position. Leaning against the hard steel bars he stared out past the branches to the night sky. While he couldn't see the moon, from the light it gave off, he could tell it was full.

He closed his eyes and sighed bringing a small pain from his chest. He flinched and placed his right hand carefully over the ribs he thought were bruised, maybe broken. He could feel them and it didn't seem like they were broken, thankfully, but the skin was soft and warm to touch which meant he probably had a large bruise under his shirt. Despite the newness of his clothes, the bandits must not have thought them worth anything special because they didn't take them.

He was about to try and sleep some more so he could try and ignore the pain when something moved out of the corner of his vision. He slowly turned his head toward whatever it was, hoping and praying it wasn't some animal or worse locked in the cage as well. Not two feet away was the shadowy outline of a person sitting against the opposite side of the cage. Two blue globes stared at him with fear from behind a long mane of hair. One of the men fell over drunk letting a little more light shine towards the cage.

A face, almost as beautiful as the Lady's, stared back at him. Her deep blue eyes were shimmering with tears, but she was trying to hold them back. Her forehead was covered by her long flowing brown hair that reached down to her back. She had tugged her shins up close to her chest. Her clothes were similar to his; a light blue shirt that looked like a t-shirt and a pair of night pants which were also light blue, but they, like the bandits', looked to be worn down. She flinched when she saw him staring at her.

This must be the girl the bandits were talking about earlier he thought.

"Wh-who are you?" she said barely above a whisper.

"James Richards." He replied in the same tone. "Who are you?"

She didn't reply. Instead she pulled her shins in closer and tried to back away farther from him.

"It's okay. I'm not here to hurt you." Again she pulled back. "You don't honestly think I'm with the bandits, do you?"

Again she flinched, but this time she didn't pull away.

"I'm Miranda." She said, even softer than the last time. "Are you … okay?"

Then he remembered that he was bleeding and probably didn't look too presentable. He shifted his weight a little, but that only made him wince. Miranda uncurled herself and placed a hand near the cut along his arm. She traced two fingers along its length, just a hair away from actually touching it.

"This is deep. If it isn't healed soon it will start to infect." She took her hand away. "I'm afraid it will scar badly enough as it is."

"Heh. It doesn't matter. I don't even feel it anymore." He motioned to his arm that was still over his ribs with his head. "These hurt ten times worse than that. Compared to these, that's just a paper cut right now."

Another bandit fell over drunk making the others laugh and shout things with heavily slurred speech. Yet there was one man who stayed away from the fire and the booze. He had black clothes and a thin black doublet with the sleeves studded by the glint of steel from the fire light. His head was hidden behind a thick mane of wiry black hair that failed to cover the gleam in his dark eyes. In the shadows and without his glasses the man looked like a shadow himself, but the light of the fire caught the steel of a long sword at the man's hip and the way he held himself suggested he probably had a quiver full of arrows strapped to his back.

"What is it?"

He looked back to Miranda and motioned towards the sentry. She told him that he did have a bow leaning next to the tree and that he was wearing black leather-like armor. He sighed. Not having his glasses was irritating and the occasional headaches he got without them didn't help his already pounding head.

"You're really hurting aren't you?" she asked. He nodded. "If I could get my hands on some herbs I could help but …"

The sentry man's head came up and he stared at the two of them like he could hear them despite their whisperings. Those dark eyes stared at them from behind the stringy hair and a grim frown was carved onto his face. Miranda looked at him oddly when James asked what the man was doing.

"Can't you see?" She asked. "I know the light isn't perfect but still …"

"I don't have my glasses." She looked at him questioningly. "They're two small pieces of glass held together by a thin metal frame that sit in front of my eyes. They help me see."

He told her how he had thrown them off before the men started beating him and she pointed towards the edge of the encampment where a large circle of grass and dirt was burnt away.

"I was sitting here wondering where the others had gone when that man's head shot up and stared off into the darkness. Then I saw something appear out of the trees and the entire placed was engulfed in fire. I could see the threads of power used, so I could tell that whatever weave was used, it wasn't meant to kill. Then the others appeared and entered into the dome. When the flames vanished they carried you, completely beaten and bloodied to this cage and threw you in.

"Before you woke the sentry came over and looked you over. He was furious at the others for beating you so badly. I think he is not just some bandit, but the leader." She glanced back over to the dark man who was still watching them from the shadows. The third and fourth bandit fell over into a drunken sleep leaving the last one talking stupidly to himself. "I thought you were dead at first, but then you started moaning quietly and shifting now and then."

She stopped suddenly and stiffened as if she had been dunked in a tub of ice water. Her eyes stared behind him at something, but he couldn't turn to see what it was. Then he felt someone move behind him and the hairs on the back of his neck rose. The sentry moved into the corners of his vision and stared at him with those dark eyes … so dark and empty …

"This is for you, girl." He handed her something through the cage and Miranda took it with a shaking hand. He turned to James as his other hand slipped something through the bars. "I think these are yours." He stood and turned away from them. "These fools will be slow tomorrow so you will have to walk on your own the rest of the way. You will need your strength." His head turned just enough to stare at them. "But if you resist or try to run I will kill you."

He walked away back to his original spot and sat down. His head was bent as if in sleep, but the shine from his eyes told them otherwise. James turned away from the sentry and looked at what the man had brought him. He almost shouted with joy when his hand found the familiar metal frame of his glasses. He placed them gently on their perch, careful not to poke his bruised eye, and welcomed them back with a smile.

Now that he had his glasses everything was clearer. He could see the trees surrounding his prison and the sentry man sitting on the ground a little ways away.

Miranda's gift was by far the better; it was a small pack of dried meat and bread, which they ate willingly and hungrily. At the bottom of the pack were some herbs, a pestle and bowl, and a bandage for his arm.

Using the stone pestle she ground the leaves and grains in the stone bowl and, after asking the sentry for water, she mixed the grains and leaves together into a sickly green paste. Laying the bowl in front of her she took a strip of cloth and used it to apply the salve. It stung like hell and sent jets of fire running through his veins, but almost immediately he could feel it working and the pain subsided. Wrapping the bandage around his arm she smiled at her work.

James flexed his fingers and saw they had plenty of maneuverability. The sentry man was now breathing with the rhythmic breaths of sleep as she placed her tools back in the small bag. James scanned the cage and found what he was looking for right next to Miranda's shoulder. Hanging on an old fashioned latch was a padlock. It was the old type of lock with a thick block of steel with an arch locking the two ends together. He couldn't help but grin.

"Miranda, do you have a pin, or something long and sharp?" She shook her head and asked why. "I'm going to pick the lock and get us out of here."

"Pick this lock? Are you crazy? This is a strongly made lock, easily the newest model. I saw them Craft it as they were locking me in here and it took three of them to complete it." She shook her head again. "There is no way to pick it."

James took off his glasses and removed one of the ear pieces' soft covers revealing a long, but thin, steel rod. He saw that the left lens was cracked—*Just my luck again!* Leaning forward he placed the metal rod into the lock and started searching for the latch. Left and right, up and down—but he couldn't find it. Then he felt something a little to the left of the rod, twisted it around, and found the latch. *Darrel if this works I will kiss you! Well ... never mind.*

Miranda watched as he fiddled with the lock and almost gasped when she heard the tiny click of the latch give way. He told her to grasp the hinges of the door so their squeak would be dulled and pulled the lock out of place. The door opened slowly and stopped against a tree giving them enough room to just slip through. Crawling on all fours and as close to the ground as they could get they made their way from the camp and into the dark forest.

James led the way through the underbrush and when they were a good distance away they got up and started running. After a few yards she pulled him to a stop and told him to wait a moment. She rubbed her hands together and a soft glow seemed to surround them, but he couldn't really tell—probably exhaustion playing with his imagination. She reached down and rubbed her hand along the bottoms of her feet (which he just noticed were bare) and then along the bottoms of his boots before saying she was ready and started off again.

Miranda held onto his uninjured arm so they wouldn't get separated and told him there was a village two days away from the forest entrance. He only half listened as he made his way through the trees searching with eyes and mind for the damn hawk he knew was still out there. As he circled a large maple the visions began flashing into his mind again and the hawk flew just over his head.

Heart leaping he asked the hawk to lead them out of the forest and got a flash of several trees bending over a trail in the shape of an X. James veered to the left and brushed past a series of bushes that were covered in berries and saw the marking up ahead. Instantly another picture of a large birch surrounded by four thick maples flashed into view. So taking Miranda he ducked under the X shaped trees and ran head long into the forest again. Despite the darkness he thought the way they were going looked familiar. Then they ran passed a tree burnt to cinders and it clicked; he was running back the way he came!

CHAPTER 4

▼

FREEDOM, FLIGHT, FIGHT

HIS ribs were throbbing and threatened to cripple him with pain, but he pressed on knowing what would happen if they were caught. Over and over he and the hawk communicated as pictures flashed back and forth. It directed him to the traveler's tree and he grabbed his pack and slung it over his shoulder before continuing through the woods. Slowly the trees started giving way to more sky and by the time the sun was just breaking the horizon they had reached the edge of the forest. The two of them, breathing heavily from running all night, stared at the sky like a refuge—a safety. Behind them the forest towered like a fortress—a prison. Taking Miranda's hand James led her out into the grassy plains that lay stretched out before them.

For miles the plains stretched, reaching far out of view in a seemingly never ending ocean of green. A tree here and there broke through the waves of grass and up above the birds were starting to wake from their dreams. There was a single mountain in the distance that loomed over the plains, but it was so far away that it looked like a blue shadow against the sky.

They didn't stop walking until they could no longer see the forest and by the time they finally sat beneath the shade of a tree it was almost mid-morning. His side was pounding so hard he was shocked Miranda couldn't hear it. The cut on his arm was stiff from the salve, but the bandage kept it from reopening. Laying there on the soft grass the two of them quickly dozed into a dreamless sleep while the hawk sat watch in the branches.

Something was pulling at the back of his mind and the hairs on the back of his neck were straight up when he woke a few hours later. Miranda lay across from him under the shade of the tree with her long brown hair spread out on the ground. In the better light of day he could see she was very beautiful, more so than he thought back at the camp, if that was possible. Above him the hawk made noises in its throat as it watched him with a big golden eye.

He almost raised his arm to let the bird perch there before the stiffness in his ribs made him think twice on it. The sudden movement made the hawk stir and lift its head off towards the direction they had come from. Reaching over James shook Miranda's shoulder. She mumbled and turned her back to him asking for a few more minutes. He burst out laughing but caught himself as his ribs shifted. Instead of letting her sleep in, he began prodding her with his foot until she finally woke with a half snort.

"Huh? Wha ... James?" She rubbed her eyes and looked around her. The realization that they had escaped came back to her and she laughed with tears shining in her eyes. "That's right ... we're free now."

"Yep. Now all we have to do is get to that village you told me about and we'll be home free with no chance of them damned bandits catching us again."

"Oh I wouldn't say that."

The blood drained from both their faces as the sentry appeared on the other side of the tree. His black armor stood out against the light sky and his face was visible with his hair tied back. For someone who looked like he could use the sword he carried he was a small man. James and Miranda leapt to their feet and backed away. The hawk shrieked loudly and flew into the sky in a flurry of feathers. The man, however, never let them out of his sight.

"I must say, for two little brats you sure know how to make tracking you difficult." His gaze flickered over to Miranda. "That was a nifty little trick you did to hide your tracks, girl. But you forgot one thing; branches and brush snap under the lightest touch and the two of you were moving so fast and clumsily that you broke about thirty twigs every three feet. If it hadn't been for that I wouldn't have been able to follow you."

He looked back at James and tilted his head. "But what I want to know is how you picked that lock, boyo. I helped make that myself and no one but we know where the latch is. How did you?"

"Maybe you're not such a great lock maker then." He replied making sure he was between the man and Miranda. "But tell me; where are the others? Still asleep? Or are they suffering from hangovers so bad they can't move?"

The sentry's face tightened into a rage and his hand drifted towards his sword. Miranda shifted behind him and he saw the hawk circling just out of range of an arrow. He sent a thought to the hawk and told it to try and find help, but when he got no reply he figured it must be out of range of him too.

"James …" His ears twitched as Miranda whispered to him so softly that he almost didn't hear her. "Can you keep him focused on you for a moment longer?"

"What?" His lips barely moving. "Why …"

"Can you do it or not?" He nodded. "When I tell you I want you to thrust your hand out at the sentry. Don't ask, just do it."

"Hmm. What are you two talking about over there?" James shifted again. "Are you thinking of trying to run? Oh, that won't work boyo. You see, if you try I have a few options; one: I can shoot you with an arrow, two: I can burn you to a cinder with a simple fireball, three: I can chase you down and slice you to pieces. All three choices are easy enough that I won't break a sweat, and I must say I prefer the third over the others."

He unsheathed his sword and held it in front of him examining the blade. It was long enough to pierce through both of them at once and still have room for a third, maybe even a forth. The steel shone in the sunlight.

"Yes, there is nothing like the feel of your blade slicing into your opponent. Nothing like it at all. But if that opponent is willing to die then it looses its grace, its lustful feeling and …"

"Three … two … one …"

Ignoring the pain in his ribs he thrust his right hand out at the bandit with his fingers spread wide. The dark man saw him and jumped to the side clutching the sheath. As he was in mid jump, however, something erupted from behind James and soared through the air. He had enough time to see it was a stream of fire as thick as his arm. In a shower of sparks the stream collided with the bandit's right shoulder, spinning him in the air and making him shout in pain.

In a flash James was running full speed at him. The bandit only had time to gasp before the bottom of his foot was hitting him full in the face cascading him back like a limp doll; unfortunately, James went flying over his body from his own momentum.

Miranda was tackling the already downed man trying to wrench the long sword from his hand as James managed to wrap his hands around the man's throat to strangle him. The sentry gasped and tried to breathe and keep hold on his sword as he lay there with the full weight of the two of them holding him down. As his eyes started to slide up into his head he growled deeply and managed to get his hand free from Miranda's grip and thrust it into her gut. James had enough time to see a faint red glow envelope the man before ...

The explosion that followed sent her and James tumbling in different directions away from the bandit who knelt there clutching his throat with one hand and covering his right eye with the other. Blood flowed from his nose where James' boot had kicked him and there was a large imprint of his foot on his face.

James cradled his ribs as he struggled to get up. He had no idea what had happened, but he knew that Miranda was hurt. He got to his knees and saw that she was lying on the ground near the tree which had fallen over from the explosion as well. He tried calling out to her but the pain made it come out in a rasp. A picture flashed into his mind of Miranda holding her stomach where the bandit had hit her, but he couldn't see if she was bleeding or just knocked out.

He sent a thought to the hawk only to get a shriek in reply. He pleaded with the creature to help, but it only shrieked again. Breaking the connection with the hawk he slowly got to his feet and looked up to see the bandit walking towards him. A glint of steel to his right made him turn to see the man's sword lying on the ground a few feet away. The other had seen it too and was now heading towards it.

With only one thing on his mind James staggered to the blade and picked it up. It was heavy, and overbalanced, but he held it straight at the man who stopped and smiled.

"What do you think to accomplish, boyo?" He stood there with both arms hanging at his sides and a smug look on his face. "Do you intend to kill me?"

"If I have to," was all he could say. The blade was too heavy for him to hold straight anymore so he let it drop to the ground.

The man laughed and started towards him again. When he was only a few feet away James lifted the blade onto his shoulder and readied to swing it. Using all his strength he lurched forward and brought the sword around with him in a slashing motion. The bandit ducked away making the heavy steel throw James off balance. But instead of toppling over he spun around on his heel and took a second swing across the man's middle.

With a shout he barely managed to dodge the sharp blade by leaping backwards. Again James spun on his heel to bring the sword around in another slashing attack and again missed by a few inches. The bandit kept hopping backwards just missing the tip of the blade. After the fourth time around James began to lose his grip on the hilt. Taking an off balance step backwards he tried to readjust his grip, but the bandit leapt for him at that exact moment and punched him in the ribs.

Pain shot through his chest making him cry out as he crumpled to the ground in a daze. His hands clutched his ribs and upper chest unsure of which was worse. He could hear his heart beating in his ears and the world was spinning again like the last time the pain had attacked him. Above he heard the man laugh.

"Well that was … fun." He said holding his long sword in one hand and twirling it around before setting it just above James' neck. "Shame all good things must come to an end, eh boyo?"

He could feel the steel hanging just above him as he cradled his chest with both hands trying not to cry. The sound of the sword being raised made his heart beat faster, which was now pounding in his ears like a pair of drums. He braced himself for the end when a loud shriek and a cry of rage made him look up. The man was backing away swatting at a mass of brown and black feathers that attacked his face.

A vision of two mice racing across a field flashed into his mind as the hawk clawed at the man's face with those sharp talons. He shoved the image away and quickly got to his feet and tackled the man to the ground, one hand to his throat, the other to his sword hand. The hawk shrieked even louder as it continued to claw at the bloody mess of a face. The man's free hand found James' throat and quickly tightened, cutting off his air.

His vision was going blurry but he didn't ease up his attack. Using his weight he shifted to the right and managed to yank the sword free. The heavy blade rose in the air and came down on the man's head. Eyes rolled into the back of his head and the hand holding his throat eased immediately. James toppled off the man with the sword still in his hand. He was shaking from the pain in his ribs and the realization that he just killed a man. Yes he'd been trying to kill *them* but he couldn't get the first thought to waver.

Getting gingerly to his feet and using the sword as a cane he hobbled over to the body. He stared at the head where the blade had struck and saw a long red welt crossing from one side to the other. There wasn't any blood, just the large mark. He looked down at the sword and saw he was holding it backwards with the sharp part of the blade in the back. Relief washed over him at the discovery. But that lasted long enough for him to remember Miranda.

She was breathing normally, but wouldn't respond to his calls. He feared she might be in a coma or something. He couldn't leave her here to look for help, the man might wake up, or a wild animal might come by and … He shook the pictures away and called up to the hawk who was circling high above. The hawk replied with a myriad of answers, but only one was acceptable. So sliding the baldric and sheath off the unconscious man's shoulder, he buckled it on and adjusted the straps. *This might come in handy.*

When the sword was secure he checked Miranda's back along the spine for any abnormalities. When he was sure she would be alright, he lifted her in his arms, ignoring the stabbing pain at his side, and started in the direction they had been heading.

Day passed into night slowly as James walked on; never stopping except to rest his arms. Hours crawled by but the scene never changed. The plains kept on and on never seeming to end, and never being broken by a road or trail. There were a few apple trees that he gratefully plucked and gobbled down. He saved a few for when Miranda woke up. *If she wakes up.* He thrust that thought from his mind faster than a bullet from a gun.

High above the hawk soared circling back every now and then and giving him glimpses of the fields behind and the fields before him. He was glad the creature was still with him, even though conversations with it were difficult at best. The hawk didn't know most of the words he used and he didn't always understand the pictures it sent him in reply. But as they kept at it some connections were made and the two of them began talking ... slowly.

The moon was just starting to deteriorate from the full white globe leaving a good chunk of it hanging in the sky. It gave off enough light for him to see, and the hawk continued to send him pictures as he struggled to keep going. Exhaustion was pulling at his legs and arms by the time the moon was at its peak and his stomach was empty. Yet Miranda continued to lay there in his arms asleep.

She must have used a lot of her strange power hiding our trails. And that damn bandit didn't help things at all.

That is correct, Young One.

James jumped as the hawk spoke to his mind again. He sent an angry thought to the beast that made it shriek as if in laughter.

How about giving me a warning before you start reading my thoughts okay? I'm still not used to talking to a bird.

Well you had best get used to it, Young One. I'm going to be here for a while.

Why are you still here? And what's with the 'Young One' stuff?

Again the hawk cried in laughter.

Mother asked me to watch you for her while she was away. And she also told me to protect you should you fall into trouble. She never told me that it would be this difficult. You get into more trouble that a hatchling, Young One. James grimaced. So he was being watched. *As for the name, I think it appropriate for someone so new to their power. Do you not agree?*

Well stop calling me that. My name is James Richards, not Young One. Okay?

Again you speak with odd words, Young One. The hawk wheeled in the air trying to act like it was ignoring him. The last two words were emphasized a little. Damn hawk knew exactly what he had said.

What do you mean by 'power'? Is this something that people in this land can do? Or am I an exception?

You are the only one capable of the Mind Speech with me. The hawk flew down closer to him and stared at him with a golden eye. *Mother gave this power to you so that you would be able to communicate with me. She may have her own reasons beyond that, but I do not know them.*

Okay … one more question. How is it that I can understand what these pictures you are sending me mean? Sure the picture of a bird evading a foe means duck or move out of the way, but what of the others?

It is the power that translates our languages to each other. Experience and time will grant greater abilities; but enough of this. Using the Mind Speech distracts you from your labor and you need to focus Young One.

James was about to break contact with the hawk when a thought came to him. *What is your name?*

I have had many names. Gold Eyes, Ravager, Kamrian. All of them are properly adorned, but I prefer the one Mother gave me, Aria.

You're a girl!?

Aria only laughed and soared back into the sky.

As the moon was starting to sink and the sky became lighter, Aria screeched with delight and flew down next to him. James stared at the bird until the vision of a village flashed into his mind. His arms felt like they were going to fall off and his legs were so wobbly anyone would think they were jelly. He was so tired, but he kept on with renewed vigor. As he approached the village the hawk fell back to the trees that settled a little ways to the right of the houses.

There weren't any people outside yet, but the dirt on the ground looked loose, like it had only just been walked on. Most of the houses were only one floor high and made of wood with shingled roofs and square framed windows. Each house had a porch made of the same wood and each was covered in different arrays of décor. Some had flowers and plants like some of his neighbors back home, while others held shelves like those in a store.

Yet a few houses, mainly ones in the center of the town, were burnt, some were still smoking while two had gone and fallen to the ground completely. This was definitely the town the slavers had attacked; those monsters …

From where he entered he could count at least thirty houses placed along several dirt roads that crossed at several intervals with one big building at the end in the center of two rows. The larger house had two floors, a very large porch that had no roof over it and an extra room to the side that looked like a stable for horses. He laughed inside and thanked all of his books for being so descriptive when it came to villages and the ways people lived. Otherwise he'd be completely dumbfounded.

Before he managed to reach the first house his legs gave way and he fell to his knees and managed to turn onto his side so as not to crush Miranda as he fell completely to the ground. His ribs were burning and his arm felt wet meaning the cut had reopened. He had no energy left to move so instead he did the only thing he could think of and, taking a slow deep breath, shouted at the top of his lungs into the silent village.

People burst from their doors with pitchforks and spades and other farming tools in their hands. They were fully dressed and some even had old leather padding strewn about them like armor. They looked around for the cause of the shout and when they spotted James and Miranda, dropped their weapons and ran forward. He felt hands take Miranda from him and rush off with words of worry. James watched as three of the men stood over him, one with a sword, and watched him as a woman looked him over. The last thing he saw before blacking out was a light orange glow emanating from somewhere out of sight.

CHAPTER 5

▼

TRIAL BY ERROR

"*I have some more news, some really great news, James.*" *He looked down at her, he forgot how much taller he was over her.* "*I have a new assignment!*" *His stomach burned, his hands started shaking in anger.* "*It's down in Virginia. Mr. Killington wants me to go down there and see if I can't smack around the guys down there into joining our organization! Just think, if they do join, we will be the largest organiza-tion in the business! I might even get promoted, which means I can ... James? James, where are you going?*"

The voice of his mother echoed in his thoughts as he lay there—wherever 'there' was. She called to him as he ran away from her down the lone beam of light that acted as the road surrounded by darkness. He ran and ran, never turn-ing back, with tears running down his face. How could she be so ... so IGNO-RANT? Didn't she care about him at all? Was work the only thing she and father ever cared about? Was he a mistake? A flaw in their plans?

That was over doing it, he knew, but for some reason that seemed to be the only thing he could think of ... and that was enough to feed his anger ...

"Who do you think he is?"

"... Don't know ... saved Miranda ..."

"... Do we know that for certain? He could have ..."

The voices flickered in and out of hearing as James lay in the darkness of unconsciousness. It felt just like back home when the pain had caused him to pass out in class. He sighed to himself. That day felt so long ago, when it was only yesterday. Then again, he didn't know how long he'd been asleep. He felt Aria reaching into his mind trying to speak with him, but everything she said was foggy and slurred.

A door opened somewhere and another voice entered, a woman's. He'd heard this voice once before now, only a few hours ago when the cloud over his mind started dissipating.

"Has he woken yet?" The woman's voice asked.

"Not yet Mistress Rosemary." Replied one of the first voices; a man's.

"I saw him stir once about an hour ago," the second man replied. "But other than that there haven't been any changes."

"Very well, you may leave me to my work now."

"Yes Ma'am." Both men replied, and the sounds of them leaving faded.

James felt someone sit on the edge of the bed he was obviously lying in. The extra weight wasn't much, but the soft mattress still sagged. The woman placed a hand on his forehead and hummed a lovely melody. A warm feeling flowed from her hand through his body and filled him with strength. Suddenly he got a message from Aria.

Young One, are you awakened yet?

Just about. He replied softly. *Do you know how long I have been out?*

Only three days. But I have been so worried I am starting to lose feathers. The hawk screeched in his mind. *What have you done to me Young One?*

"I think it is time for you to wake up now."

On command James' eyes opened and the remainder of his consciousness came with him. The first thing he noticed was that someone had removed his glasses. The second was the woman smiling down at him from the side of the bed. She had short curly red-brown hair and soft blue eyes. She adjusted a white shawl at her shoulders and stood up from the bed. James watched her from the bed, unable to see exactly what she was doing. When she came back she was holding something in front of her.

"Are you awake enough to talk, or shall I wait?" She asked.

James shifted on the bed and made to sit up. He felt something wrapped around his middle and remembered his ribs. Reaching under the blankets he felt the bandage wrapped tightly around his chest and arm. Then he realized he was wearing nothing under the blankets! He dipped back down under the covers and when he felt his face go back to its original color slid slowly up from the bed. Lying back against the wall he adjusted the sheets to keep himself well covered.

"Um … Mistress?" he asked tentatively. "Do you know where my glasses are? They're two pieces …"

"You mean these?" She held up her hands and held them out to him.

He reached out and, taking the glasses, set them in place. Surprised, he saw that the left lens was repaired to perfection, and the right's scratches were gone as well. The woman laughed at his expression and sat back down on the side of the bed.

"When you were brought to me I had no idea what they were. But I knew they must be important to you, so I had Gillian, our best glass worker, fix them. Are they satisfactory?" He nodded enthusiastically. "Good. Ah, where are my manners? Allow me to introduce myself. I am Rosemary Mallandred, Herbalist, Mid-wife, and Third in the Village Council."

"My name is James Richards." He replied with a bow of his head. "Um, Mistress, may I ask exactly where this place is?"

"Of course you may. This is the village Yattion, home of the land's finest crafters and farmers of this generation. We are only a month's travel east from the Capital of Breya and much farther from the Border of Nu'athion, where the Ice Nation, Gattar, dwells. But you needn't worry about that now. Tell me, do you feel any pain? Any at all?"

"None." He replied honestly. "I feel a little numb around my ribs, and my arm is stiff but other than that I feel perfectly fine."

Mistress Rosemary sighed and nodded like she was disappointed!

"Is something the matter?" he asked. "You don't seem too pleased at my recovery." The words came out harder than he thought, but the woman didn't seem to mind.

"On the contrary, I am very happy that you are awake and well." She looked up at him with those soft blue eyes. "But this means that you must now face trial."

"Trial?! On what charges? And who is bringing them against me?"

"The charges against you are such: being in cahoots with the bandits that attacked our village a few days past, and bringing harm to Miranda and a man named Mathwin Cormer. All of which are very serious accusations, true or not. If you are found guilty, then you will be arrested and taken to Breya where you will be imprisoned for many years."

The emptiness that filled his chest was suddenly ten fold. Imprisonment? Why him? Why was this happening to him?

"As for the man bringing the charges," he looked up from his thoughts. "It is the Second in the Village Council, and possibly the most influential man in Yattion; Mathwin Cormer. He was injured during the attack and is angry as a bull that one might have come back acting as a friend."

"It's not true! None of it is, I swear!" He was talking so fast he almost lost his hold on the blankets covering him. "I was attacked by the bandits as well, why would he think I was with them? And harming Miranda? She passed out when the bandit leader …"

"James, I believe you. I truly do, and so does half the village council thanks to Miranda's recollection. But if Cormer says you are guilty of something, then most people will believe it without a second thought. That is how powerful he is."

She got up from the bed and walked to the door. Before opening it she turned to him sadly.

"I will have food brought up to you soon." She pointed to a table next to his bed. "Your clothes are there. They have been cleaned and stitched. When they are on, tell the guards outside the door and they will bring your food in. I must get ready for the trial."

James was left lying there in the bed, stunned. Trial? But he had *helped* Miranda escape the slavers. He looked over the situation quickly, taking in every detail and saw absolutely no reason why a bandit would do what he had done. Not even in the most outrageous books did someone act like this man thought he had. Pounding a fist on the bed he remembered his clothes on the table. Making sure he had one of the covers wrapped around him, he got up and started to dress.

The room was small, but big enough to hold at least seven or eight people at once. The bed sat in the left corner farthest from the door and next to it was the table where his clothes were. He slipped his underclothes on and then the pants, shirt and tunic. Tying the belt and lacing the boots he walked over to the mirror that was at the end of the bed. His face had the shadows of the bruises and the small white scar running vertically through his left eyebrow. It was really small and hardly noticeable, but he frowned at it anyway.

He ran his hand through his hair with a sigh. It was then that he remembered the runes on his arm. The shirt covered the ones on his wrist and forearm, but not the one on his hand. Mistress Mallandred surely saw them when she was healing him … did she know what they were, or did she think they were just tattoos? He had to do something about them; he didn't want to risk anyone seeing them who might know what they were. He looked around and saw his pack lying under the table.

Opening it, he saw that some of the things had been moved; of course … they searched through his things. After all they thought he was a bandit. He didn't have any gloves, or cloth to wrap around his arm, so he grabbed his t-shirt. Hesitating for a minute, he looked at his shirt with a sad expression, turning in on its side he took it in both hands and began tearing a strip of it off the bottom. It was hard because of the cut on his arm, but he managed to tear a strip that wound twice around.

Pulling the sleeve back he held one end of the strip in his right hand while winding the rest of it around. He circled his hand twice to hide the rune there then worked his way up his arm until he was an inch or two above the third rune. Using his teeth he tied a small knot at the top and slipped his shirt over it. He looked in the mirror again and smiled slightly; at least it wasn't entirely noticeable. Better than people seeing the runes. *I'll just say its some nasty looking scar that I like to keep hidden from view so as not to disgust everyone I meet.*

When he was ready he knocked on the door and one of the guards answered. He told them he was able to accept the food and they told him to stand away from the door. The hard wood door opened revealing two men wearing brown leather breastplates and carrying sickles at their sides. They had hard faces and long hair that was covered mostly by the leather helms sitting on their heads.

It was then that James noticed something very, very odd—they were glowing! It was faint but still visible; a small halo outlining their bodies, kind of like when Miranda hid their tracks and when the bandit attacked them. It gave off a warm feeling, but not one to be thought of as safe; there was a fire in both their eyes that was ready to be unleashed if they thought him threatening.

One of them produced a tray and set it on the floor while the other never took his eyes of James. He accepted everything the two guards did; he was a suspect, and they were never treated with hospitality … only hatred. When the door closed he heard a lock click into place and the guards placed themselves at their stations. For farmers they sure knew how to act the role of a guard, but he wasn't fooled. He saw how they were both shaking and sweating.

The food consisted of a loaf of fresh bread, some strips of salted meat, a cup of water, and a small biscuit that smelled like honey. Ravenous, he devoured the food but made sure to savor the flavor, and was amazed at how good it all was. The people here knew how to cook! *Without using artificial flavoring or anything too,* he added with a laugh. As he swallowed the last piece of meat he heard someone knock on the door. The lock clicked open and Miranda walked through the opened door—with a guard behind her.

She rushed to his side and gave him a hug so hard he thought his ribs would crack again. The guard harrumphed behind them but Miranda turned to the man and gave him such a look that he actually backed towards the door a step before catching himself. Ignoring the guard she turned back to him.

"James, are you alright?" He nodded. "Oh I heard about the trial only a moment ago and rushed here as fast as I could. I tried to stop the whole thing, but Cormer is as stubborn as a goat, especially now with his leg in a splint. I am so sorry I got you into this."

"It's not your fault. And I don't regret helping you. But can you tell me something? What is going to happen at this trial?" He recalled that his books had ceremonies and traditions that had to be followed and he wanted to make an impression. "What do I do?"

"Didn't your home have a Council?" He shook his head. "Where did you live?"

He caught himself before answering. He had almost told her the truth. Instead he prepared his speech and Oscar winning performance. He opened his mouth and stopped, blinking several times before taking a step back and placing a hand to his forehead.

"I-I don't remember." Miranda gasped slightly so he kicked it up a notch and tried to look like he was going to cry. *Please let this work!* "I can't remember anything past waking up in the Gray wood. Everything ... everything before that is a blank. I—I don't remember my parents or where I came from or anything! Miranda I can't remember any of it!"

She embraced him again. This time he thought he heard her cry, but when she backed away again her face was dry and full of concern.

"Your memory is gone. Oh I'm so sorry ... No, this is all those damned bandits' fault. They shouldn't have beaten you so badly back in the forest ..."

"Miranda ... what do I do if the Council asks me about my past?"

She thought for a moment then as she was about to speak she turned to the guard who stiffened at the look she directed at him. Her eyes throwing hot daggers at the guard, she told him to leave. The guard began to stammer a response, but she silenced him and went so far as to push him out bodily. Closing the door behind her she turned back to him.

"Okay, leave the part about your memory to me. But before I am able to say anything there are some formalities that will occur first." Pacing back and forth she began to explain the ceremony.

James took everything in and felt Aria doing the same. *I can assist you if you forget anything,* she told him.

Thanks.

The first thing that would happen would be …

About half an hour later when Miranda was making him recall everything she had told him, again, someone knocked on the door and Mistress Mallandred stepped into the room. She was wearing a long dark robe that covered her almost completely, but he could see a hood hanging at the neck. She nodded to Miranda and told them it was time.

Taking a deep breath James followed her, with one guard in front and one behind him, out of the house and into the street he'd seen when he first arrived. With the sun completely up and his glasses repaired he saw that the village houses were not made the same. Each one had something different about it that seemed to define it somehow. One had a porch with a sign hanging over it with the picture of a chisel and log. *That must be the crafter's house and store.*

Other houses had more obvious things that just a sign. One had several glass displays covering shelves and hanging on wires from the overhang. Another had hundreds of strange flowers and plants sticking out of every possible place where one could be placed. The windows had even more plants in them and he wagered that there were even more inside.

When the procession reached the large house at the end of the road there was a crowd waiting to receive them. The people were as varied as their houses. They were blonde, brown haired, black haired, a few were even red heads. Their clothes were similar in style, but not in color or condition. Most of the men were wearing pants like his; brown or black or lightly tanned. Shirts varied from white to blue and beige with the laces undone and a vest here and there covering shoulders, but none of them wore a smile.

The women had dresses that all came within an inch of the ground and stopped at the waist where a dress-top would continue. While the older women had their hair in a bun or a single braid, the ones who looked no older than he, let their hair fall untied down their backs. The littlest girls had a ribbon tied around the tops of their head. James noticed that the procession had stopped just short of the large house he'd seen when he first arrived and he was standing in the center of the crowd.

Standing on the tall porch of the house in front of him were seven people dressed in dark robes that skimmed the ground and covered them from head to toe. Large hoods covered their faces hiding them from view, but he recognized one of them as Mistress Mallandred by the way she stood. Six of the people were centered on the seventh who had a white symbol on his chest. The symbol showed a flame with two swords crossing before it. He was obviously male by the size of his shoulders and the way he stood.

"Will the one on trial step forth and present himself to the village Council." Every head turned to the center man who had spoken. His voice was deep and carried an air of authority similar to that of the Lady's.

Taking a steadying breath James took three steps forward and stopped. Taking his right hand he placed it over his heart and, keeping his other hand at his side, bowed to the Council. He heard Aria speaking to him, going over everything Miranda had told him.

"Council, I present myself. My name is James Richards and I am here to defend myself against the charges brought against me."

The man in the center stepped forward. "So you are to plead innocent? Very well, rise and enter my court."

Before he had a chance to rise, Miranda stepped forward from behind him and bowed in a similar fashion.

"Speaker, I am Miranda Se'Cruz[1]. I present myself and ask for a moment to speak before the trial."

A few people shifted in the crowd. It was rare that anyone spoke before the Council's trial. The Speaker nodded his consent. Both of them rose from their bows.

"I wish for it to be known that the accused, James Richards, is unable to recall his past." People shifted again. So did a few of the Council.

"Explain yourself." The Speaker said.

James nodded. "Speaker, Council, I am unable to explain this very clearly because I do not understand it entirely myself. But, I cannot remember things from my past." No one spoke so he went on. "The only thing I am capable of recalling clearly is waking up in the center of the Gray Woods, unaware of where I was at first and how I'd come to be there. Before that I see only a cloud of nothing."

"Do you know who your parents are or where you have come from?" He shook his head without looking at the Speaker. The latter turned to the others of the Council and they spoke for a moment. "Very well," the Speaker said finally, "We shall continue with the trial now." James heard Miranda curse under her breath. "Enter my court."

Inside the large house it was dark except for a few candles placed in a circle on the floor. Beyond the candles were seven chairs in a half circle. They were all nor-

---

1. Se'Cruz—Sounds like Seh-Crew. The Z is silent.

mal looking chairs except for the one in the center. Its high back and padded seat made it look almost like a throne. The seven Councilmen circled around the candle ring and stood before their chairs and waited. James stepped into the candle ring and watched as the Speaker seated himself.

When all were in their chairs, the flames on the candles turned an icy blue and rose up around him like a dozen pillars. At first he thought they were going to encase him in the fire, but it subsided back to its original size. Their colors, however, stayed at the icy blue. Suddenly remembering what Miranda had told him James knelt, slowly because of his ribs, towards the Speaker with his left hand on the floor and his right on his knee.

"James Richards," The man on the right of the Speaker said in a strained voice, "You are here to face trial on the charges of kidnapping Miranda Se'Cruz, being in cahoots with the bandits that attacked our village, and brining harm to me, Mathwin Cormer. You have said to plead innocent, but I grant you one last chance to change your mind. Be warned that this will be the only time you may do so."

"I do not wish to change my plea."

The person on the left of the Speaker rose and the one on the right sat down.

"Do you have any evidence to your innocence?" James looked up and saw Mistress Mallandred's face staring at him from beneath her hood.

"Some. But whether or not you shall accept them is questionable, since the man who brought the charges against me sits in such a high position of power."

Watch yourself Young One. You tread on the edge of breaking the ceremony.

"Master Cormer's position and opinion are only a part of the trial process." Mistress Mallandred said sternly. "You may proceed to show us your evidence."

Taking a deep breath he started to explain what had happened to him in the Gray Woods. He didn't mention the Lady or Aria, for fear of them thinking he was lying, and because Aria warned him not to. So he told them how he woke up and started wandering through the woods. He told them about finding some berries on a bush near the traveler's tree and falling asleep. He spoke of waking up with a bad feeling and how the slavers captured and beat him and threw him in the cage.

When he came to the part where he first noticed Miranda, the Speaker told one of the Councilmen to allow her inside. Together he and Miranda spoke about the bandit leader and how James had picked the lock and managed to guide them out of the forest. As Miranda spoke about the fight with the leader the Speaker seemed to become pale beneath his hood and his breathing quickened with every detail. James took over when she got the part where she'd passed out. And when he was done bowed his head.

"An interesting story." The Second, Cormer, stood up and made his way to the fire ring. He had a bit of a limp from the leg that had been injured. "But do you really expect us to believe such a ridiculous tale? Do you take us for fools?"

"Not all of you." He replied staring directly at Cormer.

"You dare insult a member of the Council!?" He shouted. "So tell us; which of us do you dare say are fools?"

"An easy question; but before I say anything I wish to know one thing. Why are you the one pressing charges against me? Shouldn't Miranda's parents be doing that? She was the one who was taken from the village and I was the one who brought her back. So if anyone should be accusing me of harming her, it's them. I heard all about your injury from Mistress Mallandred and I feel bad that you were hurt.

"But what I really want to know is this: Which is hurt more? Your leg or your pride? How does it feel to know that your entire village was beaten and overcome by only seven men?"

The Council sat completely stunned. No one, *no one*, ever dared speak to a member of any Council in that manner or tone. But, this boy had not only insulted them, but Mathwin Cormer, the most dangerous among them. Who was this boy to say such things? And, 'seven men'?

"Dear boy!" Every head turned to look at the Councilwoman speaking. The long dark robe hanging loosely on their shoulders and the soft, but sharp, voice made it obvious this person was a woman. "What makes you think that there were only seven men who attack us? I was there! I saw the attack and I can assure you that seven men could not have executed it! There was fire flying through the air from every direction. The ground was enveloped in flame and easily a hundred men were around us threatening us with their weapons. I saw their faces and I most assuredly saw the sword that was pointed at my son's neck!"

"And I'm telling you that there were only seven bandits, Madam." James replied quickly and with a sharp note to his voice. "I saw their encampment and all those who were in it! Seven men; six lackeys and one leader, that's all. That's why they only took Miranda and not every woman and child they could find! But if you are so sure that there were hundreds then tell me: where are their footprints? Surely that many men would have left plenty of footprints on the road in your village.

"And here is something more for you to think about! Can everyone see what their opponent is going to do as they do it? How do you know that the seven men didn't just throw their power in several directions and unleash it in several places? Am I wrong in saying this is possible? As for the hundreds of men, is it not possible to create heat waves to project images and make it seem as though there are more people around than there truly are? Is this possible? Well, answer me!"

His voice echoed in the dark room as everyone there took in what he said. The woman who had shouted at him sat down and looked at the others. They all had the same look on their faces. He was right, and they all knew it to be true. Turning back to Cormer, James took a step closer to the man, but the ring of candles stopped him from getting too close.

"You asked me which of you I thought was a fool, and now I'll give you an answer." Cormer and the others looked at him. "I think you ALL are fools! I cannot even begin to think how people with such a low capacity of thought made it to such a position! But you Master Cormer are easily the biggest of them all. And so, as not to break ceremony ..." He bowed with his right hand over his heart.

Cormer was glaring at him from beneath his hood. He opened his mouth several times to speak, but shut it instantly. Miranda was staring at him with a look of awe and fear. He had spoken to the Council like they were nothing! Aria was shaking her head, but he could tell that she was holding back her laughter. Finally Cormer spoke.

"Boy," he said with a hint of laughter, "you say that you cannot recall your past, true? Then tell me this: How is it that you can recall the ceremony of trial? How is it that you know all of the formalities and traditions that need to be met if you cannot remember your own parents?"

"Miranda came to me before the trial. That was when I realized that my mind was clouded. Taking pity on me she schooled me on the proper etiquette."

"So isn't it possible that the two of you, could have made up this entire story?" the old man continued. "Or perhaps you used some type of power or herb stashed away to make her think you had lost your memory."

"That's not true!" Miranda said taking a step forward. "James doesn't have any powers! And his clothes had been searched before being given to him!"

The Council all started talking rapidly to each other. He caught some of what they were saying.

"... no power ..."

"... must be lying ... at his age ..."

"Silence!" The Speaker rose and made his way down to the fire ring. Cormer watched with apprehension plain on his face. "James, Miranda, is this true?"

"I—I do not know, Speaker. I ..." He replied choosing his words carefully.

"Speaker," Miranda said, cutting him off. "While the two of us were locked up at the camp and while James lied there, unconscious, I delved him. I was shocked when I didn't find anything, not a drop of power at all."

Delved? James had no idea what she was talking about. He knew what 'to delve' meant, but what did *she* mean by it?

Again the Speaker turned to James. "Is ... is this true?"

"I am not entirely sure what this 'power' is," James continued, "but I do not believe I have it."

"I knew it! He is lying!" Everyone turned to Cormer as he spoke. "Speaker, everyone knows about the power. Everyone *has* the power. There is no way that this boy has not manifested yet."

The Speaker turned back to James and studied him for a moment before motioning to two Councilmen. Both nodded and stepped over to the candle ring. The three of them, the Speaker included, formed a triangle around him and raised their hands to each other.

"James, we are going to put you through a test that everyone goes through when they come close to the age of manifesting. It is a painless ordeal and will be over in a moment, I promise. But it is necessary to this trial to know the absolute truth. Do you consent?" He nodded. "Very well. Let us begin."

Good luck Young One.

The three Councilmen's hands began to glow softly with a light similar to those of the flames and he felt the feeling of their power wash over him. At first nothing seemed to happen, but slowly he began to get a twitch in his arm and it felt like the runes were growing hot. In a flash of red light his entire body was lifted off the ground and every muscle was frozen stiff. He heard everyone gasp as the three Council members fell to their knees, still glowing with their power.

James heard a faint beating in his ears that seemed to beat just out of sync with his heart. Deep down, he saw a bright light. He reached for it, feeling its cold depths become warmer the closer he got. But before he reached it, before he could take hold of it, he felt something block his way. As his mind hit this 'wall' he was pushed back, hard, and found himself standing back in the dark lit court room.

Miranda was helping the Speaker to his feet while the other Councilmen helped the other two sprawled on the floor. He tried to go help them, but again he hit something that threw him away. Shaking the stars from his sight he tested the air again. Reaching out with his hand he felt the air around it become steadily thicker until he couldn't help but retract it. The only person who was looking at him was Cormer, staring at him from underneath his hood. The Speaker placed a hand on Miranda's shoulder and bade her let him go.

"I hereby find the accused, James Richards …" Everyone turned to the Speaker. James' heart was beating twice as fast. "Clear of all charges."

Cormer swore loudly rounding on the Speaker.

"Silence Master Cormer!" The old man gritted his teeth and fell silent. "There is evidence enough that this boy has spoken the truth. During the testing I felt his power and he is correct; it has not manifested itself yet. He is as powerless as a newborn in the ways of the powers. I cannot say yet whether he is an Intaruan or a Gattarian, but I believe that he is one of us. I am sure that Majhra and Ralco will concur with me up on this."

The two Councilmen nodded making Cormer turn to James in a rage. The new, but oddly familiar red-orange aura surrounded the old man and tendrils of it crawled towards him. James watched, scared, but intrigued as to *what* this light was as they crawled around him to the candles surrounding him, turning them back to their original color of red, yellow, and orange. With the barrier down, Miranda leapt into his arms with a shout of joy. He gratefully accepted the embrace and returned it.

"James." He released Miranda and turned to the Speaker. The man had removed his hood and stared him in the eyes. His own were a deep brown and deep set like a man who'd seen much and held years of experience, despite the thick mane of brown hair's lack of gray. "There are some things that must be discussed about what to do now. With your memory gone, we do not know where you are from and are not about to send you out into the world in your current condition. Do you wish to stay here, in Yattion?"

"Master Se'Cruz, Speaker, I would be honored." The man's eyebrows lifted a little. "It was obvious. The way you tensed in your chair while Miranda described our flight and battle with the slavers was something only a concerned parent would do. Am I wrong?"

"No, you are correct. Miranda is my daughter. And I am in your debt. But for now, Miranda, I must ask you to leave so that we may speak with James." Miranda complained but in the end she complied.

Miranda stepped through the wooden doors out into the village where everyone still stood waiting. Several people rushed up to her asking her questions. Is it over? Is he guilty or innocent? What happened?! Pushing her way through the crowd she started explaining some of the things that went on. When she told them what James had said to the Council everyone gasped. When she told them *how* he had spoken to them, some fainted. But she heard quiet laughter coming from the children and her friends.

She continued to explain what had happened and was about to tell them he was clear when the doors opened behind them. Everyone turned to watch the Council walk out with James following behind the Speaker. No one breathed, except Miranda.

"The accused has been found innocent of all charges." The Speaker said in a booming voice. "I am sure Miranda told you everything that happened inside so I shall get to the next topic. It is true that James has no recollection of his past and does not know where he comes from. So, to repay the debt that I owe him for saving my daughter, he has accepted my invitation to live here in Yattion."

The entire crowd applauded the young man who blushed and tried to hide his face with a cough. Miranda laughed and so did many of the others. That was the best thing about the peoples of Yattion; they were quick to forgive, if they were accepted that is. A forgiving people, but also very confusing at times too.

"Since he is too young to live on his own yet we have a few things that need to be taken care of first." The crowd quieted. "First, he is in need of a place to stay. Is there any among us who would have him live under their roof until the time comes for him to leave or until he is old enough to have his own?"

People looked to their spouses and husbands and children and whispered to each other about the matter. But someone spoke almost as soon as they began.

"I shall take him under my roof."

A tall blonde man stepped forward and bowed to the Council. He was a big man, but was very gentle too. He was Dannil Gashain, the renowned wood crafter. He wore a light blue shirt under a vest of green silk. The man was easily the richest of them all, but the fact that he had room and gold was not the reason he volunteered. Everyone knew that his son had gone off to fight in the war and died at the hands of a Gattarian Commander. Not only that, but shortly after his wife had died leaving him alone.

"James, do you accept Master Gashain's offer?"

"Master Gashain, I am grateful. Thank you very much."

The crowd burst into applause again. But Miranda saw that Cormer was nowhere to be seen. She wondered where the Councilman had gone too. *Probably licking his wounds.*

"Since it would not be right that he stay here free of charge, we also need someone to take him in as their apprentice." The Speaker's voice took on a humorous note as he added, "That way he can pay back the enormous debt he now owes me."

The crowd laughed and then settled into a steady chorus of chatter. Three people stepped forward after a moment and presented themselves. The first was Master Greg Ignatius, the farmer. As his apprentice, James would plow, plant, tend the animals, and learn many things about them as well. Second was Rosemary Mallandred who wanted someone to help care for her herbs, learn the trade of healing, and reach the plants on the higher shelves. And finally, Elyas Se'Cruz, the Speaker, stepped forward.

"I run a forge here," he said to James, "You might not think you're strong enough for the job, but that won't matter for a while. I'll teach you how to keep the fires lit, clean the area around the forge, and everything else you need to know."

Before he had a chance to answer, someone shouted something from the back of the crowd. People moved aside, or were moved, as Neru Tellis struggled to get to the Speaker.

"Neru, I'm sorry." Elyas said to the boy. "But you are by far the laziest apprentice I have ever known. I cannot apprentice you again."

The people were muttering under their breath things like "rude young man" and "should be ashamed of himself" as the dejected boy made his way to the back of the crowd again.

James turned to Elyas and said something to him so the rest of the crowd couldn't hear. The Speaker nodded and motioned him towards the crowd.

"Thank you for offering to take me under your wing," James said with a bow of his head to Mistress Mallandred and Master Ignatius, "But I have decided to take Master Se'Cruz up on his offer. I hope you won't be offended by my choice."

The other two said they weren't offended in anyway and wished him luck before stepping back to their places in the Council.

"I have also agreed to train him and prepare him in the ways of his powers." Elyas said to the surprise of everyone. "Yes, his abilities have not yet manifested, but in time and with training it shall. Until then he will be under my command in that matter." People applauded, though some had skeptical looks. If his power hadn't manifested yet, then how did they know if he was enemy or ally?

"This concludes the trial." Everyone made the bow with hand over heart and broke off into groups back to their homes. Se'Cruz looked down at James and smiled. "James you may go with Master Gashain if you wish. I am sure you will want to see your temporary home. When you feel fit enough, come here to my house and I shall begin your instruction in both apprenticeship and your powers."

"Thank you, Master Se'Cruz." He said with a small bow of his head. He turned to Miranda who had stepped up next to her father. "I'll see ya later then."

James and Dannil made their way to a house in the center of the village. The large man told him what he did and all about the fine art of carving and crafting. He sounded like a child wooing over a new toy through the store window. When they got to the house James noticed there was a basement door a little off from the main entrance. According to Dannil that was where he stored all of his completed works as well as the ones he kept safe until merchants came through to buy.

The first room he saw as they walked into the house was a living room. A few chairs sat in random places. A large fire place worked in stone sat at the far end of the room. It was empty now, but the size of it told that it would heat the entire room, maybe even the house. There was a plain rug spread in the center of the floor, and a couple of portraits were strung above the den.

The first was that of Dannil, the man was smiling broadly, looking almost foolish with his hair neatly combed. The second portrait was that of a woman. Her hair was just like Dannil's, blonde and shining in the sun light. But her eyes were different; they were green while his were dark blue. Her face was lightly toned and she smiled warmly almost with a sense of royalty to it.

But it was the third picture that caught his eye the most. It showed a young man, no older than James, smiling timidly with blue eyes like his and long blonde hair that he had tied with a single leather string. His sharp features spoke of a strong build, obviously from training with the army. James saw Dannil looking at the two pictures and felt a pang of pity for him. They were very much alike right now; both without a real family and both families taken from them without warning.

Dannil lead him from the room and the pictures and showed him the rest of the house. Dannil kept the place very tidy. There wasn't anything on the floor that shouldn't be, and the shelves were decorated with hundreds of wooden carvings. The house had at least seven rooms all on the one floor, two of which were bedrooms. Dannil's was closest to the living room and directly across from it was the room that must have belonged to his son.

"This will be your room." He said steering him into the room.

It had a single bed that was easily long enough to fit him. The headboard had the most intricate designs he'd ever seen carved into it. The walls were bare as were the shelves hanging just to the side of the bed. There was a window leading out into the road with curtains pulled back to let the sunlight in. It was indeed a magnificent room. But he felt uneasy using a room that must have held much importance to Dannil.

"Never mind that," he said when James had voiced his thoughts. "Jacob was a good man, and a brilliant fighter. But he won't be coming back. Seems a shame to let his room go to waste. Go ahead, it's all yours."

That night James lay awake staring at the ceiling. His mind wandered to Aria, but the hawk was either fast asleep or too far for him to feel. He couldn't clear his mind of all the things that had happened so far. They kept playing themselves over and over until he could have retold the entire story in such detail ... he sighed. He kept thinking about Dannil. The man had lost so much, but was a very giving man ... kind of like his own father. He stopped himself ... he didn't want to think about those two right now.

Slowly his eyes started closing as sleep began creeping up on him. He thought about Darrel and Chris and wondered what they were up to. Darrel would probably be playing one of his games right now and Chris would be sleeping or reading. He laughed quietly. They were comical in so many ways ... His final thoughts before finally dozing off were about his mother and father. *I hope they aren't too worried* he thought despite his attempts not to.

CHAPTER 6

▼

TASTE OF A NEW LIFE

WHEN James woke up the next morning it took him a moment to realize where he was. It wasn't until he put his glasses on and saw the room did he remember. His mind wandered again to the thoughts he had the night before, but none of them came easily. Pushing the covers off, he began dressing. Since he didn't have any other clothes he put the ones the Lady had given him back on. Leaving the boots off he strode out of the room only to find Dannil standing just outside.

"I was about to come and wake you. It's almost time to eat." He motioned for him to follow. "I have some things for you to do today, if you don't mind helping and old man."

"Master Gashain, you're not old and you know it." He replied laughing. "You just say that so people will tell you how young you look."

The big man laughed and clapped a hand on his shoulder.

"How right you are. But you needn't call me Master Gashain. That's too formal for me, but I allow the Speaker and Council to use it for ceremonial reasons. Everyone calls me Dannil, and if you started calling me otherwise, people would start to take advantage of that and copy you."

Breakfast was laid out on a table in the dining room, which was separated by a single archway from the living room. There were two chairs sitting around the small table which had five dishes on it. Two were empty, but the other three held some cooked ham and sausage, baked bread, and other assortments. As they ate Dannil told him about the chores he had for him.

"Well, I need only a few things and then I'll let you be on your way." He said swallowing a piece of ham. "I wrote everything on a list so you won't forget. Oh, and take it easy out there or Rosemary will have my hide strapped to her front door. She gave me explicit instructions not to let you work those ribs of yours to much. Oh, and she wants to see you at the end of the day to reapply your bandages."

James shivered. "Do I have to go to her?"

"What, are you scared of her? Well," he leaned in closer. "Truthfully I can't blame you, she scares me too. But yes, I think it would be best." James sighed in defeat. He couldn't rightly explain. "Ah, it'll be good for you to get yourself fixed up right and quick. Trust me."

When they were done eating, James washed the dishes and put them on the drying racks while Dannil got his list and started preparing his work desk. The list he gave him was small enough and didn't look like it would take too long. Before he left, Dannil handed him a belt pouch of money.

"There's a little extra in there so go buy yourself some clothes and necessities."

Thanking the man again, James left him to his work and headed out into the village. The sun greeted him with a warm burst of light that made him blink from the sudden change. Blinking, he waited for his eyes to adjust; when they did he saw that people were out and working already. One man was dipping large pieces of something into a barrel and pulling them out. The material turned a light brown and dried quickly. As soon as the stuff was decently dry, the man dipped it in again.

The tanner ... cool.

Next to the tanner a group of women were sitting in a circle with large amounts of wool at their sides and the *click click* sounds of sewing floating through their gossip. One of them noticed he was watching and smiled. He waved back with a smile and continued down the road. After asking the farmer, Master Ignatius, where he should go, he finally found the place first on his list: the baker.

Sweet aromas of bread, meat, and sweets drifted from the store as he approached it. A few of the children were staring at some of the things displayed in the window. One of them he remembered from his trial. She had been wearing a red bow in her hair, now she had a deep blue one tied in the same fashion. When they saw him coming two of them gasped and pointed whispering to the others. But it was the smallest one that actually approached him.

The boy had big green eyes half hidden behind a curtain of light brown hair. He stared at James with his mouth hanging a little open and his hands hanging at his sides. He had a tiny little beige shirt that was unkempt from neat little shorts. He didn't have any shoes on so his feet were dirty, but he didn't seem to mind too much. James smiled at the child making him blush.

"Can I help you?" he asked raising an eyebrow.

"You are the guy who spoke mean things to the Cownswil, right?"

James couldn't help but laugh. The little child blushed again but waited for an answer. Kneeling down he looked the kid in the face, still laughing.

"I wouldn't say they were mean things. But," He stretched his smile a little wider and motioned for the boy to come closer. "I did tell Master Cormer he was a fool."

All the children laughed and started asking him more questions. Where are you from? What was your name again? What's your favorite color? Do you like bugs? He knelt there answering some of their questions truthfully while others he would say something mysteriously making them go wide-eyed and 'ooh'. They kept up the tirade of questions until their mothers came out of the bakery. They apologized for their children's behavior, but James said he didn't mind. Waving goodbye to the kids he stepped into the bakery.

The aromas wafted in the air twice as strong as he closed the door. Piles upon piles of breads, pastries, meats, and sweets stocked the shelves form corner to corner. At the back was a counter with a set of weights and a few sample trays. Taking a few steps inside he heard someone grunt behind the counter. A tall dark looking man stood up with a heavy box in his arms. Pitch black hair covered his head and hung loosely over his ears. Two black eyes were scrunched up with strain from holding the box.

"Hey, can you help me o'er here?" he said, the strain obvious in his voice. "Just get the other end of this thing."

Ducking under the counter flap, James took the other end of the box and helped carry it into the back. For something that only held some meat, it was heavy! By the time they finally set it down on the shelf they were both massaging their arms.

"Thanks, lad." He said leading him back into the front. "I usually don't have any trouble with that stuff, but my back's been hurtin' lately and well ... Ah, listen to me complainin'. Welcome to me shop. What can I get for you?"

Taking the list out James read the items off the little piece of paper while the baker, whose name turned out to be Kyle, went and got the food. When the bread, meats, and sweets were wrapped, James took out the coins that Dannil had given him and paused. He didn't know how the currency worked! He started trying to come up with some excuse to have Kyle show him, but nothing came.

"Ah, that's right, you don' remember things, right? Here let me show you." Taking a few of the coins from the pouch he laid them in a row on the counter.

The first coin was bronze and about the size of a nickel. On the front was a picture of a first crescent moon and on the back was a single number that looked like a fancy five. The second coin was also bronze but a little large than a quarter. It contained a picture of a crown with two stars over it and one below while the back held a fancy number twenty. The next two coins were silver and varied in size like the two bronze and held similar pictures on the front; the smaller one with the moon, the larger with the crown and stars. The small silver had a number fifty on the back and the larger a one hundred.

"The small bronze is called a penny; it is the cheapest coin among them all. The larger bronze is called a crown. It takes four bronze pence to equal one bronze crown. The small silver coin is called a silver penny. Easy enough right? And the larger silver coin is a silver crown. Its two silver pence to a silver crown. Also, and this is where it gets complicated, it is two and a half bronze crowns—or two crowns and two pence—to a silver pence, and five to a silver crown. I won't get into the more detailed stuff, but that's about all you'll need to know. At least in a place as small as Yattion."

"Do people use gold coins? Or does it just stop at silver?"

"Oh, people use gold, but only the more wealthy of us of course." He scooped the coins back into the pouch and handed it back to James. "I tell you, I haven't seen a gold penny or crown here in over fifteen years! Merchants rarely carry it, no matter how many guards they have, and royalty never comes here. So you see my point."

James looked back into the pouch and took out the price Kyle asked for. Placing it back at his belt he went to take the things from the counter when he realized he didn't have his pack to carry it all in. So, gathering the wrapped parcels in his arms he left the bakery and made his way back to Dannil's. He placed the food on the table and placed them in the cabinets and shelves that encircled the kitchen. Grabbing his bag from his room he swung it over his shoulder and left.

Back and forth he went, from stop to stop, gathering what he needed and when his pack was full, carrying it back to the house. The middle stop on the list was for some blankets and a rug from the 'wool women'. That was an experience he hoped never to repeat. The wool women were a group of elderly ladies who, when he entered, greeted him with their soft and old voices. They reminded him of the old ladies from his books and his grandmother. They asked his how he was, whether Dannil was feeding him right because he looked so thin, did he have a pretty girl back home, everything he answered stammering back and forth between them and asking again and again for the things because he had to finish his chores.

"Nonsense." One of them replied taking his arm and pulling him into a chair at a table. "You just rest yourself there for a moment and I will see if I can't scrounge something up for you to eat."

He tried to tell her he wasn't hungry but she ignored him while the others continued asking him questions. Half an hour later he stumbled out of the house with not only the blankets and rug, but a bag of sweets and things they said would taste delicious. They invited him back anytime, and he replied saying he would if he could find the time, but deep down he swore never to go there unless it was a complete emergency.

Lower on the list was Mistress Mallandred's. He stood outside her door for a few minutes wishing he didn't have to go inside. Taking a deep breath he went and knocked on the door. A muffled voice told him to come in. Closing the door behind him, James thought he jumped into a jungle. Plants hung from the ceiling and walls, from shelves and shelves, and they covered the floor enough that he had to be careful where he walked lest he step on one of them.

The light was horrible too. There weren't any candles burning or lamps shining anywhere, making the sunlight that managed to creep through the windows the only source. The air was stuffy and hot making his glasses start to fog a little. Weaving and ducking through the plants he finally found Mistress Mallandred in the back leaning over a table with a pestle and bowl that held a brown mixture that reeked like a sewer.

"Ah, James, good of you to come." She turned to him and smiled warmly. He shivered anyway. "Have a seat over there and I will be with you in a moment."

The small stool was hard and uncomfortable to sit on, and the light was even worse there because there wasn't a window that he could see. How does she find her way around in here with so little light? On cue the herb woman appeared around a corner with a small flame alight in her palm. It took him a moment to realize that the flame wasn't on a candle or lamp, but just sitting there on her open hand.

"I don't trust candles and lamps around my herbs and plants." She let the small flame hover in the air just above them. No sparks or smoke fell or rose, it just hovered there giving enough light for him to see the tray of tools on the table he hadn't noticed before. He felt his blood run cold at the sight. "Well are you ready?"

He didn't trust himself to talk, so he just nodded and closed his eyes.

"Oh don't be scared child," she said with a laugh. "I'm not even going to use these on you. They are there to cut the bandages so I can take a look." She tilted her head to the side when he didn't move. "Are you okay? You're as pale as a sheet."

"Suffice it to say, I don't have good relations with tools like that." He said before he could catch himself. The cutting knife in her hand was distracting him.

"Something from your past haunting you?" He nodded but said no more. "Well don't worry. I don't know what happened but I assure you, I am a well trained hand and won't hurt you at all. Now, take off your shirt and tunic so I can have a look."

He didn't bother taking the tunic all the way off; instead, he just parted it down the center and let the two sides fall to his waist. Unlacing the shirt he slipped it over his head and placed it on a peg that was on the wall behind him. Mistress Mallandred paused as she bent to examine his arm and looked at his right instead. He stiffened when she asked if there was something wrong with that arm too.

"No, no." He said quickly remembering the story he'd thought up. "It's just a nasty scar that I have from long ago that I keep covered so people won't sick up when they see it."

"Ah … wait I don't remember seeing any scar when I was caring for you when you first arrived. Unless I'm mistaken I remember seeing some interesting symbols. What are they?"

This was bad. He had expected people to buy the first story so he didn't have another ready for this!

"Um, well … they're … I think they're runes of some sort." His mind was working double time trying to piece together some little white lie. "I'm not sure what they mean, but I think I may have gotten them a while back because they looked … er, interesting. I can't be sure though because everything is a little fuzzy."

"Ah, that's right; your memory problem. But, you managed to recall something, so that's a good thing I guess. Alright," she clapped her hands together, "let's take a look shall we?"

The bandages were cut away and set on the tray in a heap. James dared a peek at his ribs and saw a large bruise. It was an ugly mix of blue and purple, and hurt like hell when she placed a light hand on it. Rosemary didn't stop there. Taking the brown mixture she had been working on she spread some over the bruise and told him to hold the rag in place while she went for something. The mixture smelled worse than before, but was warm and comforting against his tender skin. When she came back she had another roll of bandages in her hand.

"Now lift your arm while keeping a hold on that salve."

As she slowly began to wrap the bandages around his middle and a few times over his shoulder she spoke to him about his condition. He knew that all the running he'd done had hurt more than helped in this case and of course fighting with a broken rib or two was not the healthiest decision. And of course it would take some time for the bruise to go away.

"But I will say this; you are a quick healer." She finished tying the bandage and he began putting his shirt back on. "Your ribs mended themselves awfully quick even with the salves I used. I have never seen a more stubborn body in my life."

"I usually don't get sick," he told her slipping his arms through the tunic's sleeves. "I never got into fights or such trouble before so I never broke any bones or had my arm sliced open. But, yeah, I admit I have quite the immune system."

"Another fact about your past coming to the surface." She said with a smile. "At this rate you'll remember everything in no time!"

The trouble is I remember everything already. The problem with that is I don't know when to shut up.

You should think before speaking Young One. Aria said with a laugh. *It will cause you less grief in the future.*

How about you stop interfering with my thoughts, Aria?! He snapped back. *Geez, I can't get a second to myself anymore it seems.*

Ah, the curse of the Mind Speech. In time I hope you will learn to guard your thoughts and keep them from wandering so often. It's distracting.

Mistress Mallandred bade him farewell and closed the door behind him. It was odd walking at first with the new bandages, but they broke in quickly.

The second to last thing on the list was the seamstress, Baraque[1]. Master Horacio Baraque was still dunking sheets of leather in the odd smelling liquid when he came up to him. He was a skinny person with long limbs and a boney face. He was completely bald, which didn't help make him look any better, and he had beady little eyes that sparkled in the sunlight. His wife, Mistress Anasandra Baraque, was a cheery woman with a completely different build than her husband. Where he was tall and skinny, she was plump and stout. They looked an odd pair, but according to Dannil, there wasn't a couple more in love.

---

1. Baraque—Sounds like Bar-Uhk-way.

"Ah, Master Richards, it's good to see you." Horacio said dipping the leather into the liquid again. "What can I help you with?"

James said that he needed a few more sets of clothes, since all he really had was what he was wearing. Horacio laughed and nodded towards his wife.

"She be the one you want to see about that. I make the leather, she makes the clothes."

Mistress Anasandra steered him into her house and asked him if he knew his measurements. Again, like he told the Lady, he didn't know. The seamstress laughed like her husband and began measuring his hips and waist, shoulder width and arms, chest and neck, even his ankles. Jotting everything down on a piece of paper she fumbled through a list of things, talking to herself. In the next room she asked him to pick out what color material he would like.

"Now, pick something you can work in, something for everyday use, and something for special occasions and Sundays. And of course you'll want extras incase the first ones tear or become dirty, so I'd say about seven pairs should do for now." She looked through the materials for a moment before adding, "And don't worry about the price. Dannil has done me so many favors that it's the least I can do."

James looked at all the different colors and picked out the ones he liked best. For his first pair, which would be for Sundays, was a deep blue with a hint of aqua on the other side. His work clothes were plain brown and beige, and for everyday wear he chose colors similar to the ones he had on—greenish brown. Mistress Anasandra was 'happy to help such a nice young man' and told him to come back tomorrow for his first fitting.

Outside, the sun was beaming high, meaning it was about noon already. He was still full from breakfast and the snacks earlier so he headed down the road to the big house at the end. The last thing on the list just said: *Se'Cruz. He knows what I need.* Stuffing the paper back into his pouch he trudged along the dirt road. Before he reached the front porch the hairs on the back of his neck rose and he felt an odd itching in the back of his mind.

Behind him he heard something move and turned around to see three boys all about his age staring at him. One of them he remembered from the trial, Neru, he thought the boy's name was. His lightly colored hair was cut short and pressed flat on his head. He was tall, just about his own height, and held himself with an air of authority, though James could tell it was just for show. The other two were almost identical to each other. Their dark brown hair was cut short like Neru's but parted down the middle. They were rather small but had chests and arms at least twice the size of his own.

"What can I do for you?" James asked as politely as he could. The way Neru stood spoke of possible trouble, and he wasn't in the mood or in shape enough for that.

"Oh, nothing …" he said in reply.

"Well, if you'll excuse me, I have to find Master Se'Cruz. I'm running an errand for Dannil and I need to speak with him."

"An erran', huh?" The boy on Neru's right said. His voice was deep and slightly slurred. "Look a' that Marad, Dannil has him runnin' chores already."

"Hmph. I can see for myself, Daz." Marad said without looking over.

"Shut it both of you." Neru said. "I'm sure that Master Gashain has plenty of good reasons for sending Se'Cruz's *apprentice* out on an errand."

Now he remembered. The incident at the trial when Neru had come forward after Se'Cruz announced his apprenticeship; he said that Neru had been trying to become his apprentice for the past two years. He was probably jealous that James had gotten the position.

"Well, if you don't know where Master Se'Cruz is, I'll be on my way." He stepped off the porch and headed around the back.

A shuffle of feet was all the warning he had before James realized the others were coming for him. Steeling his ribs, he bolted away from the house and began running full throttle towards the small enclosure of trees that backed the village. His mind reached out for Aria and started relaying messages to the hawk. Ducking into the trees he started dodging left and right past trees and brush alike, remembering what the bandit had said and making sure not to break too many twigs. Behind him he could hear the others not far behind.

I am ready Young One.

Good, I'm almost to the rendezvous point. He replied ducking under a low branch. *Just make sure to go easy on them. Don't gash up their faces like you did the last guy okay?*

Very well. She replied.

The trees became thick all of a sudden dulling the light and making it harder to see, but with Aria guiding him he was able to keep up the pace and the lead he had over the others. Ducking around a thick pine James called up to Aria who flew past and landed in the tree opposite his. As she settled into the branches, Neru and the others appeared looking completely winded. Perfect.

Alright, wait until they are in range then start.

Very well.

Neru took a few steps forward and stopped. James looked over to the hawk and nodded. *Let's go.* In a flurry of feathers and shrieks Aria took flight into the air and started diving at Neru. All three screamed and covered their face with their arms. Using the distraction James leapt up into the tree he was hiding behind and positioned himself above Daz and Marad, making sure he was covered by the pines. With a thought he told Aria to start the next step, and the hawk dove once more at the three frightened boys before flying off.

"Wh-what in the Fires was that!?" Marad said massaging his arms. There were a few scrapes from Aria's talons up and down them.

"How should I know?" Neru said holding a hand out at the retreating hawk. His forefinger was curved and his thumb was placed inside the arch. Probably some sign against evil spirits. "And watch what you say! Cursing with the Fires like that. You want to bring the Flames on us all?"

"It was just some crazed bird." Daz said calmly. James could see he was shaking.

He was having too much fun. When the others started to leave he set the next part of the plan into motion. Shaking the branches of the pine with arms and legs he laughed maniacally, in a deep foreboding voice. The others whirled around in alarm, Neru making the sign with his finger and thumb again, the others just staring at the tree with open mouths.

"I AM THE SPIRIT OF THE WOOD!" He cried. "LEAVE THIS PLACE, MORTALS! YOU HAVE ANGERED ME AND MY CREATURES OF THE FOREST!"

Daz and Marad shouted at the top of their lungs as the tree started swaying towards them. Neru was watching in stunned silence.

"NOW GO! AND NEVER COME INTO MY DOMAIN AGAIN! OR NEXT TIME YOU SHALL FACE MY WRATH!!" Daz and Marad looked at each other. "I SAID GO!!"

The twins turned tail and bolted with their arms waving over their heads and their shrill screams echoing through the forest. James called to Aria and the hawk appeared again and started dropping worms and other insects she'd caught on them. He heard the hawk laughing at them as she flew after. James looked down and saw Neru staring after the twins.

"Very funny!"

James burst out laughing and half fell, half jumped from the branches onto the ground a few feet in front of the tall figure. Righting himself he stared him in the eyes waiting to see what he would do. Neru just stood there with his back to him, hands tightened into fists at his sides.

"Serves them right, don't you think?" James asked. Neru could really hold his temper.

"What makes you think you had the right to do that kind of thing to us?" he shouted back rounding on him. "I thought it was a real spirit! Do you have any idea what you have done? Why did you scare us like that?!"

"Because you were chasing me for no reason!" he snapped. "I thought you were going to beat me up or something with the way you came after me. Then there's that fact I was terrified you might actually start using your power on me!"

"We wouldn't use our powers against someone in our own village. Especially not on someone who doesn't have them himself." He took a step forward. "What kind of people do you think we are?"

"How can I answer that? I don't even know you! I just did what I thought would keep me from being beaten again!" he placed a hand near his side where the bruise had started to ache from all the running and yelling.

Neru just stood there looking angry, furious, and maybe a little hurt. But James didn't care, he was in such a rage that he wanted to rip the kid a new one! When Neru didn't speak James considered the conversation over and started walking past him. When he was at Neru's shoulder he stopped.

"It's because I'm Se'Cruz's apprentice isn't it?"

"I've been trying to get that position for four years now. But he just won't give me a second chance." Neru turned to him. "I had the job when I was thirteen. I thought that because of my … anyway, I wasn't good enough it turned out. I worked my best, but it wasn't enough for him so he asked me to leave."

Apprenticed at thirteen? I didn't have my first job until I was sixteen. What could possess him to do that?

"Why did you apprentice yourself at such a young age? At thirteen you should still be playing with all the others, maybe even starting to look at a girl or two." He added with a laugh.

Neru didn't answer. James didn't wait long though. If it was a private matter, then he didn't need to know. Calling up to Aria to see where she was, James left Neru standing there in the forest. The hawk steered him out of the woods before saying goodbye and flying back to her place in the trees.

The door to the smithy was in the back of Se'Cruz's house. The smithy itself looked like a large rock jutting out from the ground with a door, windows, and chimney. It was in the shape of a dome and connected itself to the rest of the house by another door in the back. The sound of a hammer hacking away at metal could be heard through the open window and the smell of the forge wafted in the air. Stepping up to the door, he knocked.

"Come in!" James opened the door and was blasted by a wave of heat so intense he thought he was under attack. "Ah, James it's you. Come in, come in."

Elyas Se'Cruz was as big a man that there ever was. Without his Council robes he looked like a competitor for the World's Strongest Man. His arms were twice as thick as his and twined with sharp muscle. The veins in his lower arms were showing from the strain of the attack on the metal piece he still hammered. His back was like a wall of muscle and skin covered only by a single leather apron. The hammer he used had a head the size of James' foot and about twice as wide with a long wooden handle protruding from one end.

The thin piece of metal he was working was lying on an anvil that looked to be part of the floor. Its deep black surface was unscratched despite countless beatings from the hammers. Elyas had the metal pinned down with one hand wielding a large pair of pliers while the other hammered away. The glow from the metal drew his eye like a moth to flame almost immediately. But before he could admire the work, Elyas set the hammer down and using both hands with the pliers dumped the metal into a barrel of water that hissed and sent up a cloud of steam.

"So, have you come to start your training?" The smith said setting the pliers on the table next to the wall. "Or perhaps your apprenticeship?"

"Actually, I'm here to run an errand for Dannil." James took out the paper and read aloud what it said. "I really hope you know what it is he wants because I haven't a clue."

"Yes, yes I know what he needs." The smith dusted his hand on his apron and went to the back of the room.

It was then that James noticed how messy the place was. The table was covered in items and pieces of metal that needed working. The walls had hanging clips, but nothing was on them, it was all strewn about the floor in clumps here and there. The area around the anvil was decently clean, but outside the little circle of cleanliness was dust and debris in all directions! He had a horrible feeling that it was going to be his job to clean this place up. Luckily he had plenty of practice from home.

"This be what Dannil requested." Elyas came back holding a wooden box about the same size as the hammer head. "Heh, a new set of chisels and carving knives. His old ones were getting on in *months* and their edges were actually getting dull." The man sighed. "If only he would stop using them for a day or two and take the time to sharpen them, he wouldn't need another set for another year or two."

Elyas gave him the box and was leading him to the door saying, "Watch your step there," and "Be careful of that metal piece." When they finally got to the door James couldn't help but ask.

"As your apprentice, it's going to be my job to clean this place up isn't it?" The large man bellowed a laugh so loud that James felt himself jump.

"You bet your bottom it is." He said in between laughs. "I'm a very busy person and don't have the time to go around cleaning this place up everyday. And I don't let Miranda come in here because she can't lift the larger hammers. Well, that and she has her own chores to do. Ah, but don't worry. Keep at it and the place will be good as new. When that happens I'll make sure to dirty it up a bit more."

James sighed inwardly and smiled to himself. *What have I gotten myself into?* Se'Cruz was laughing again, as they stepped outside.

"Cleaning the place isn't all you'll be doing here, so don't get too down. I'm going to teach you how to light and keep the forge at the right temperature, how to heat the metal, and when your power manifests I'll teach you how to Shape the metals. Not to mention, during your free time we will work on Awakening your power. Plus," he added with a wicked looking smile. "No apprentice of mine may work in my forge without combat training."

"Combat Training?! You never said anything about that!!"

"Think of it as a fun way to build muscle, stamina, and physical strength. And trust me, you'll need them if your going to keep *this* forge lit. And I'm sure you don't want to be defenseless the next time Neru chases you? Yes I saw the whole thing, until you vanished into the forest." He leaned down closer. "By the way, what did you do to make Marad and Daz come running out of there like that? They looked like they'd seen a spirit. Not to mention I think they went and wet themselves in there."

James told him about how he hid in the tree and spooked them into thinking it was a spirit. He even showed him his deep evil voice. Elyas stared wide-eyed at the sound his voice took on and made a gesture with his hand. It was the same thing that Neru had used.

"Master Se'Cruz, what is that sign?"

"Oh this? It is a sign to ward off evil spirits and foul luck; though I have yet to see the latter come true."

"Oh, that's what I thought. But I have one more question." James felt something pull at the back of his mind, towards the other side of the forge. "What happened to Neru when he was your apprentice? I mean, why take on the job so young?"

"I thought you might ask me that. Well, I'm not sure if it is really my business to tell you his reasons for starting the job, but as to why he stopped ... well, suffice it to say his heart didn't seem into it after a while. I can't really blame him, but I needed and still need an apprentice who can keep his mind in one place and concentrate on his work."

"Master Se'Cruz ... I truly don't think I can complete the tasks you want me to do adequately enough alone ... Do you think ...?"

"You want Neru to come back and work for me, don't you?" He nodded. "Well, I don't know. How do I know he won't slack off again? Give me a reason, a good one and I will think on it."

"A good reason? Well I know one way to get him to work harder: A rival." He turned his head a little so his voice would reach the back of the forge. "If he knows that someone else has the same job he does, he might try all the more harder to be better than that other person."

Se'Cruz saw what he was doing and smiled. "Well I said I needed a good reason, and I am willing to take that one, but then again ..."

"Master Se'Cruz!"

Neru came hurtling around the side of the forge and stopped as they were both already staring at him. He faltered for only a moment before rushing up and kneeling in front of the smith.

"Master Se'Cruz, please, please! Take me on as your apprentice again! I swear I will work harder! Harder than this newcomer! My parents worked it out and ... I will be able to concentrate on the work. I won't slack off, I will make you proud! Please!"

Se'Cruz laughed. "How can I say no to a plea like that?! Welcome back Neru."

"Really?! I can comeback to the forge?" The smith nodded. "Oh thank you, thank you Master Se'Cruz! I promise I won't let you down again!"

CHAPTER 7

▼

TREASURES AND PROMISES

ELYAS was as good as his word and the day Rosemary said he was healed; James began working at the forge. Together he and Neru picked up the tools and metals and dust and slowly began to make the dirty place seem a fit workplace. It was tiring work, but James showed Neru how to sweep up the dust without stirring it into the air and in return Neru showed him how and where to place the metals and hammers. When they weren't cleaning the forge, Master Se'Cruz would take them outback to the field and put them through the most rigorous training.

He had them run around the field as fast as they could, and then see how many times they could make it around without collapsing. James was faster than Neru by a lot, but he couldn't keep up his pace for more than one and a half laps (but it was a big field!!). Neru knew how to pace himself better and managed five whole laps before he was too tired to continue. After that, he had them do push-ups, sit-ups, and pull ups on bars he had placed on the side of his house. Next came hand to hand fighting, but for that he only showed them the proper way to punch and kick, a few grapple holds, how to tumble if you were thrown, and even some very painful 'pressure points'.

The first day of real combat practice had been the most fascinating day he could remember. The sun was high in the sky, a few clouds dotting the otherwise clear day. The three of them went around to the side of the house where Elyas kept a shed of weapons and things he would sell to merchants. Since he was the only one who knew how to use them, there wasn't any other use for them. Normally farmers and craftsmen didn't need to use a sword or battle axe. For most a bow was fine.

"Okay boys," Elyas said as he opened the door to the shed. "It's time to pick your weapon."

They both stared wide-eyed and open-mouthed at the arsenal. There were swords, axes, halberds, maces, flails, shields, bows and arrows, anything and everything that a man could fight with was packed here in this shed. James started towards the swords but was stopped when Elyas grabbed his shirt.

"Whoa there," he said hauling him back to the door, "I don't want you to go and pick the weapon you think is the most deadly or well crafted. I want you to pick the weapon that was *meant* for you." He pulled two handkerchiefs from his pocket and held them out to them. "Put these on."

"But Master, how are we to see which weapon we want?" Neru asked taking the cloth.

"I'll explain after you're blindfolded." He waited until he was sure neither could see. "Now I am going to send Neru in first. While you are inside I want you to think of nothing. Clear your mind of thought and reach with your mind. The weapon that is meant for you will call you to it."

Neru took a deep breath and stepped inside. James waited patiently for him to come out, but not being able to see couldn't say what was going on. He heard Neru's footsteps walking across the hard wood floor and the sound of his breathing as he began to slow down. The sound of metal sliding against metal sounded and Neru let out a 'whoop!' James heard him run out of the shed and to Se'Cruz's side.

"Good, now James."

Without waiting to steady his breathing he stepped into the shed. He tried clearing his mind, but there was too much confusion in it that pictures and memories kept floating up. He stopped in the center of the shed and turned this way and that feeling with his mind like he did when searching for Aria. But still nothing seemed to happen. He was about to give up when Aria spoke to him.

To clear your mind, think of something calming from your home.

Something from my home? What will that do?

Trust me. Think of a song, a poem, a person, something that you find calming.

Pushing aside some of the useless junk swimming in his thoughts he thought of a song he heard when he was little. It was a lullaby his mother used to sing to him, but it was the most calming thing he could think of. He began humming the song and slowly everything began to settle down. Never stopping the song he let the weapons call to him. After a moment something pulled at him from the right. He slowly turned and walked towards the feeling ... now it was higher up, almost out of reach. His hand clenched around something wooden and he pulled it from the shelf.

"You may now remove your blindfolds."

Using his free hand he tore the cloth from his eyes, put his glasses back on, and gazed at the greatest wooden staff he had ever seen—the only wooden staff he'd ever seen. Its surface was shining, like it had been polished, and it was as smooth as glass. Setting it next to him its length broke his height by a few inches. It was then he saw four runes crafted into the top of the staff. They drew and mesmerized him as he stepped out of the shed. He felt like he should know them ...

"What an amazing weapon." He said twirling it his hand.

"That staff is one of my best weapons, though it wasn't I who made it. It was Dannil. He made it for a powerful man long ago. He spent weeks making it perfectly balanced and smooth so not even the smallest error would be seen. The man who wished to buy it left specific instructions and drawings of those runes so Dannil could carve them. But he made one mistake and never told him in which order to carve the runes, or so we think. So instead of allowing the man to channel his power through the staff, it became resistant to it. Any Intaruan who tries to use their power against that staff will find themselves at a terrible disadvantage."

Aria might know what these runes mean. After all, she can speak with the Lady, and she definitely knows things.

Neru's weapon turned out to be a wicked looking double-edged sword and shield. The hilt of the sword was black with a single red line snaking its way from top to bottom. The hand guard too was black but had silver markings on it. Yet it was the blade of the sword that James didn't like. It was a normal looking (but kind of thin) sword at first glance, but when it moved, the steel seemed to multiply in number making it seem there were three swords instead of one.

"Another interesting pick." Elyas said when he saw Neru's weapon. "That blade was made by me, but again, it had been requested by a powerful Intaruan—a soldier. The steel he gave me to use had already been endowed with some of his power, which is what gives the sword the illusion effect. Yet the man never came to retrieve it, so it has sat in my shed for seven long years."

Taking the blade and shield Neru turned to James and thrust the blade at him. Hopping to the side he swung his staff at the other's side, but it was blocked by the heavy shield. Back and forth they went swinging and blocking, dodging and parrying until they were breathless. Elyas just stood there and watched them the entire time with his arms crossed, checking for flaws and places of improvement.

"Neru, don't try to be so flashy with your attacks." He said taking the apprentice's sword arm. "Move it with quick, targeted strokes. That's how you use a sword like this. It is meant to be fast and deadly, not slow and flashy."

He and Neru went through a few stances and exercises. It looked like an odd dance to James who stood there leaning on the staff. Aria was munching on a mouse a little ways off, but it reminded him how hungry he was.

"James, that staff isn't meant to attack outright." He slipped the weapon from his hand. "Use it to defend and buy yourself time to see the flaws in your opponent's technique. When you see it, strike!" He tossed the staff back to James. "However, sometimes you may be fighting more than one person at a time. With a staff like that, it isn't as hard as you might think.

"Use both ends to deflect the blows by swinging it around between your arms and around your back if you need. Also, use its length to thrust past your opponent's defenses. Now try attacking Neru again. But remember … defend and strike. Also, Neru, use this practice sword. I don't feel like explaining to Rosemary why James had his arm cut clean off."

Again the two of them danced back and forth swinging sword and staff in unison. The few notes and stances Elyas put Neru through made an improvement on his form, but James saw something that looked promising for his own counterattack. Batting the sword away using one end of the staff, he whirled around using the shield as a platform to spin behind Neru and clotted him on the side of the head.

"Good! That's what I'm talking about!" Se'Cruz said kneeling next to Neru's unconscious form. "Ah, he'll be alright in a minute. See he's already waking up."

James was relieved to see Neru standing and even more so when he said that he just had "one flaming headache!" Elyas sent him off to Rosemary's with Miranda there to make sure he got there okay. He kept James behind to work on his power. Setting the staff against the shed and sitting on the ground he listened as Se'Cruz told him all the properties of the power and how to summon and control it. It was fascinating!

The power was like a large pool of energy that people had born in them. The size of this pool never changed during their years of Vacancy as it was called, but when a person started training and practicing with their power the amount they could wield grew. To use one's power they had to find it, deep within, and summon it to them. Depending how strong the person was would determine how much of their power would come when they called.

When the power was coursing through them, it was up to the person to manipulate it and focus it. How and with what they used their power with determined the outcome. For instance, an Intaruan didn't just make fire appear out of nowhere. What they did was manipulate the air around them so it became flammable and then using their power ignited it into the flames they would throw about. The younger Wielders had to use something that could produce a spark in order to use their powers at first, but with time they could dispose of them and use it like anyone else.

Elyas told him to watch carefully as he summoned his powers. The mountainous man took a few steps back and took a deep breath. James sat there watching, never blinking, as Elyas just stood there for a moment. Then he saw it; a red orange glow enveloped the smith, outlining his body like a kind of light barrier or something. From where he was sitting he could feel the warmth emanating from the light, like a bonfire. Elyas looked pleased at the discovery of James' ability to see the light, but didn't say anything about it. Then it was James' turn.

He led James through some mind exercises that helped him clear his mind of thought. Then he told him to look for his power. That part was easier than he thought it would be. Without the distractions of random thoughts he was able to feel his entire being, everything it did and everything that happened to it. Down, near his heart he saw the power hovering just out of reach. It wasn't just a pool of energy, but a beacon of light that beckoned him and it called for him to use it. He reached out to it and …

"Aack!"

Elyas caught him as he fell back. It felt as though he'd been thrown from his power by a powerful force. His breathing was rapid and he felt physically exhausted. When he caught his breath enough to speak he told Elyas what had happened. He didn't seem too surprised.

"I knew it. When we were in your trial and we put you through the test to determine whether or not you were telling the truth, the three of us ran into that wall, which we call a Seal." He was pacing back and forth in front of James. "I have never felt a Seal so strongly made and securely placed. Whoever made it was incredibly powerful. Perhaps someone from your past knew that you would be exceptionally strong and so determined to Seal your power so it wouldn't manifest."

"Is there any way to break it? I don't want this Seal stopping my power!"

"No one likes being Sealed." he replied looking down at him with a serious stare. "But I'm afraid no one can get near it to remove it without being completely drained. I had been Bonded to Majhra and Ralco when we tested you.

Oh, Bonding allows one to combine their power with that of another, and up to eight people can be Bonded at once. While Bonded, all their power is put under control of the one leading the Bond, the Leader. Simple names, yet effective."

"So why not try a full Bonding then? You say eight people can Bond, so that must be enough to break the Seal!"

"It wouldn't work. James, that Seal would drain all of us. And besides, Bonding takes a lot of skill and only five people in the entire village can do it. And our powers combined couldn't dent that Seal. I'm sorry."

With the day so far along, Elyas sent him on his way and told him to come back the next day bright and early. Dannil wasn't at the house or in the shop, so James went to his room and flopped down onto his bed. Who would place a Seal over him? He couldn't be that powerful ... could he? Se'Cruz said it would take someone of great power to make the Seal ... It couldn't be ...

Aria! Come quick I need to speak with you!

No need to shout Young One. I am here.

The hawk fluttered in through the open window and landed on the end post of his bed. James sat up and stared the hawk in the eyes.

Aria, did the Lady place a Seal over my power?

What makes you think that ...?

Se'Cruz said it would take someone of immense strength to make it, and she is the only person I have met thus far who meets that description. Did she make this Seal?

Mother had her reasons, you must understand that. She replied almost hastily. *When you spoke to her in the Woods about whether or not you would have the power she thought that might be why you were brought into our world. So when she had to leave you, she searched for your power and found it. She was amazed at the amount of energy you had and knew then and there that was why you were brought here.*

I want to speak with her! I know you can communicate with her even from this distance. Tell her I want to talk now!

Watch your tongue! Aria screeched and flapped her wings at him. *Mother cannot be summoned by anyone! She comes when she feels it necessary or important.*

~Aria, it is alright. I am here.

Both of them jumped as the Lady's voice echoed in their minds.

~You wish to speak with me, James Richards?

Yes. Why did you put this Seal over my power?

~Aria has already told you. He got the impression she was smiling, but couldn't be sure. Her emotions were completely blocked from him. *Before I left, I felt your power and knew that it was the true target. Not only that but I knew that if your*

power manifested itself while you were on this continent and it was not that of fire, you would be hunted and killed. I didn't want that to happen so I placed the Seal.

But I can't go around living this way. He replied seriously. *Not in* this *world. If I am going to survive here I am going to need every advantage I can get. And besides … I trust these people. Even if I am a Gattarian, I know they won't kill me. It wouldn't be right for a farmer to slaughter me.*

The Lady didn't answer right away. Impatient as he was, James managed to hold back on repeating his demand.

~Very well. But I am unable to reach you now to remove the Seal. I am very far off taking care of things that need to be seen to. When I am able to come back to the Gray Woods, I shall contact you. But I am unable to stay in one place for too long, my powers are needed all over. So when I call, you must come as quickly as you can.

Really? You'll remove the Seal? She nodded, *Thank you … My Lady, I'm sorry I was rude. I—I shouldn't have acted that way. Please forgive me.*

~It is alright James Richards. Now I must go. Take care of yourself and Aria. Goodbye. And she was gone.

Dannil knocked on the door and entered. He said that he had some food ready. James, remembered how hungry he'd been during training, hurried out of the room. He remembered Aria and when he turned around she was gone. She must have left when Dannil knocked. Clever bird …

Time went on in Yattion as normal. People woke up, went to work and made a living. James became used to waking up with the sun and cleaning the forge. Sometimes he had to run to Neru's house and wake him up so he wouldn't be late, but that was soon remedied after Elyas had them both lug wood and coal from his storages all day for being late. After that Neru and James were at the forge each morning with time to spare. Yet sometimes he would have them lug wood and coal anyway.

When they weren't working they were training. Sometimes he would have them spar, while other days he would train them one on one. Neru slowly got used to the fast motions of his practice sword and learned to use it in combination with his shield. James, however, grasped the concept of the staff almost at once. His long arms and height helped to balance the length of the staff and allowed him to pull off maneuvers that Elyas could only describe for him.

His training in the power didn't go nearly as well. While he couldn't summon his power he could find it now without having to search. Also, he could clear his mind of thought instantly if he needed and then he would be able to prod and poke mentally at the Seal. He never attacked it outright but kept his distance and searched for a weak point. Then one day while he was prodding the Seal again he noticed something.

He was sitting in his usual spot a few yards away from the forge under the evening sun. Elyas was sitting a few feet away from him, watching his every move and occasionally speaking to him with hints or suggestions. Neru was long gone, he didn't need to work on his powers, but, unfortunately, James did and that was what he was trying to do.

He was focused entirely on the bright light that called out to him from the other side of the Seal. It was infuriating! The only thing that stopped him from being able to use his powers was a seemingly paper thin barrier of power! Every-day after combat practice, he and Elyas tried to find a way past the Seal and every day ended in failure and James feeling completely exhausted.

His mind was hovering just above the Seal, not touching it; that would drain him and repel him from the light and back into complete consciousness. There *HAD* to be some way … Like so many times before, James pressed up against the Seal with his mind and felt his energy begin to drain away and the feeling of the repelling began to push at him; he tried calling out to his power like Elyas said one did to summon it to them. Incredibly, the light responded and began stir-ring! It hovered over to him and crashed into the Seal.

They were so close now that he could feel the force of the power course through him. The over all effect left him stunned and wide eyed with Se'Cruz crouched over him; he'd fallen over. The smith was calling to him and when he responded began asking what had happened.

"You were sitting there one minute," he said quickly, "and then the air around you began to shift, like the waves of heat that fly from the forge and distorts our vision at times. I felt nothing, at all, but I *knew* it was your powers. What did you do?"

James told him how he had pressed against the Seal and called his powers to him and how the force of it had been flowing through him. Elyas told him to try again … he complied before he finished the request. This time he held on tight to the energy that coursed through him and tried to use it somehow. Elyas began walking him through the steps for controlling the power.

"The power is not a sentient force." He said as he paced around James. "It is only a force, one that needs direction and only you can conduct it. Tell the power what it is that *you* want *it* to do and then will it to comply."

James grasped the power from the other side of the Seal and held on tight! The repelling of the Seal pushed at him with strained force, almost like it was failing to repel him and it knew. Above him, he heard Elyas talking again.

"I know that your element is unknown, but I'll put you through the basics of Fire Wielding. I don't know if this will work or not, what with the Seal and all, but we have to try. Ready?" He nodded in response. "Okay. Concentrate on the air around you while keeping a grip on the force. Draw the air in around you. When you feel it, change it the same way you control the power—with your will. Change it so that your power can ignite it!"

Try as he might—and he tried harder at this than anything else—he couldn't do what Elyas said. The air didn't respond to his call; the force pulsing through him like a second blood kept all his focus and all his concentration on it and it alone. When he diverted his attention to drawing in the air his focus slipped and he touched the Seal completely.

"Damn it all to the Flames!"

Elyas looked askance at the curse that burst from his apprentice's mouth. A little ticked at the new failure, he attempted it again. After five more tries that left him completely drained of all energy—he had to be carried into the house to recover—he still didn't quite have the hand on the force. It took a good two weeks before he finally learned some control over it. Though he couldn't make fire with it, he could make some nifty barriers that protected him from the power.

He and Elyas kept the news of the new power a secret from Neru (and everyone else for now) until they were sure he could control it completely without fail. Then one day Elyas had Neru and James spar; this time Neru was allowed to use his powers.

"But, Master," Neru said as he was handed the wooden practice sword and metallic shield, "If I use my powers, James could get hurt. Even with the staff he won't be able to stop the flames from scouring him."

"Don't you worry about that." James said as he slid into a fighting stance. "I promise I won't embarrass you completely."

That got Neru's blood boiling and made him slide into his fighting stance. Elyas stood back and with a shout the battle commenced. Neru was quick and deadly with his sword and kept his shield up to keep James from countering. The wooden blade flew through the air like a bullet as the staff hit the hand guard, knocking it from Neru's hand. The boy looked shocked for a moment before he remembered the new rule. A bright red halo enveloped the apprentice and a fireball formed in his hand.

"Last chance to back out, James." He called as he backed a few feet away with the fireball hovering just above his palm.

"Just throw the damn thing!" James shouted as he readied his new power.

With a sigh and a shrug Neru tossed the blazing fire at him. The flames burned through the air but left no smoke in its trail. When the energy was flowing through him, James crafted it with his mind so it encased his entire body. With a small explosion the fireball collided with the barrier. Neru cried out as it hit James and started running towards him before he realized he was perfectly fine. The fire had slid right off without burning either skin or clothes.

"How in the Fires …?"

Elyas and James looked at each other for a moment before they burst out laughing. Neru just stood there trying to figure out what had happened. When he got his breath back James told him everything.

By using this force he could slow, even sometimes deflect the fire crafted from the power. It was tiring and drained him of strength quickly depending on how much he used it and to what degree, but it was all in preparation for the day when his powers would fully manifest.

The apprentice was amazed—a little flabbergasted—but still amazed.

One day when he was washing up from another day of work, errands, and training, he looked in the mirror and was shocked at what he saw. His face had grown harder and achieved a sharper looked to it. His arms were still the same size, but more defined and had the hints of muscle starting to appear from all the lugging and combating. Then there was the shadow of a beard that was creeping up on him. It was in his blood to grow beards slower than most, but his lack of shaving had started taking its toll.

After his first year in Yattion, Se'Cruz allowed him and Neru to start working at the forge, not just clean it. Learning how to pump the bellows and keep the fires at the right temperature was arduous work, but compared to hammering the metal from one shape to the next it was a cake walk! The giant hammers were so heavy that by the end of the day he willingly went to Mistress Mallandred's to get some pain relieving herbs.

But he didn't work all the time. There were days when Elyas would say that he didn't need them at the forge and sent them off to do whatever. These times they cherished and spent hanging out with others their age (Daz, Marad, and Miranda) that'd gotten the day off. Neru said that the parents organized these days so there would be others to 'play' with. The pond was easily the one place that they went to the most because it allowed them to relax and 'play', as Neru put it, at the same time.

But no matter how tired he was, at the end of everyday he would lie down in his bed and just stare at the ceiling thinking about home. His stomach writhed at what his parents must be going through, and he didn't want to know what his friends thought had happened. *I just wish I could tell them I was safe ...* would be his last thought before nodding off.

CHAPTER 8

▼

FAREWELL AGAIN

ANOTHER full year passed by without anything interesting happening, unless you counted a myriad of merchant's wagons, the occasional tax collector, and the holidays that popped up out of nowhere. One such holiday was Summer's Eve, or Summer's Fest as some called it. Summer's Eve was, of course, held on the day before the first day of summer.

It was a day of relaxation where no one would work for one full day, sun up to sun up. Reason being: there was a time when the Emperor of Intaru was a real tyrant. He was a ruthless man who made everyone work at inhuman paces for little to no pay. The Emperor was overthrown by a peasant man who wanted it all to stop. The outcome was that the peasant man became the new Emperor and, with the help of some officials who had experience in the matter of ruling a country, managed to bring the place back to order. The celebration of relaxation was held in his honor.

The other holiday that amused James the most was Year's Birth—or New Years to him. Despite the fact that this world and his were different in so many ways, there were a few occurrences where they seemed alike; this was one of those times. Everyone stayed up all night waiting for the moon to hit its peak at midnight thus ushering in the New Year. Events that could only be held at night were, again, like some of the games he'd played when younger and even sometimes when he was older.

Capture the Flag, or The Flag War was one of them and James was a natural. After the first game where he'd captured the flag in record time, everyone fought over what team he should be on next. In the end to stop a fight, he backed off from the game and watched instead. Another game, one that he wasn't a master in was simple hide and seek. While he wasn't the first person to be found, he didn't know the layout of Yattion as well as everyone else and thus had a harder time finding hiding places for himself and where others could hide while he was 'it'.

On his twenty-first birthday the entire village held a celebration in honor of his true entry into manhood. Now he could legally have his own house, though he said Dannil would miss him too much if he left. The carpenter smiled at the comment and turned back to the banquet. James smiled at his friend's back ... he had seen the small tear.

It so happened that his birthday was on the same day as a famous and renowned holiday called Harvest of Souls. It was the equivalent to Veteran's Day (and held on the same day too) where everyone would have a day of silence in honor of souls of soldiers who died in the war. This was a day looked forward to by everyone in Arollay because it was the start of a month of Peace.

According to the villagers, the day allowed the spirits of the dead soldiers to come close to the living world and the Land's power permitted no violence. No one, soldier or not, could lift a hand against another for one full month. People came home from the front lines to be with their families for a time before they had to go back. But this didn't stop people from having fun and being of good cheer.

The celebrations held during Peace time were the greatest of the year, and his birthday was no exception. They danced and paraded and sang and drank. People told stories about legends and myths from generations past. James even got up and told a story from a book he'd read—though to everyone else it was made up on the spot. It was about a boy and his dragon (he had to explain what a dragon was) and how they had to save the world from an evil that threatened to destroy everything. The people applauded when he was done and asked for more, but he wouldn't say anything more until the next time they celebrated.

The gifts he got were excellent. Elyas and Miranda went and made him a shaving kit. She said he looked funny with the 'fuzzy rug growing on his face.' Dannil made him a wooden carving of him wielding his staff. The detail was amazing! He could even see the little runes carved at the top end of the staff. The Wool Women gave him one combined gift; a cloak made of wool to keep him warm in the slightly cooling weather. It was a mix of browns and blacks and came with a bronze circular brooch that held it closed.

He was also given a saddle by Baraque and Anasandra, with a holster for his staff and a new set of clothes too. Then it was Master Ignatius who gave him the greatest gift by far. It was a Nordic horse, he said, leading it into the village center. It had a mane of golden hair that was flat and messy on its head. Its coat was a beautiful dark brown with a single white diamond on its forehead.

"I bred him myself." The farmer said. "I was surprised he came out as well as he did; horses not being my best specialty. But there is one small problem; his back just isn't strong enough to do the work I need him to and I figured that you could make good use of him. He doesn't have a name yet, so I leave it to you to decide."

Setting the saddle on the stallion and hoisting himself into the saddle, which he needed a little help for considering the size of the horse, he rode in a slow walk. Ignatius led him into a canter and James learned the ways on how to hold the reins and steer with his knees. The horse liked to prance around a bit after standing still for a few moments he noticed. Swinging back to the village center he hopped off the saddle, well, fell would be a more appropriate term …

Aria, do you know of some type of language or something that is here in Arollay? Something besides the common tongue.

Yes, there is a language that the creatures learned from the land at the world's making. Why do you ask?

I'm looking for the word which means …

"I'll call him Trae'len." He said.

"That's a nice name. Does it mean anything?" Someone asked.

"It means Strong Hero. I heard it once a long time ago."

Thus he and Trae'len began their riding and practicing together. James modified his battle skills to accommodate being on the horse. It was harder, but the staff's length was a big factor.

The weather in Intaru was very warm all year round, and didn't get cold enough to have need for more than a single thick blanket at night. And so the winter season passed by without much damage to crops and herds. But it was six months after Peace that something finally happened. Something that would forever change the course of Arollay's future.

It was night. The entire village was asleep in their beds dreaming of whatever their imaginations could come up with. There was a merchant's train just outside the village, loaded down with the supplies it brought and the ones it had bought from the villagers. Once again Dannil and Se'Cruz had managed to sell every-thing they had prepared and also managed to haggle up the prices to quite a sum.

James was tossing about in his bed trying to wake up from the odd sleep, but found he could not. Something held him in his dream ...

Visions flashed through his mind, one after the other, too fast for him to see clearly. Some lasted long enough for his mind to translate, while others vanished as soon as they appeared. Something was pulling at the back of his mind, some-thing he knew well enough. He could sense when people were using their powers and could also see their power as they summoned it and used it to whatever pur-pose (that, he found out, was the red orange glow he could see surrounding peo-ple sometimes), but being surrounded by Intaruans all the time he had learned to ignore the feeling. But now it surged through his mind demanding he listen to it!

Still locked in sleep he cleared his mind of thought and feeling, and listened to the feeling. *Danger ... enemies ... death ... awaken ... must fight ... Danger!* James sat up in his bed with a shout. His pillow was soaked with sweat and his sheets were crumpled up at the foot of the bed. Fully awake he was able to feel out what the problem was and with heart stopping fear gripping him, he leapt out of bed. Not bothering to put his shirt on he grabbed his glasses and staff and ran out of his room.

Stopping long enough to pound on Dannil's door and shouting for him to wake up, he ran through the house and was flying across the road to the center of the village where the warning bell sat. Since the first attack, the Council prepared this bell as a warning system against attack and every night someone would be chosen from the 'young stock' to act watch guard. But where were they and why didn't they start ringing the bell already? From the feeling's intensity, the enemies were very close, almost just outside the village.

Skidding to a halt at the bell he reached for the hammer that hung on a string, but his hand only grabbed air. He groped around on the ground but the hammer was nowhere to be found. *Wait! The handle had broken and Cormer had taken it to Elyas to be fixed! Damn it!* Without the hammer he had no other choice and, tak-ing his staff in both hands, began attacking the bell. Lacking the weight and size of the hammer, the staff didn't make as much noise as it could, but all around the bell lights in people's houses burned into life.

Again and again he swung the staff against the bell praying that everyone could hear it. As he reared back something flew past him, nicking his upper arm. He felt warm blood trickle down his arm as his other hand gripped the cut. Behind him he heard the sound of a bow string being pulled back and just barely managed to jump out of the way as the arrow flew into the bell with a loud clang.

Behind him shouts erupted as the invaders charged into the village. Dozens of auras burst into light as some of them began lobbing fireballs into the houses. Before he could bring up a barrier the others began attacking him with swords and axes. His staff flew through the air knocking away blade after blade, striking where he could, but no matter how many he knocked away, more came to take their place. Elyas had trained him to fight multiple enemies but there were too many! He didn't give up. He had to keep as many of them occupied as he could long enough for the villagers to get ready.

Sharp pains shot up from his sides and arms as a few of the blades got past his whirling staff. A foot flew through the air and knocked the wind from him. Falling to the ground, James knew that he was dead.

Above him he heard battle cries and felt more power being summoned. A tunnel of fire as wide as a trailer blasted through the attackers, searing them and burning them to cinders.

The smell of burnt flesh and death wafted through the air making him gag and vomit, but the fires did not stop. Over and over, the villagers, five of them Bonded, continued the assault. Steel clashed above him as he tried to get up. Feet were trampling all around him missing him only because he was rolling on the ground. Twice someone tried to stab him only to miss and have their shin broken as he struck out with his foot.

He needed to help, needed to fight! A hand grasped his arm and hauled him to his feet. Neru's battle hardened face stared into his own before turning back to the battle; his steel sword flashed through the night sky, fires blazing left and right through the enemy.

Whirling his staff he charged into the fray. As he clubbed and jabbed the attackers he noticed something familiar in the way their armor faded into the shadows. Three of them ran at him with swords raised and cries of rage. James blocked the first one with the top of the staff and turned it away as he brought the bottom up to meet the second blade before batting it away and jumping back as the third sword hit only air. Quick as a flash he hurled himself back at his assailants.

He kicked the sword out of the left man's hand before cracking one end of his staff on his head. The other two tried to attack him again, but he deflected their blows and slammed each end of his staff into their groins. As they fell to the ground clutching themselves with tears in their eyes he saw a flash of steel to his left. Spinning as fast as he could, he aimed to deflect it. Wooden staff met steel long sword in a clash of strength. James pushed against this new attacker as hard as he could, but the other didn't budge.

James shifted the sword to the side and backed away before charging back in. As he brought his weapon down the enemy raised his sword and his face to meet him.

Long strands of black wiry hair fell over a gaunt and scarred face; one he knew he couldn't forget. The black leather armor was studded and the quiver was gone from his back, but the bandit leader he had beaten two years ago stared into his eyes with recognition. They leapt apart again, holding their weapons ready.

"You! What are you doing here?" James demanded.

The slaver looked at him and smiled wickedly. His face was a mass of scars from Aria's talons from two years ago and the smile contorted his face making them look even worse.

"Why to take all the women and children and sell them to the highest bidder. What else?" he replied. "I am surprised to see you made it here alive. Shame it was all for naught," he said with an evil grin, "and like I said two years ago, 'all good things must come to an end'!"

He launched into a tirade of swings and slashes that were so fast he barely managed to block them. *Down, left, up, left, right! He's too fast!* The blade found its way past the staff only twice and the only thing that kept it from dealing a lethal blow was a lucky roll to the side; but it still managed to cut him! James backed away from the duel long enough to try and regroup, but the slaver wouldn't let him. The red halo of energy surrounding the man flared and a blast of fire erupted from the ground like a volcano. The bandit laughed wildly as he watched the pillar of fire.

"That won't work this time!"

James leapt through the fire swinging his staff with all his strength. Two years of training and apprenticeship met the steel blade forcing it from the other's hand and into the night. Again and again he attacked the dark man, hacking away at anything he could reach. Try as he might, the man couldn't use his powers against the barrier he'd placed around himself and the staff's own resistance.

"Like you said, 'it's been fun, but all good things must come to an end!'" James shouted still hacking away.

Taking the staff in both hands, lost in the rage of battle his mind a fountain of fury and hatred, he thrust the wood into the man's gut as hard as he could. The air burst from his mouth accompanied by a spurt of blood. Doubling over, the dark man crumbled to the ground. Breathing heavily James started back to the fray when he heard a scream from his right.

"Help! Someone! I'm …"

The voice was muffled as a hand was clasped over the mouth. It was all he needed to recognize the voice though.

"Miranda I'm coming!"

Pain flared up his side as steel pierced his skin and dug in deep. Behind him the bandit leader held the hilt of a dagger, its sheath protruding from his belt. James felt blood trickle down his side as the blade stared getting hotter. He was going to be burned from the inside out! Forgetting pain and death, thinking only of saving Miranda, he whirled around making the dagger slide from his side, taking more skin with it. Staff flaring with power he rammed it as hard as he could at the man's chest.

At the last moment the leader moved to evade the attack, but shifting his weight James redirected the attack. The flat end of the staff rammed into the air pipe with a sickening crunch. James could only watch with bile rising in his throat as the man clasped his throat trying to breathe. No matter how he tried, his wind pipe was closed and he heard rasps of air, not enough to keep him alive.

What have I done?

Young One! Get Miranda!

Tearing his eyes away from the corpse he turned and ran through the night to Miranda's voice. Twice he was intercepted by a bandit, and each time one of the villagers took them down with a pitchfork or some other weapon. Dannil was plowing through the men with a pair of knives as long as his forearms. The large man was nimble on his feet and managed to crush one of the men with his arms alone! Elyas was swinging his largest hammer around like it was nothing; anything that got in the way of it was completely destroyed.

James burst through the melee and saw a group of slavers trying to subdue some of the women they'd caught. He saw Anasandra, Yalli, Ignatius' wife, and several others. Three men alone were trying to restrain a flailing figure; Miranda. Staff in hand and barrier at the ready, he charged in. Two of the men met him with axes, but they were too slow and he knocked them aside with ease, cracking them on the backs of their heads. The third man, however, grabbed Miranda and hauled her up placing a knife at her throat.

"Stay back or I swear I'll cut her!" the man said. "And don't you try to use your powers either!"

Aria! Where are you? I need you quick!

I come!

Almost at once the hawk dove at the man wrenching the blade from his hand with a shriek. The man dropped Miranda and started throwing fire at the bird. James rammed his staff into the man's gut making him double over before he swung it upward into his face breaking his nose. Using the distraction, the other women jumped onto their attackers and began clawing at their faces and fighting with a ferocity James would never have guessed they had.

When he was sure the man was unconscious and the women were all running to aide their husbands, sons, and fathers he turned to Miranda. She had a bruise on her bare arm and a cut was clotting on her forehead. But she looked to be alright.

"Miranda, are you okay? You're hurt; let me get you somewhere safe."

"James I'm fine! Get back into the battle! They cannot hold out much longer. You and Neru are the only ones capable of fighting!"

True, the only thing keeping the slavers at bay was the Bonded circle, but he could see they were tiring and there were still a lot of enemies left.

"Right. I'll …"

"AHHH!"

James spun around and shouted as Dannil stood with his back to him, arms stretched wide with a sword sticking through his middle. The man on the other side of the blade had a knife wedged into his neck. Both men collapsed to the ground, the bandit dead, Dannil dying.

"Dannil! NO!"

James and Miranda knelt over the man's dying form unable to do anything to save him. They both had tears in their eyes. *This feeling of helplessness …* Memories flooded his mind of the past two years; Dannil sitting at his desk carving little figurines and even larger statues … *GOD how I hate it!* The two of them laughing over a few mugs of ale … sitting in the common room at night beside the fire, reading or talking about the other's day … *I have to do something!* The day two years ago when Dannil took him into his care when he didn't have anywhere else to go. The man had sacrificed so much for him … *PLEASE!* There had to be some way to help him … he couldn't … he couldn't … *SOMEONE HELP!*

Pain scored through James' chest making him cry out. The pain had come again, the one he thought had left him when he came to Arollay. He felt as though someone were squeezing his heart while it was still inside his chest. Dannil placed a shaking hand on his shoulder, breathing in sharp slow breaths. But he didn't notice. All he could do was clutch his arms around him as the pain seared through every pore in his body, threatening to eat him alive! Above he saw Miranda summon her power accompanied by the dying Dannil.

"James, listen to me!" Miranda shouted, sending her power into him. "You are manifesting! Concentrate on my power and Dannil's. We have to Guide you, or you will die! James can you hear me?!"

He heard a beating in his ears, kind of like a second heartbeat. It was his power, he knew, attacking the Seal separating them. Faster and faster it beat, trying to break free. Slowly he felt the Seal start to weaken and only just grasped Miranda's power as his burst through. In a torrent of power his body writhed and twisted as it tried to cope with the amount of energy surging through him.

His insides burned hotter, his mind was going crazy, and he couldn't feel anything except the pain of the power. It pressed against his skin from the inside; every pore was on fire as it tried to escape. He breathed in short quick gasps between grunts of pain … Then he heard it.

Let me guide you.

Who are you? He replied weakly.

Let me Guide your power. The man's voice said again.

Let me Guide your rage. A second said in reply.

Let me Guide your mind. The third, a woman, finished.

Who are you? He asked again, but the voices only repeated themselves. Again his body writhed as his power fought with Miranda's. If this kept up he would be destroyed! Again the voices spoke their requests. He didn't know if he should trust them. But if he didn't do something soon … *Guide me.*

At once the battle inside him ended and everything went black.

Miranda poured more of her power into James. She was using everything she had just to hold his power back long enough for him to focus, but she wouldn't be able to hold it for long. Dannil had assisted as long as he could, but the man lay still at her feet. She didn't look at him; if she did she would lose her concentration. She had to help James … he could be helped.

As she poured even more power forth she was suddenly thrust back by an opposing force. Staggering back she watched as the aura around James glowed like a beacon! But something wasn't right. The aura was a light blue color and giving off an air of coolness. *Oh no! It can't be! He's … he's a Gattarian!*

The aura swirled and pulsed like a beating heart with James at its center. Faster and faster it pulsed until it was a solid orb of power surrounding him completely and shielding him from view. *So he is a Gattarian … after all …* A loud snap interrupted her thoughts. Running down the middle of the orb was a crack and slowly it was opening, revealing James. Slowly he stood up from the ground, arms at his sides; his head bowed hiding his face from view.

The orb didn't vanish however; instead it warped and twisted so it looked like blue fire in the shape of wings. Tongues of energy were flickering along the light and into the dark sky. The air around her became suddenly frigid as the glowing figure knelt down next to Dannil and placed a hand over the wound. Miranda gasped as she saw the tendrils of power float down into the wound. In a flash of light the power retracted itself leaving no mark where it had been.

Dannil took a sharp breath as life quickly flowed back into him. His eyes stared around and stopped on James who stood there above him. But James didn't look down at either of them; he was staring at the crowd of people in the center of the village. Everyone had stopped fighting and gazed in horror and disbelief as the Gattarian started walking towards them. They all shook as the wings flapped, lifting him into the air.

Screams erupted from the villagers as they scattered and shouts came from the bandits as they raised their weapons and summoned their power. All at once, the thirty or so still left exploded in a blaze as they sent combined fire streams into the air. The heat from the attack forced Miranda back a few steps, but she never took her eyes off James. He simply hung there in the sky as the fires engulfed him. She cried out and started towards the bandits, but stopped as they screamed.

The pillar of fire split in two as a shaft of ice appeared out of nowhere and hurtled down at the men, cutting through their attack. They tried to run, but their legs and torsos were suddenly encased in a block of ice. They watched as the shaft soared through the air at them.

"James, stop! Don't do it!"

Dannil ran forward, blazing with his own power, and attempted to drive James' attack away. Fire met ice in a burst of energy, fighting each other in mid air. Dannil didn't back down, he pushed with all his might at the ice spear, the tongues of fire doing nothing against the cold ice, and at the last second it swerved to the side. The glowing figure dropped to the ground in front of Dannil in a flurry of coldness and anger.

"It's over!" Dannil said. "They cannot fight. There is no need to kill them. They can go to prison at the capital like everyone else. Please, don't waste your life becoming a murderer on their account."

The once calm blue eyes that everyone had come to know now shone with fury and power as he spoke. Miranda's heart sank as she heard his voice. The pain she felt in it was unbearable. What was happening to him?

"They would kill you without a second thought, old man. Why would you show them mercy? Especially after one came within seconds of killing you tonight?"

"I know that!" Dannil replied placing both hands on James' shoulders. "James, I love you like a son! I cared for you these last two years as if you were my own … but I will not stand by and watch my fellow Intaruans die at the hands of the enemy!

"Not like my son …"

The last four words drove home as the rage began to dwindle and fade. James staggered back with his hands to his head. He was in so much pain … his aura was flaring with every step he took away from the bandits and Dannil. *He couldn't control it. That's why he hurts. He doesn't know what he is doing!*

"James, please …!" His head came up as she rushed into his arms. "Stop it, now. I don't want you to hurt anymore. The fighting is over, you can let go now. There isn't need to kill them." She looked up into his eyes, so soft and blue. "Let it go …"

Out of the night a hawk soared down onto his shoulder and cooed in his ear. He looked at the hawk with tears streaming down his face. He whispered something to it, "Aria …" Miranda held him tighter as his aura flared again and he cringed in pain. She wanted it to stop; she wanted it to end … now. *Bring back the James I know and love! Bring him back now!* Once more his aura flared higher into the sky, bringing with it a shriek from the hawk and a cry from James.

Then it vanished.

The two of them fell back to the ground. The hawk took flight and circled once before landing at their side. The villagers gathered slowly around them, dropping weapons on the ground and silently watching … the bandits stood there now completely encased in ice. The last flare of power had sealed them in completely. Elyas and Dannil pushed through the crowd with Neru at their heels. All three of them were covered in blood, but only Dannil's was his own.

No one spoke. No one moved. The night was frozen in time …

The three of them stood around his bed watching him with concern. He sat there half covered by the warm covers with his head bowed trying to go over everything that had happened. Elyas and Dannil stood at the side if his bed while Miranda sat next to him with a comforting hand on his. He didn't look up at them; he didn't want to see them look away like he was some monster. *Then again, that's exactly what I am.*

He had told them how his powers had broken through the Seal and even about the three voices he heard speaking to him. When he got to the part when everything went black they told him what had taken place. He cringed and cried when he heard what he did and said and looked like he was ready to scream when he heard what Dannil had said to him.

After he had regained control over his raging powers they had carried him to the room. Rosemary told them that he was alright, that he'd just used too much of his power too soon after manifesting and a little rest was all he needed. She was only slightly surprised that the injuries he had taken were already healed; after she had seen him heal Dannil's wound, it shouldn't be any shock to see he could heal himself. The rest of the village was quiet while people cared for the wounded and buried the dead. Thank the spirits that none in the village had died, some attested to James' power for that miracle as well.

"The worst news is yet to come." Se'Cruz said folding his arms. "I went to the merchant's train this morning and found they had already left. Plus I saw separate tracks among their wagons so that means they sent forerunners to spread the word of a Gattarian enemy in Intaru. Knowing how the army will react they will probably send the Elite."

"You can't be serious!" Dannil shouted as he staggered over to the blacksmith. "The Elite? They can't possibly think that James is so strong that the Elite need to be brought in!"

"Dannil, I cannot see a Gattarian's aura or the threads of their energies, but last night I saw James' power shine like a beacon!" He turned to the window. "I can promise you that everyone within five leagues of here felt his power last night. The Elite will come for him."

"Yes," they looked down to Miranda as she spoke, "They will come. But they will not find him. He will already be in Gattar by the time they get here. Right?"

"No ... I cannot go there yet."

"But you have to!" She made him look at her. "James if you are caught by the Elite, they will kill you!"

"I have to go to the Gray Woods first." He told them looking away again. "I have to have the Lady of the Grey Woods remove the Seal over my power. She is the one who placed it there and she is the only one able to take it away."

"But after last night, surely the Seal must be broken."

"No, it only gave way last night. But now that my power has fallen back into the recesses of my mind, the Seal is back and stronger than ever."

The three of them looked at each other. If someone like the fabled Lady of the Gray Wood would place a Seal over his power, then who was he really?

Elyas and Dannil left the room to tell everyone the plan leaving Miranda and James alone. They just sat there, staring in opposite walls for moment after moment before one of them spoke up.

"Do you hate me?"

James' head was ringing from the impact of Miranda's fist to his face. He covered his cheek with his hands as he glared up at the fuming figure standing at the side of his bed.

"How could you ask such a thing?" She demanded. "How can you even *think* that I would hate you?!"

"Because I'm the enemy." He said stoically. "Because I am a monster to the rest of your country. Because I *killed a man!*"

The air was charged with the rampant emotions streaming from both of them. Miranda stared down at James not knowing how to react. She had seen the slaver's body being carried off as she was waiting for Rosemary to check on James. She knew it was James that had killed him. She knew he had done it … to save her. She clenched her fists again and threw another punch at his head. He caught her fist and effortlessly forced her down to the floor.

"Don't … do that again." He said with a calm fury.

She shifted her body on the floor so her arm wasn't being pulled from her shoulder.

"James, you can't … you can't beat yourself up over that." He let go of her fist as she spoke. "You did what you had to do."

"No! There was no need for …"

"If you didn't do it, he would have killed you!" He sat there silently. She could feel the tears flowing down his face.

"I—I didn't want to." He said as she cradled his head in her arms. "I only meant to stun him, but he … but I …"

"Shh, its okay, it's okay." She hugged him to her as he sobbed. This was the first time she'd really seen him cry. "James, listen to me. Sometimes we have to do something we don't like to help those we care about. We know that what we need to do may be wrong, but we do it anyway because if we don't then we may lose everything. You did something you hated to save me, and I cannot thank you enough because I know it was a terrible thing to you. But listen to me, Life is not always going to go the way you want it. Sometimes you need to change the way you think even if you think it isn't the right thing to do."

Silence fell upon them as they sat there, holding each other. She still felt him sob every few seconds but she let him get it all out.

Plans were made to make sure that James had as big of a head start over the Elite as he could get. Everyone in Yattion helped prepare for his trip. Kyle gathered as much meat and bread and cheese as he could and packed it all away in a bag. Mistress Anasandra packed several pairs of clothes while Master Horacio prepared his saddle and Trae'len. Master Se'Cruz re-shod the horse and said he was working on something that would help greatly, just in case. Dannil took his staff and smoothed it out so it wasn't as beaten and old looking and even gathered a purse full of silver for him.

Morning, the next day, was cloudy and murky and carried a feel of rain in the air. The entire village was gathered at the north end to see their friend leave. Elyas came forward and handed him a parcel wrapped in a green cloth and said to open it when he was a good distance away. He said, "I pray you won't have need of it, but I like to be prepared."

Some came forward and gave him a last minute farewell hug before retreating back into the crowd. No one spoke the hard words that they knew would come sooner or later. Miranda handed him a small ring on a small chain and told him to keep it for luck. The band was silver and the jewel a red diamond shape. It had a pattern carved into it and polished black of a rose and its stem.

"This is my favorite ring." She said as he pulled it over his head. "I want you to have it so you will always remember us and know that you always have a home here waiting for you."

They embraced and he turned towards his mount.

Neru was standing next to Trae'len, holding his reins while James climbed into the saddle and placed the staff in its holster. The two embraced briefly and exchanged a few words that no one else could hear. Dannil stepped up and held his hand out to James who took it in his own.

"I can't find the words to thank you." He said to the big man. "You have been like a father to me these last two years. And the rest of Yattion has been a big dysfunctional family." A few people laughed while others started crying. "Thank you. All of you."

"Now, don't go getting all emotional on us." Elyas said. "You get going before we tie you to that horse and lead it away ourselves."

With a smile and a single tear that fell, he turned in his saddle, and with one final wave of farewell, he flicked the reins and left Yattion.

▼

PLOT DEVICES

THE glowing mists floating in the air swirled once more before dissipating. A sturdy hand was tapping a finger on the arm of a throne-like chair. It was made of the finest mahogany and polished to a shine; the carvings were exquisite and done by a professional hand. The two claws at the end of the chair's arms mimicked those of a bear and curled around to show the gruesome claws. The back was thick and dark with carvings of runes lining the sides up to the top. Of course it was padded; the large dark blue cushioning was very comfortable.

With the mists gone, the room seemed much darker; that was easily remedied. The same sturdy hand flicked once in the air and torches and chandeliers all around the room burst into life. The marble walls were a nice mix of white and black mica, set in perfect succession all around the room without a single error in the design. Several windows broke the pattern, their stained glass throwing a myriad of colors against the floor. A long, blood red carpet ran along the floor from the throne to two very large wooden doors with the same runic carvings. Only the best for the soon-to-be ruler of the world.

Ten years of searching; then two more, and now he had found his prized tool once again. A wicked smile slowly appeared showing white teeth set in perfect rows. Twin blue eyes shown in the fire light as they watched again the wondrous events that had transpired the night before. Oh, this was only too perfect.

He had lost the boy when bringing him through the barrier and again, as he always did when he recalled that shameful day, he cursed his weakness. His powers couldn't hold up against the strain of using the forbidden spell contained in a book that no one even knew about. The Spell of the Worlds; a most interesting find, and one he had put to good use. The Spell of the Mind; another nifty find that had helped in his search for the perfect tool. But he was only mortal and his powers were limited, stronger than any living mortals, but still limited.

But now that he had found him once again, how to bring him to his humble abode? The three spirits were still close to him and were ready to assist him if they felt he was threatened. If he went there himself, he would die. He laughed at the strangeness to that phrase. He had to constantly remind himself, he was ageless, not immortal. *Ah, the Spell of the Body, easily the best spell of the entire book.*

Gripping the arms of his chair he decided to walk to the ancient text this time instead of bringing it to him. Boots of the strongest and softest leather strode across the marble, their soft thuds doing little to hide the rustle from the pant legs as they brushed against each other. His kingly vest had been sewn by a maiden some eight hundred years ago and it still looked good as new. Its dark threads matched perfectly with his room. A crown was a bit too pompous so he had kept things simple for a change and wore only a golden circlet with his insignia of a falcon over his forehead.

Stopping at the dais where he had kept the book from day one, he looked once again at the plain leather bound cover with only a few words inscribed on the front; *Darr Juntav's Book. Do not open on pain of death!* He laughed at the last words. Pain of death indeed. He had been hesitant at first and went so far as to have some slave he found open the book first just to be safe. The poor soul had been destroyed the instant the book was opened. At least he wasn't able to tell anyone else about him; he was a private man.

Gripping the cover, he opened to the first page and ran a finger down the contents. *Spell of Manipulation … Spell of Extraction … Spell of the Law …* Ah ha! Here it was; *Spell of the Shadows*. Running through the pages, he stopped at the fiftieth and began reading over the neat writing. It was always fun to learn something new, and by the looks of this particular spell, things would be so much easier. The script was handwritten, but easily eligible.

To make the shadows come to life
Gather your power and your strife
Focus on the form and keep a steady hand
This spell will give you an army o'er the land.
Bring together the shadows of night
And gift them with your power and might

They will be your servants true
To do whatever you will them to.
Repeat the phrase one times thrice
And make sure your prowess can pay the price.
Shai'lun klana ov uhr
Uen ov jar ae le uhr jaunul
Vonig haan ytr shain
Comolyn uhr tuum Kalyn.[1]

Well that is quite a mouthful, but it's kind of catchy. Positioning himself besides the dais he raised a hand and pointed two fingers to the corner where the torches' light didn't reach. Without thought, a bright red aura, visible only to him and the Intaruans of the world appeared around him. He recited the spell. The first time made the light in the room darken, the second made the red tendrils of energy snake their way over to the shadows that now completely encompassed the wall, and the third time began forming the shadows into solid forms.

He felt his power draining away, but he had plenty to spare and this was a rather simple spell compared to some of the others. The red aura around his body finally blinked out as he gazed at the two figures standing before him. They both wore long dark robes with the hoods pulled up to hide their faces. One had a sword hanging at his hip, while the other had a very large axe. Oh these two would be perfect.

"Master." The one with the sword said in a high raspy voice as they both dropped to a knee. "We live only to serve you. Please, tell us how we may be of service to Your Excellency."

He smiled. *Oh yes ... they would be perfect,* he thought again. With a wave of his hand the glowing mists appeared in the air before him again. He motioned for the two Shai'lun to step closer.

"This is a very important mission." He said to them with a smile. "I need you to bring me this boy."

"Is that all, Master?" The second shadow said. Its voice was deep and dark sounding. "What is so special about this boy? And why do you need us to get him for you?"

---

1. Man of Shadow, come to me. Bend to my will and do my bidding. Rise from the dark. Lend me your Power.

He narrowed his eyes in anger at the remark and put it aside; these creatures were stupid fools compared to him, they could never understand the complex machinations of his mind.

"This boy is very powerful." He said with an edge to his voice. "So much so that he cannot fully control his powers. At the moment he is being watched by three spirits that will come to his aide if he is threatened. Because of this I do not dare risk my own life to bring him here. I will live only once, but if you die, I can bring you back as many times as needed. These spirits will not always be with him, but I dare not wait too long to act. The later I wait to acquire him, the stronger he will become, so I need to act now. That is all you need to know for now."

The two Shai'lun watched the vision of the young man closely for a few moments more, making sure they knew who he was by look alone. They bowed and burst into twin plumes of smoke that flew through the walls and into the world. He watched them go, a little impressed at their traveling abilities. They still had a ways to go, but they would catch the boy quickly. He went to close the book and stopped. There was more writing after the incantation … *Just great, fine print.*

A word of caution to this spell:
By creating the Shai'lun,
You give birth to creatures with their own sense of attitude.
Loyal they may be, they will think on their own
Yet the spell will hold them to their orders
Time may slow where they gather
Making them virtually undetectable.
Most important: Their powers are only as great as their creator's!

Attitudes of their own huh? *Well I found that out on my own already.* Closing the book he turned back to the glowing mists. James Richards was still riding that confounded horse of his, and that hawk was circling in the sky, watching his surroundings. But most annoying of all were the three spirits that still hovered around him, unseen by all except him. He would acquire the boy's powers and he would complete the ritual and he would rule over this land for the rest of time! Nothing could get in his way now. It was only a matter of time, and he had all the time in the world.

CHAPTER 10

▼

MEETING ON THE ROAD

"WELL, this is just wonderful." James said to no one. "First I'm ripped away from my real family like some dog, now I'm being forced to leave my second because of my powers."

Keep complaining Young One, and you might actually get my pity.

Stuff it bird.

Trae'len, don't say things like that to Aria.

The horse whinnied and shook its mane of golden hair. Patting the stallion on his neck he stared around at the surroundings. In the two years since he'd last been here, the plains leading to the Gray Wood hadn't changed at all. They still stretched in all directions with only a few trees here and there breaking the never ending waves. The clouds over high kept the sun off his back and he was grateful. Se'Cruz had shown him a map of all Arollay once a long time ago and he knew that it would take him possibly a month or two to get to the Dead Lands. *If* he kept a good pace.

He didn't want to cross the forsaken lands that acted as the Border of Nu'athion. That in itself would take him weeks to cross because of the terrible terrain and weather. Yet the Border acted as one of the mostly used battle grounds between both kingdoms and so had many outposts along the ways. If he could just find a way to sneak past the Fire army fortress at Belayn's Crossing, the smallest part of the Dead Lands, he would be able to find shelter in the Ice fortress until he could leave.

He didn't know what he would do once he was actually inside the Ice Kingdom, and he didn't have a map that showed the most up to date villages and towns and such. Yattion hospitality was a one of a kind thing and he doubted whether he would be welcomed with open arms in the next village he tried to live in. Shaking his head he tapped Trae'len into a canter to clear his thoughts.

The dark stallion leapt into a gallop instead, but he didn't stop him. The horse was too impatient and didn't like taking his time. A bad habit, yes ... but right now he wasn't too worried. From what Elyas could tell, it would take a few days for the news to reach the capital (if the messengers were ungodly quick) and then the Elite would start out and that would take them some time to catch up to him. Though, he said that news would travel to towns faster than the wind and guards would be on the look out for anyone suspicious. Aria flew above in the sky as James and the stallion blasted through the plains.

Run, run, run, run! I love to run! Am I going to fast? Please say no.

Run as much as you want, he said to the overly energetic horse, *but save your strength, we have a long way to go.*

Aria screech high above in agreement as the horse slowed just a little. Again his thoughts floated to the surface and began their ritual spiraling through his mind. He had been shocked when he found he could speak with Trae'len. But Aria had told him that the Lady had opened his mind to any creature he chose. But he "had to be careful of how many partners he took" because his mind might not be able to handle so many intrusions. That, and the hawk said, "Animals can be stupid at times and never stop talking."

By the end of the day they had covered almost the entire distance between Yattion and the Gray Woods. Making camp under a single tree he unsaddled Trae'len and brushed him down before placing the fodder in the feeding muzzle and slipping it over his head, went to making his own dinner. The tree provided plenty of wood, but he didn't take too many so as not to ruin it completely. When the fire was hot enough he took some of the meat that was packed and started cooking it. Aria arrived a little later with a large field mouse already half eaten clenched in her beak.

When the fire was out and his sleeping roll was ready and waiting he thought about the parcel Elyas had given him. Digging through the packs, he found it and took it out. Untying the knot and setting the green cloth to the side he stared open eyed at a marvelous pair of ... *Oh, damn, what are they called? Um ... oh yea! Armlets, duh.* They were made from a shining metal with leather padding inside them. They weren't broken by a hinge, so he slipped his hands through and placed them over his forearms. They were amazing and even covered the rune on his arm. *These will be better to wear than the piece of my old shirt.* He kept the cloth anyway … for sentimental reasons.

They were up with the sun and riding the rest of the way to the Woods, which already started looming up from the plains. Trae'len wasn't happy at the fact he couldn't run through the trees, and even more so when James dismounted. They didn't have to go very far into the forest before a bright light began making its way towards them. When the Lady came in full view from behind a tree the three of them bowed. James looked up at the face he had seen two years ago when he first woke in Arollay and smiled.

"My Lady," he said, "I thank you for seeing me on such short notice. I know you are needed all around."

"You are very welcome, James Richards, Gattarian." He flinched at the last. "Do not hate your powers, James, for they shall save you more often than not in the future. This is why you have come to me. You want the Seal over your power removed, yes?"

"Yes I do. I will need it if I am to make it to Gattar alive. And for when I get there I may have need of it as well, if not more so."

Mother, may I speak with you a moment?

~Yes Aria, you may. James felt the connection between him and the hawk become shielded. Trae'len snorted at the feeling too, but he whispered to him and calmed him down.

"James, Aria has told me the rest of what occurred in Yattion. And I must say I am worried." She turned to Trae'len and patted his nose, which he enjoyed thoroughly. "According to her when your powers manifested you had no control over them, correct?"

"Yes." He replied recalling the incident again. "I felt it pulsing through my body like lightning through a metal wire, threatening to overwhelm me. Then just when I thought I was going to die I heard something …"

He stopped. Would she think him mad if he told her about the voices? Most people didn't hear voices in their heads unless they were crazed or trying to contact the dead … in that case they were raving! Then he remembered that the Lady was able to read his thoughts and he grimaced. So now she knew.

"Tell me, what did these voices say? Tell me exactly how they spoke to you, it is very important. Word for word."

"They said, 'Let me Guide your power. Let me Guide your mind. Let me Guide your spirit.' At first I didn't want them to get anywhere near me, but I knew without their help I would have died." He looked up at her. "Lady, who were they and what did they do to me?"

"As I thought." She released Trea'len's nose and turned to him. "Those voices were spirits, three spirits that managed to cross the barrier of the living world. They were there to help you through your Awakening, and you are right: without their help, you would have died. For no Intaruan can Guide a Gattarian or vise versa. But how they managed to guide you is beyond my knowledge. Yet, maybe I do know. By chance, did the rune Tuhugara shine or burn when you manifested?"

"I-I think so. Tuhugara is the rune of death, right? Wouldn't amahyl be better then? After all it is the one that means strength."

"Perhaps, but think of this. Those voices were spirits from the land of the dead. What better way to communicate with the living than through something from the Words that means death? As for the spirits, I think I may know who they were. If I am correcting in saying so, there were two men and one woman, yes?" He nodded. "Ah yes, Marlao Blood, Kinran Death, and Tiana Paine ... why am I not surprised?"

"Wait, I know those names!" James said stepping closer to her. "Marlao Blood was the first man whose power was so vast that he died while manifesting in an explosion of energy that shook the entire land. Kinran Death was the second to be born with such power. He died at the age of thirty battling an entire division of Intaruans in the Border ... in fact he created a large chunk of the place in the battle! But he didn't die from blade or fire or arrow, but from summoning too much of his power at once and blasting the entire area in one big eruption!

"And Tiana Paine, the first person with that strength to live out a full life, but only by never drawing on her power for any reason after manifesting. Despite that she was the strongest of the three by far! And you're saying that these three spirits entered my mind and Guided me through my Awakening? Why?"

"Again, I can only guess, but I believe that these spirits saw you as a possible totem between this world and that of the dead. Your strength rivals theirs to such a degree that they were able to connect to you through it as well as through the rune. They may have felt pity and sadness at the thought of another dieing from their power like they did and so helped you through the Awakening. Again this is only a guess."

"Well that's one hell of a guess." He said throwing his arms over his head. "Geez, why do you bother trying to hide how much you know? I can tell you aren't saying everything you know. I can see it in your eyes and the way you don't seem to be staring at me directly. Come on, tell me what you know."

Young One you go too far! Aria landed on his shoulder and gripped it hard with her talons making him wince. *Remember who you speak to! Mother cannot say everything because the Law of the Land holds her. That is the Highest power, one that cannot be broken by any means and any attempt means destruction! So hold your tongue!*

Well excuse me for not knowing there was a Law! If you want me to not do something, tell me about these things okay!

"Enough, both of you." The two of them jumped and broke contact. "Aria, it is okay. I do not mind, and neither should you. Try putting yourself in his place: trapped in a world apart from your own, a new power that threatens to destroy you if you do not control it coursing through you, and not being raised on the ways of the world. And James, if there is anything you need to know about the ways of the land, ask Aria. She is well schooled in them and can teach you everything you need to know.

"Now, unless you would like the Elite to catch you before you even leave the woods, I suggest we get on with what you came here for. James, are you ready?"

He had completely forgotten about the Seal. Aria took flight, the tunic taking most of the sharp talons' scrapes with her. The Lady stepped up to James and placed her hands on both sides of his head and closed her eyes. He was about to brace himself for the Seal's release when he jerked his head away from the Lady's grasp and pushed the pulsing energy away.

"Wait, my Lady, I can't have the Seal removed yet! I can't control my power at all. If I try to summon it without the Seal, I may lose control again and next time it might not subside until it's too late. I ... I don't think this is a good idea."

"Do not worry," She said patiently. "Aria told me everything that happened. I am not going to remove the Seal completely. Instead I am going to weaken it enough for you to summon a percent of your powers at a time. It will stop you from losing control as well. Plus I have a final farewell gift for you, though this will not be the last time we meet. Now come ..."

Again she placed both her hands on the sides of his head and closed her eyes. Like so long ago, he felt like he was being dipped into a warm bath slowly as her powers coursed through him. The feeling lingered longer than it had last time, but he didn't mind. When she released him he felt stronger, and the glowing pool of energy within felt closer, but the Seal blocked him from touching it with his mind.

"I have placed the Seal as well as some knowledge in the ways of the power." She said as she led him over to Trae'len, who nudged his nose out for another pat. "From what I know of man's abilities you will be able to use what my Seal will allow to enough effect that no one will doubt what you are when you show them. I believe the knowledge is simple enough too. As to how to use them, that all depends on you. While you travel, train your power and learn what it can do, it will help you in the long run."

Bowing once more James took Trae'len's reins in hand and made to leave. The Lady placed a hand on his shoulder and held up a finger with a smile. With a snap of her fingers the world spun and blurred and twisted so it looked like a kaleidoscope. When everything righted itself he saw he they were at the other end of the forest, pointing directly towards the Border. Aria shrieked and Trae'len whinnied in thanks and farewell as the three of them again started on their journey.

As he rode, James summoned his power to see what he could hold. To his surprise it came easily, though the amount he could hold was barely a spark compared to what everyone said he had been using that night. He tried to mentally use the power, but nothing happened. He thrust his hand out and tried to focus his energy through it, but still nothing. What was he missing?

Remember what Elyas taught you. Aria said. *The power doesn't create things, it manipulates them. Think, what makes ice?*

Wait … what makes ice? Water, duh! He rapped his knuckles on his head. *But where am I going to get spare water from? I don't dare use the amount I brought, and there isn't a lake or stream close enough for us to reach by the end of the day.*

Water is not only in lakes and streams, Young One. Water can be right in front of you for all you know.

Again, DUH!

There was moisture in the air, even in a place as dry as Intaru. So, reaching out to the air he tried to draw in the moisture from the air around him. Again it came easy enough, and when he felt the water hovering around him he prodded it with his power and commanded it to form ice. Slowly a thread of blue light crawled from his hand and wrapped around the moistened air. As soon as they met, a chunk of ice appeared in his hand. It felt exactly like normal ice from an ice dispenser, but the shape was too messy.

Again he tried and this time attempted to form the ice into something, but again, he got a misshaped chunk. Aria tried to help him by giving ideas and possibilities, but only a few worked. He kept ending with blobs of ice with no discernable shape. By the time they stopped for dinner that night he had managed to make the ice into four different shapes, all of which were still a little sketchy, and could even made it hover in the air for a while, though that took more energy.

While he was waiting for the food to cook, he began gathering the moisture around him again. He needed something better than misshapen blocks of ice; he needed something he could fight with. The Elite would crush him if he had to fight them using only his staff. He gathered more water than before and tried to form it before he froze it. *What would be a good weapon? Something that could fly obviously, so maybe a dart, or perhaps an arrow would do.*

His mind felt the water, almost as if he were molding it with his hands, and started shaping it into a point. When he was satisfied with the shape and size, he focused his powers into the moisture and commanded it to freeze. Just as it had with his first tries, the tendrils of blue light crawled from his hand and wrapped around the moistened air. On contact it froze and a half foot long icicle appeared in his hand. He breathed a sigh; that took a lot more energy and time, but it looked better. Channeling the energy like he did when he made his barrier, he made the icicle float in the air a few inches above his hand.

"Okay … now I need a target." He looked around and saw a few rocks a little ways off. "Those should do for now."

He aimed with his hand and then focused what was left of the power that was allowed by the Seal. *I need to unleash it all at once, in one big burst so it'll rocket through the air like a missile.* Focusing the energy behind the icicle he unleashed it all at once. Quick as a bullet from a gun, the ice flew from his hand and pierced the rock! It hadn't shattered or cracked, but pierced the rock instead. Happy as he was, the effort had drained him of much of his strength. He smiled and went back to cooking the meat … he'd try again tomorrow when he was refreshed.

After three days of traveling they came to a road. There wasn't anyone on it, thankfully, though, as Aria pointed out, there wouldn't be word of a Gattarian this far already. He didn't think she was right, but kept it to himself. He'd read books in which rumor spread like wildfire and in Yattion things would reach them from the battle field only a few days after it had happened. Yet no one seemed to be on the road so early in the day, so taking advantage of it he practiced a little more. His icicle missile was still slow and took a lot of energy, but he was getting the hang of it … sort of.

They stopped at midday so Trae'len could rest and eat. There were three huge boulders randomly placed in a pile lying on the side of road and everything else around it was just like the plains; empty and grassy. Though, here the grass wasn't very green, it was more like a yellow green instead. He felt the ground with his hand and saw that it was dry and brittle; it must not have rained out here for some time. Trae'len didn't seem to mind the dryness of the grass because when the feeding muzzle was taken off he went to work on the grass like a lawn mower.

James took out his staff and went through some basic forms Se'Cruz taught him. His moves were slower because he hadn't practiced until now, but Aria said it looked good anyway. The wood whirled around in his hands as he imagined the fight with the bandits again. He saw their black armor on all sides, swinging their swords and axes and holding their powers ready to use just in case. He shuffled his feet in a spin and jabbed, swung up into one's face, and tripped his feet out from beneath him.

He was about to draw on his powers and practice with it and the staff together when the hairs on the back of his neck rose and an itch formed at the back of his mind. Gripping the staff, he concentrated on the feeling; it was an Intaruan, and they were close ... behind him! Whirling around and striking out with the staff he hit only air. The feeling was moving to his left and was lower, like the person was crouched or crawling. Turning to his right he acted like he was going to attack the ground on the opposite side. Bashing the staff against the ground away from the feeling's source he thrust it backwards.

The runes on the staff cut through the barrier surrounding his stalker. The camouflage broke revealing a young man only a few years younger than himself with shoulder length brown hair and similar brown eyes. He was tall and lean like James, but he lacked the muscle that being a smith's apprentice gave him. His black shirt was tied up to his neck and the belt which held two short knives all looked to be worth quite a sum. There was an ugly brown cloth wrapped around his right forearm as well.

Realizing he had been discovered the kid tried to run, but Aria shrieked and dove into his face making him trip and fall. As he tried to get up, James placed the end of his staff at the place of his neck where it met the skull. The man stopped moving and placed his hands above his head in surrender.

"Who are you?" He demanded shifting the staff a little. "Why did you try to sneak up on me?"

"My name is none of your concern." The other said with his face to the ground. "I was trying to figure out who you were without being seen."

"Why didn't you want to be seen?" He asked pressing the end of the staff tighter. "Are you some kind of criminal?"

He didn't answer. He seemed to be struggling with the fact he was backed into a corner. Aria spoke to him asking if she should tear him to pieces while Trae'len asked if he should sit on his back to keep him from moving.

"Okay, okay! I was hiding from someone and I wasn't sure if you were one of them! That's why I cloaked myself. Happy?"

"For now." James replied curtly. "But who are you hiding from?"

Before he answered the hairs on his neck rose again and the feeling in his mind changed direction. Both of them looked to their right to see two men on horses not twenty yards from where they were. Both men wore red coats embroidered with gold on the sleeves and chest. A black baldric crossed their chests and held the sheath of their sword at their backs. Each man was clean shaven and had the same burning red hair kept tidy and combed.

They watched James and the stranger for a moment before riding down next to them. The man on the right had a light scar across his right cheek and a mean look to his dark brown eyes. The man on the left had no noticeable characteristics, but his eyes looked like they were clouded over and out of focus. The stranger James had pinned was now on his feet with two knives in hand. How'd he get up so fast without him noticing?

"Damn it." He said just loud enough for the wind to carry his voice to James. "These are who I was hiding from."

"Good day, sir." The man on the right said. "I am Ryol Yashir, and this is Bren Talra. We happened to notice that you seem to be having a little trouble with this man here and decided to assist you. We are Elite ranks and have been looking for this traitor for sometime and thank you for finding him."

ELITE!!! YOU'RE KIDDING ME!!

They don't seem to know who you are, Young One. Do not let them see your fear. And hide your power from them in case they can feel it out.

Yea, no duh! He bowed slightly to the Elite. "Well, I am glad to be of assistance to you, Master Yashir, Master Talra." He said as calmly as he could. "I am always happy to serve the Elite in any way I can."

"How kind." Bren said shortly. His eyes were still clouded over and he wasn't looking at the stranger which worried him.

The stranger, however, wasn't as courteous. He whirled his knives through his fingers and jumped at Yashir's horse. The brown stallion reared as the blades cut its sides. Yashir barely managed to hold onto the reins as his horse bucked and fell over. Trae'len cried out in anger and shock at seeing one of his own slaughtered mercilessly. James managed to hold the horse back with his thoughts. He didn't want to risk losing him.

Yashir roared in rage as he pulled himself free from his dead horse and drew his sword. Bren simply sat where he was and never took his eyes off James' back. What was he staring at? Could he know? He felt the hairs on his neck rise as the stranger and Yashir both summoned their powers. They seemed to be equally strong, but James didn't think the stranger had any sort of chance against that sword with only a few knives. As the two of them launched their attacks Aria cried out to him.

Look out!

He barely managed to duck as the steel blade whizzed past his head. Behind him Bren leapt down from his saddle and held his sword in both hands. Turning around he faced the Elite with his staff and almost summoned his power. Bren knew, but he didn't think that Yashir could feel him out as easily. Bren advanced slowly. Again Aria cried out to him.

The other one behind you!

Again he barely managed to duck as the steel blade swished over head, brushing a few hairs. Bren lashed out with his sword but missed as he rolled to the side and struck out with his staff. Yashir fell to the ground as the wood swiped his foot out from beneath him. Bringing it up, he blocked the second attack from Bren and countered with a blow to the side. Slowly backing away he could only watch as both men began their assault again. Aria was screeching in the air, but he held her back. He couldn't lose her either.

Behind the men the stranger stood there stunned that they had left him to fight this other guy. Over and over James blocked attack after attack managing to hold off the steel long enough to memorize their attack patterns. He could hear Elyas' voice as the old lessons repeated themselves in his mind. Bren would attack first at the upper torso and then Yashir would follow through with a low attack to the thigh, but that left them open. He only had one chance to strike and he had to make it count.

But when they began their attack, and he tried to counter, they vanished from sight. Stunned, he stumbled forward and whirled around and only by God's own luck had his staff in the right position to block both swords. Knocked off balance he watched as the men vanished again. The hairs on his neck were up and he felt them moving to both sides of him. Spinning the staff in a wide circle he bashed Bren on the head and cut through the waves surrounding Yashir before thrusting the staff into his chest.

As Yashir clutched his chest something big and black collided into him sending him tumbling into the ground. Where the Elite had been now stood the stranger with his knives in hand. He glanced over at James and smiled before charging down Yashir again. Bren roared and began swinging his sword like a mad man. Engulfed in rage his moves were sloppy and missed every time. Attacking him again and again didn't seem to be doing much to slow him down, even when the side of his face was red with welts. Then he began using his power.

Forming his barrier he cut through the stream of fire like it was nothing and continued hacking away at the Elite. Bren tried blasting the ground beneath him, but again his barrier absorbed the impact and again Bren came out with another welt. The man didn't know when to give up! Thinking of how to use his own powers without attracting the stranger's attention he summoned the pool of energy to him. With his body coursing with the cool power, he struck out at the ground.

The little moisture in the dirt was able to act as a conductor and a sheet of ice materialized beneath Bren's foot as he charged in. With his footing gone, James lashed out again with staff and power, channeling the energy like he did with his barriers. The threads of energy flowed along the staff and when the wood hit the Elite, a shockwave erupted from the blow sending both of them through the air. Tumbling to his feet he readied himself for another attack, but Bren was lying ten feet away in a heap. Right next to him was Yashir, clutching two knives sticking from his chest and stomach.

The stranger went up to the dieing man and yanked both knives free before slicing his throat. He didn't seem to mind the blood that splattered onto his clothes and, wiping the blades on the Elite's coat, sheathed them.

"Damn, I didn't think that they'd catch up to me this quickly." The boy said walking over to Bren. "Good spirits what a mess! You sure did a number on this guy."

"Is he alright?"

"Don't sound so worried." He said curtly. "Remember, he tried to kill you too. So I don't think he deserves much pity on your part."

Aria flew down and perched herself on his shoulder.

Young One, I have bad news. These two men, these Elite, can talk with the Mind Speech. That is how the other knew about you while fighting Black Fang.

Black Fang? How come he gets a cool name? Wait! You said they can use the Mind Speech? Like we do?

Yes, but theirs is much stronger since they are the same species. What's more, before they died, they sent a message.

To who ... oh god. They told the other Elite where I am!

I am afraid so.

"Hey, what's with you? Your face just went white as a sheet. And what's with the bird?"

"Thank you for helping me back there, but I have to go now." James said with a small bow. Running over to Trae'len he jumped into the saddle. "If I were you, I would get as far from here as I could. There will be more Elite here very soon."

"What?! How do you know that? Damn it. These guys won't leave me alone!"

"You don't have to worry. It's me they're after."

"But if they see me, they'll kill me without a second thought. Wait there one second."

The stranger turned and whistled. The hairs on James' neck rose as a horse walked into view from behind the boulders. It was a deep brown horse with no markings on it anywhere. Its tail and mane were black and hung long like Trae'len's. It was a small horse, but compared to Trae'len who was still young, it was about the same height. He'd never seen a horse like it and didn't know what it was called. The stranger leapt into the saddle with experienced grace and turned the horse towards him.

"If the Elite are after you too, then I might as well stick with you. After all I can't fight them alone anymore."

"You can't be serious!" James said leaning in his saddle and placing the staff in its holster. "I can't travel with anyone. It's too dangerous. And besides I …"

"Don't talk to me about dangerous!" the stranger replied sharply. "I've been in danger since I was four! I have run from the Elite for the last few years and only now they …" He cut himself off. "What's more, like I said, I can't fight them alone and neither can you."

"Yea, but … I don't … oh damn it all!" He was stuck. "Alright then, but don't slow me down. I have a long way to go and I can't have some stranger holding me back."

"Long way to go? You sound like you know a place where the Elite can't find you. Now I'm really interested. Don't worry about me falling behind. She may be small, but Haenya can keep up with the fastest of stallions."

"Alright then let's go."

"Hey what's your name?" the strange asked pulling beside the trotting Trae'len.

"I'll tell you mine, if you tell me yours."

"Huh. Alright then, I'm Alamar Janury. This is my faithful companion, Haenya."

"I'm James Richards. The hawk is Aria, and this feisty guy is Trae'len."

CHAPTER 11

▼

RENDRO YTR SHAI

ALAMAR wasn't the most talkative person, but he did provide some company and Trae'len seemed to like having Haenya close by. The horse was such a pain. Aria kept circling them high above and sent pictures of the road behind them and before to act as warning. Neither of them trusted the other enough to say why the Elite were after them so neither bothered to ask. In silence they traveled, never within sight of the road and always hiding if they saw or sensed someone coming.

Every night they would agree to take turns keeping watch for the Elite, with Aria watching with Alamar at her own request. But he never did anything that spoke of treachery or suspicion. He would just sit watch with his knives loose in their sheaths and stare out into the night. Another thing was the dirt brown cloth he kept wrapped around his arm; it looked just like James' did (he wore the armlets all the time now, but used his own cloth to keep the rune on his hand covered).

Four days after the battle with the Elite, they came to a town. According to Alamar it was called Malken and acted as a center of commerce between the towns and villages closer to the border and the capital. There were tall stone walls surrounding the town with parapets dotting the corners. Men could be seen walking back and forth with crossbows and swords. There were arrow slits in the walls too, making the place look like a fortress rather than a town. James was all for dodging the place entirely, but Aria reminded him that they needed to buy provisions.

"Just don't do anything to attract attention." Alamar told him as they neared the gate. "If they don't think you're up to something they'll leave you alone. Oh, and don't give them your real name at the gates."

"Gee, I didn't think of that one." He replied easing himself in the saddle.

The guards stopped them at the gates and checked their baggage. They stared at Alamar's knives suspiciously but went on to James next. His staff drew a few glances, but nothing much. Alamar waved up to the guards watching them from the wall who leered back.

"Names." The guard said holding a pen and pad.

"Tristan Callaway." Alamar told him politely.

"Darrel Black." James said in the same manner.

"Okay, Tristan and Darrel. Very well, you may go in." They flicked the reins and started in. "Oh one more thing." The guard looked at Alamar's knives and James' staff. "If there are any disturbances, know that there will be serious consequences."

"Yes, sir. You needn't worry about us. These are only for protection against bandits on the road. And the occasional cutpurse."

Malken was a lively town. There were people walking in the streets, which were made of cobble stone, looking at wares at shops and hawkers crying out their prices. The buildings were all two stories, some even went to three maybe a fourth. The place looked completely different from Yattion. The stores and houses were separate buildings, not combined, and they ranged from things like selling amulets and good luck charms to heavy armor and weapons. There was even a place where you could buy fletching for arrows and strings for bows!

It took a lot of control to keep from staring at everything like a child in a toy store, but he couldn't help it. All his life he had read about places like this and here he was finally seeing it in real life! Sure it wasn't under the best circumstances, but still! It was hard navigating Trae'len and Haenya through the crowd, but Alamar did a good job of winding through the back ways between stores and buildings. He led them past dozens of inns and taverns that looked good enough to stay at but he simply shook his head.

"Staying at an inn would make it easier for the Elite to track us." He said as they past a place called the Blue Crown. "I'm trying to find a nice stable or something we can hide in. I hate sleeping in stable hay, but we have little choice."

"If you say so. But I still want to explore the town, and I also need to stock up on food and other things."

After an hour of riding back and forth through the alleys, Alamar finally steered them towards an inn called the Lady's Maid. He dismounted and told him to wait while he checked the stables. The three of them waited there for a minute while Alamar was gone … until Haenya suddenly trotted forward into the open. He tried to grab her reins, but she was already out of reach. What made things worse was the fact that Trae'len followed her. They rounded the stables and found Alamar talking quietly with a small boy who looked no older than twelve.

"Huh?" The boy asked as they approached. "Why do you want to stay in the stables, sir? It's much warmer and cozier inside."

"We don't exactly have a lot of money to go and buy a room, kid." That was a lie. James had plenty of money from the purse Dannil had given him, and he was sure that Alamar had some money on him. "If we stay in the stables, it'll be cheaper. Besides, you know as well as I do that they hay in there is much warmer than any of the beds in any inn."

"Yonre, what's going on out here?"

All of them jumped as a big man in a dull red shirt and black pants walked out of the inn. He was balding on the top and tried to hide it by combing over … it didn't work at all. At his waist he carried a cudgel and what he thought might be a sword breaker. James highly doubted they were just for show.

"Master Gil, these men want to sleep in the stables because they can't afford …"

"SLEEP IN THE STABLES?!" They all jumped again. "Boy, get back to mucking out the stalls, they're filthy!"

Yonre bowed and ran back inside. The innkeeper turned his attention to James and Alamar; his dark eyes were creepy.

"Now, I want the two of you to get out of here before I call the guards." He gripped his cudgel; he wasn't planning on waiting for the guards to arrive. "I let none sleep in my stables unless they got four legs and look like those pathetic mounts you're riding."

Pa-pa-pathetic?! I'll show him pathetic!!

Down Trae'len!

But he …!

I said DOWN! Let us handle this.

Fine, but if he calls us pathetic again, I'm going to kick his fat gut so hard he'll …

"You better calm that horse down before it does anything it might regret … pathe …"

"Master Innkeeper!" James said quickly. He didn't want Trae'len to kick anyone; though it might prove entertaining ... "We do not have the money to stay in one of your rooms, and since you won't let us stay in your stables, *and* since you run the cheapest inn around, what would you say to us working for a room?"

The fat man eyed him for a moment before releasing his cudgel. Alamar turned slightly and glared at him out of the corners of his eyes. *He* had a hand on one of his knives ... crazy moron!

"What kind of work can someone like you do? You don't look like you can perform, and by the sound of your voice, you can't sing either."

Got that right ...

Shut up Aria.

"I have been known to be quite the cook." He said turning his attention back to the man. "I am well schooled in the art and can assure you some of the best cooking you've ever had. If that isn't what you need, I can clean effectively, I can take orders, I can even tell stories to the other guests. I have quite the collection." The last part was a lie; they weren't really his stories ...

"And what about you?" He said turning to Alamar.

"I can clean ... and serve food. I don't perform for anyone, so don't ask."

James shot him a death glare. *Idiot! We're trying to get on his good side!!!*

The innkeeper stared back and forth between the two of them for a few minutes. James could see thinking wasn't the man's strong suit. He was weighing the possibilities of having a gourmet chef, and a possible bard and some kid who said he could clean. What would that do for his business?

"Let me see what you can do first. If I like it, then you can stay in a spare room I have upstairs. You can stable your horses at three bronze pence a piece and *if* you work hard enough, I'll let you have your meals for free."

James hopped down from the saddle and handed the reins to the stable boy, handing him the money as well. Taking his sleeping pack and staff from the saddle he set them aside while he went to work trying to convince the innkeeper that he could tell stories. He thought of a short story he'd read once long ago about a girl who came upon a magic lamp and found the genie, or mystic magic man since neither the inn keeper or Alamar knew what a 'genie' was. He seemed impressed and turned to the subject of cooking. James asked if he could use a stove inside.

The Lady's Maid was a large inn, despite the minimal cost, which meant it had a large kitchen. There were ten people working at ten stoves around the room, all wearing the same white apron with the inn's sign on the front. The innkeeper motioned to an equally large woman with black hair tied in a tight bun and mean, deep set eyes. Mistress Zala, as the woman was called, handed him an apron and shoved one of the other cooks away from their stove.

Fifteen minutes later, she was staring at a dish of potatoes, carrots, peas, and small chunks of beef with thick, dark gravy on the side. She and Master Gil tested the food and said they were surprised at how good it tasted. Mistress Zala wasted no time in handing him two sheets of paper with two orders and telling him to get to work. Then she rounded on Alamar. Digging in her apron, she pulled out a pen, pad of paper, and a small booklet of available meals. Grabbing an extra apron, she threw it over his head, 'to hide those horrible looking clothes' and pushed him out the door to take orders.

It was hard work, trying to make several dishes at once with only a handful of others to help. The stern woman kept a close watch on all of them, but always loomed over James as he mixed and rolled and cooked. Order after order came in and went out in a seemingly never ending cycle. Alamar would come in carrying dishes and leave with others loaded down with food and drinks. People were cheering at the pretty girl standing on a table swinging her dress about and singing a song.

While he was waiting for the sauce to a dish to finish cooking he got a bad feeling at the back of his mind. It felt like someone using their powers, but there was something different about it he couldn't identify. He contacted Aria and asked her if she saw anything suspicious outside. She said there wasn't anyone or anything out there besides a few delicious looking mice. Thinking it must be his powers acting up, he shoved the feeling aside and went back to cooking. After a few hours, Mistress Zala told him to clean up take a break.

Gratefully setting the apron on the hook next to the door he sat down in a chair in the common room and listened to the dancer. She was standing on a table and dancing, swishing her dress around in beat with the song. She was pretty looking, and had a nice voice, but she didn't seem to be looking at anyone except a big, muscle bound guy with a long scar running along the right side of his face.

Why oh why have you left me, my hubby?
Did I act badly or did I act funny?
Come back to me my hubby
For without you my life is not lovely.

The sun rises and you are not there
Lying by my side, snoring away

Come back; oh come back, my hubby!
I need you to be near me today!

It was a catchy tune and sounded similar to something he heard in Yattion. A serving girl came up to him and asked if he would like something to eat or drink. *She* was very pretty and had the most beautiful auburn hair and brown eyes. He said a little water wouldn't hurt and she smiled when he asked if she would like to join him a little later for dinner.

"Why, sir, I would love to." She winked and went to get his water.

Alamar flopped onto the chair next to him with a heavy sigh and looked like he was about to fall asleep. His hair was messy from all the walking and serving he'd been doing. He eyed James evilly for a moment before leaning back against the wall in the chair and began watching the dancer. A few minutes later the serving girl came back with his water. She set the glass on the table and with a smile walked to the next table.

Under the glass was a piece of paper that had a perfumed scent to it. Alamar smiled and started to take the paper before James punched his arm. Taking the paper, and making sure Alamar couldn't see he read:

Mellanie Kirstan. I will meet you for dinner at closing.

SCORE! He folded the paper and placed it in his pocket with a smile. He turned to Alamar and smiled widely. The other pulled back his lip like a growl and turned back to the dancer who was now singing about a boy and his dog. The real context of the song was something entirely different.

Mistress Zala came out and told him his break was over a little while later and after another four hours of cooking and cooking he was finally allowed to go to his room. He flopped onto his bed, which was very hard, but he didn't mind at all. He'd been sleeping on the ground for a week already and this bed felt wonderful. Recalling he had a dinner date he decided to wash up and put something a little nicer on. Taking out his favorite tunic of dark blue he washed his face, shaved, and made sure his hair wasn't sticking out in all directions. He dug through his medical supplies and brought out a new wrapping for his arm. He set the cloth he'd been using into the bag for another time and wrapped up the runes.

Because the silvery metallic gleam went well with the dark blue, he reequipped his armlets after giving them a quick polish.

Closing time came and he went down to meet Mellanie. She was wearing a very nice dress of red with her hair done up in a neat little bun with a few loose strands hanging over her forehead. She had makeup on, but that only emphasized her beauty even more. One of the other serving maids came out with their food before bidding them goodnight and heading out the door. They sat there and talked for a while, eating and drinking. It was all very good.

"So tell me, James, what brings you to Malken?" She twirled a strand of hair in her finger. "You don't look to be a merchant and I doubt that you're looking for permanent work here."

"I'm just traveling with a friend to meet some family a little ways north of here." He replied with a sip of wine. "I'm afraid my aunt has fallen ill and I wish to see her before …"

"Oh, I'm so sorry." She reached across the table and held his hand. "Is it really that bad? Oh, I wish I could help. Is there anything I can do to help?"

"That's very nice of you, but it'll be alright. She's lived a good long life, and this illness has been plaguing her for sometime."

As they sat there in silence the feeling that something wasn't right came back. The hairs on his neck rose and the itch appeared in the back of his mind. Quick as a flash he grabbed the dinner knife from the table and spun around. The knife flew through the air and stuck in the wall with a twang. Inches from where it struck, a figure loomed out from the shadows.

He wore a long black robe with the hood pulled up, hiding its face. The dark material faded in the shadows. The way he moved spoke of a weapon, but in the dim lighting he couldn't see where or what it was. As Mellanie started to scream another figure cloaked in black appeared behind her and clamped her mouth shut. He felt his power trying to rise, but the Seal kept it at bay. He readied his barriers over him and Mellanie and grabbed the other knife off the table. He called to Aria but she wasn't close enough.

"Well, that was a very touching moment between the two of you." The first figure said in a high raspy voice. "I didn't want to ruin it, but you had to go and start throwing knives around."

"Who are you?"

"Just some travelers going to see their sick relatives to the north."

The other laughed wickedly. Why didn't someone upstairs hear them? And where was Aria? Something really wasn't right about all this. He just didn't know what! The man moved in closer, while the one holding Mellanie backed out of the way. If they thought he would go down without a struggle, they were dead wrong! Summoning his power he rushed at the first man.

Drawing his sword, the shadow slashed through the night. Rolling to the side he missed the blade by an inch and, focusing his energies into his fist like he did his staff, punched the guy straight in the face. Bones crunched and blood splattered as the shockwave burst forth sending them both into the air. James, who'd been practicing with this, tumbled in the air and landed on both feet. The dark man crashed into the wall and vanished in a puff of smoke.

His dark laughter, however, stayed in the room.

"Oh that was clever." The voice said. "Using your power as a force instead of its physical form so we can't see it. Very clever. I underestimated you."

"Where are you? Show yourself!"

"I'm right behind you."

The darkness molded into the man a foot behind him with his sword raised high. He ducked under the initial slash but caught a boot to the face in exchange, rolling into the table and knocking the chairs over in a loud clatter of wood. *That should wake someone up!* He looked up and saw the man raise his sword again. Grabbing a chair he used it as a shield to take the hit; the blade stuck in the wooden seat. Wrenching the chair and sword away from the man he aimed a kick at his stomach.

Again the shockwave erupted sending the man across the room and James skidding across the floor. He was getting tired quickly; using his power like this was draining and he'd never had to use it so offensively before. The man reformed like he did before, and started towards James again. He passed by the other dark man who was holding the now fainted Mellanie. If she was out, then he could use his power openly … but would that work? These guys seemed to be able to absorb any attack thrown at them.

The shadow man raised his hands revealing long claw like fingers. James got to his feet and tried to think of someway to stop them; the only question was … how? He ducked and dodged the claws easily as they came. He managed to catch one of the hands and wrench it out of its socket, but again the man became vaporous and righted it instantly. That's when he got an idea. Slowly making his way to the back of the room he found the knife he'd first thrown lodged in the wall.

Yanking the metal out, he focused the remains of his power into it like he had done against the Elite. The shadow laughed at the puny steel and launched into another series of attacks. Rolling to the side he thrust the knife into the other's side and let the power burst forth. This time the shadow screamed in agony as its side exploded from the inside out. The one holding Mellanie dropped her and grabbed the other as he fell back with a hand to the gaping wound.

"Well, for someone only a few weeks into his power, you sure have developed it quite well." The uninjured shadow said in a deep voice. "Tuum kalyn dras al uhrna! Rendro ytr shai! I shall see you again, James Richards."

And in two plumes of smoke the men vanished leaving through the roof. He stared at the spot for a moment. That thing had spoken with the Words! But the Lady said only the animals and she could … What was that thing? He reached through his connection into Aria's mind and found what the shadow had said: Your power will be mine … Beware the shadows … A warning he would take to heart.

Sagging from the effort of holding his power he rushed over to Mellanie. She was out cold. He tried to wake her up, but nothing he did worked. Finally, he picked her up and carried her upstairs to his room. Alamar was asleep on the bed, snoring away. He set Mellanie on his bed and tried to wake her; when she didn't he pulled the covers over her and went to fetch Mistress Zala.

The cook was outraged at the mess downstairs and demanded to know what happened. He told her how the men and he had fought, and how no one seemed to wake up even we he crashed into the table and chairs. When he got to the part where they kept vanishing in plumes of smoke she dismissed him for either mad or exhausted.

"Shadow men?! What nonsense is this, boy?" Mistress Zala asked folding her arms.

"But madam, it's the truth." He stepped closer to her and stared her in the face. "I wouldn't lie about this!"

But the cook wouldn't hear it and went to wake Mellanie. She took the large wooden spoon she seemed to carry with her everywhere and began tapping her on the head lightly, ordering her to wake up. When she didn't, the cook turned her over and whacked her hard once on her bottom. She woke with a shout and clasped her hands over the dress. Without waiting to see if she was alright or even to hear her story, Mistress Zala shooed her out of the room and closed the door.

Alamar was fast asleep on his bed and snoring the night away.

CHAPTER 12

▼

THE PLOT THICKENS

SITTING once more in the throne like chair, he stared down at the two forms before him. He was tapping a finger on the arm of the chair again, but this time it was in frustration. He couldn't believe that a spell from the book had actually failed. The Shai'lun were supposed to be a force unparalleled, yet these two had lost to one boy! He may be the strongest Gattarian to ever walk the land since its making, but he had only manifested a short time ago!

"How do you plan to explain yourselves?"

The two shadows bowed their heads deeper at the tone in his voice. Frustration was only a part of it. He had watched the entire thing through the Mists of Revelation and saw how they had been tossed about like rag dolls.

"Master, it was my fault ..." The first said in his high raspy voice.

"Of course it's your fault!" He roared. His fist pounded on the arm of the chair to emphasize his anger. "You thought you could handle the boy on your own, even when I told you how strong he was. You thought that he didn't know how to use his powers effectively because of his recent manifestation, right? I made *two* of you because I knew it would take *two* of you to handle him! Why did you disobey my orders?!"

"Pardon me, Master," the second lifting his head a fraction, "but we did not disobey your orders. You never said to ..."

The entire structure shook from the explosion that engulfed the Shai'lun. Its dark body evaporated in the fire that rose from the marble floor to the ceiling.

The other was thrown to the side and landed so that the hole in its side was visible. The room was thrown back into the dim lighting of the lights as the fire vanished as quickly as it came, leaving the floor as spotless as ever. He turned away from the place where the Shai'lun had been seconds before and looked at its brother. He recalled the fine print that had been under the spell. *A word of caution to this spell: By creating the Shai'lun, You give birth to creatures with their own sense of attitude. Loyal they may be, they will think on their own.*

"Now, while I let your sibling sit for a time in Hell's Fields, I want you to go back and capture the Gattarian!" He stood up and towered over the cringing figure. "I don't care if you kill him, I can bring him back, but I want his powers and I want them soon. Now go!"

The shadow burst into a plume of smoke and flew through the window. It had better not come back without either the boy or news of his untimely death, or it would join its brother in Hell.

CHAPTER 13

▼

SOME FRIENDLY ADVICE

JAMES and Alamar left Malken the next day after buying a few supplies. They rode in silence again with Aria relaying their surroundings to him. He wasn't sure if he should mention the shadow men 'to Alamar or Aria. If the cook didn't believe him, would they? The Lady had said Aria was wise in the ways of the land, but he wasn't sure if she would know about these.

The days dragged on as they continued riding north. Alamar asked where they were going one time and James said he didn't really know. All he knew was that he had to get as far north as he could.

"But if we keep going directly north we'll run into the Masjr Fortress, the stronghold of the Fire army at Belayn's Crossing."

"I don't plan on going there." He said looking up at the sky. "I just know that I have to go north for now."

"Is there something you aren't telling me, James?"

He didn't answer. As much as he hated admitting it, he was beginning to like having Alamar around. He might not be very forth coming about who he was, but traveling with someone was better and safer than traveling alone. And besides … they were both outlaws; *always stick with your kind,* he thought. He didn't want to lose this friend just yet by telling him what he was. Maybe in a few days … maybe.

Days passed and so did the distance. After three and a half weeks of travel from Yattion, James started wishing he had a pad to sit on. *A car wouldn't do to badly either.* He was getting tired of sitting in a saddle all day, and with Alamar around he couldn't practice with his power to pass the time. So instead, during breaks and after camp was set up and the food cooking, he would go to work with his staff. Flying from stance to stance, form to form he maneuvered across the ground in a trance. Alamar watched from the fire as he sharpened his knives on a whetstone.

As he always did when practicing alone, he imagined the bandits surrounding him with their weapons and shadow like armor. The odd thing about being in life threatening danger was that afterwards, you could recall every little detail to the point.

The blades cut through the air, his staff hitting them aside before whirling around and bashing someone's head or chest. He saw the leader try to attack him from the side before they began their one on one fight in the middle of the battle. Down, left, up, left, right … again the blade was moving with incredible speed and he was only just able to get out of the way as it tried to slice his head off.

He bashed the staff against his chest and then went to help Miranda and the others when the knife was plunged once more into his side.

He stopped for a moment and placed a hand where the steel had pierced his side. There was a very thin scar there, hardly noticeable and it didn't hurt at all. Despite the fact that a number of swords had nicked him, that was the only mark he had from the whole affair. Gattarians were known to be able to heal with their powers, but he was clueless as to how he had done it. *Probably the spirits …* he thought.

"Don't thrust so often." Alamar said suddenly, interrupting his thoughts. He twirled a newly sharpened knife in his hand. "It gets obvious what you're going to do after a while. Try something else like swinging and parrying. A few feints here and there wouldn't go amiss either."

"How the hell am I supposed to do those?" he asked leaning on his staff. "I don't even know how to feint, and I can't parry what I can't see. As for swinging, that leaves me open on one side and sometimes even throws me off balance. Do you know how long this thing is?"

Alamar got up and took the staff. Twirling it about for a moment he showed him how to feint. He was very convincing. He looked like he was going to attack one way, and then would do something with his hands and strike out in a completely different direction. He led James through the steps and then pulled his knives out.

"Okay, attack me."

"Fine," James replied, sliding into a fighting stance, "but don't be a poor sport when I beat you."

They both chuckled evilly.

The staff whirled through the air but missed every time. Alamar was quick and painfully nimble. He crouched down like a cat or leopard ready to spring, and when he did, it was with deadly accuracy. If they had been fighting for real in the brief time, James would have died twelve times while only managing to tap Alamar once or twice. When they were done they sat around the fire tired and breathing hard. He might not have hit him too many times, but he'd managed to keep the little man moving the entire time.

"Who said who shouldn't be a poor sport?" Alamar said as he wiped his face with a wash cloth.

"Damn, where did you learn to move like that?" James asked slipping his tunic back on.

"I learned by watching my aunt's subordinates …" He stopped and went back to cleaning his face and arms.

"Subordinates? Who was your aunt?" Alamar didn't answer. "Never mind … But, um, you may want to think about trying to be more precise with your movements. You took too long to think where you should move to next. Look at what your opponent is doing and at what angle the attack is coming from and then move."

"Ah, but what if they feint? Then I'm dead." Alamar pointed out as he placed the wash cloth in his bags and pulled out a piece of bread and some cheese.

"That's where I think some actual blades would come in handy." James replied, motioning to the small blades at his sides. "Those are good, yes, but they don't have enough length to hold off an attack if you need to defend. If I were you I would get a pair of long daggers, to work with. That way you can guard yourself and deal more damage to the enemy in one swing."

"And when did you become such an expert?"

"Since I saw you fight." He replied sitting down next to the fire. "I was trained to defend and look for flaws in my opponent's technique before striking out. During our spar I memorized your movements and saw the flaw. That's how I managed to hit you those two times."

Alamar stared at him for a moment with the bread and cheese halfway to his mouth.

"That's pretty amazing. You really memorized my movements?"

"Well, not entirely, but I found enough of a pattern to counter in the end."

They sat there for an hour eating and giving the horses some drink, all the while talking about fighting techniques and ways on how to improve on each other's fighting.

Later that day they went hunting for food. There supplies weren't low, but they wanted to make sure they could rely on them in case of an emergency. If there was one thing James couldn't do, it was hunt. Finding tracks in the ground and following them required a keen eye and even with his glasses, he didn't have a keen eye. Alamar wasn't too great at it either and they both started getting worried.

Luckily, James had a companion who was queen of the skies and an excellent hunger. Aria pointed out a group of deer a ways off and helped James track them down. He put on an act to make it look like he'd suddenly gotten the hang of the sport. Alamar bought it.

When they came within sight of the herd it was just a matter of a single fireball and a nice buck was soon roasting over a fire that gave off no smoke.

That night the sky was clear and the stars were out in all their glory. He loved nights like these when he could see all the stars. The light pollution at home had been too great for this many to be visible except through a telescope. Oddly enough he was able to find Orion and the Bull, Libra, and Scorpio all cluttered in the night sky. He's never seen the last two except in a book before and didn't know if they normally were out together, but he enjoyed the sight none the less.

Aria was perched on his shoulder looking up at the stars as well while Alamar slept next to Haenya and Trae'len. The hawk brushed a wing against his face and he nudged her back in return.

The night is very beautiful. She said after a moment. *The heavens shine like a thousand worlds.*

I wonder if my world is out there.

I'm sure it is Young One. She nudged his head with a wing. *And I will make sure you see it again someday.*

Thanks. He ruffled the feathers on her head. *I just hope that when the time comes, I am not too attached to this world. Already I am starting to wonder whether or not I'll stay or go.*

What about your family and friends? She turned her head to him completely. *Surely you miss them.*

Of course I do but ... I have other friends and family here in this world now too. I don't want to just up and leave them. It wouldn't feel right. And of course I don't want to leave you behind, Aria. You're like a big sister to me at times, you know.

Always bothering me when I want to be alone and never around when I need you.
She tightened her grip on his shoulder in response.

I'm honored you think of me that way, Young One. She stopped for a moment
and looked at him with her golden eyes. *Perhaps it is time I stop calling you that.
You are no longer just a hatchling.*

*Actually, I've gotten used to it. I like it, to tell the truth. But if you were to give me
another name, what would it be ... for curiosity's sake.*

Mi'retone. It means He Who Brings Hope in the language of the Land.

He Who Brings Hope? I haven't brought hope to anyone, Aria. Why that name?

Before she could answer, the familiar feeling in the back of his mind returned
and the hawk became very still. Alamar woke with a start and grabbed his knives.
His eyes were livid as he searched the area. He looked over to James and then in
the direction he was staring and gasped. Standing only a few feet away was the
shadow man that had attacked him at the inn, but neither he nor Aria knew that
yet.

"We meet again, James Richards." The shadow said. He glided forward and
stopped as he saw Alamar already crouched and ready to spring. "How pathetic,
you have yourself a bodyguard. What a little worm."

Alamar cried out as he was lifted into the air by an invisible force. He grabbed
at his neck like he was being strangled and kicked with his legs. Aria shrieked and
flew into the air but was also grabbed by the invisible energy. Try as she might,
she couldn't get free.

"Let them go!" The shadow looked over at James who was burning with his
power. "I said let them go NOW!"

He lashed out and shot three of his ice darts in the man's torso. He laughed
and vaporized, letting them fall to the ground.

"Fool. Do you think you can harm a shadow with physical power and weapons?" The shadow laughed again. "Mortals should know their place! You cannot
harm me with your meager attacks. I am ..."

The dark figure was sent sprawling across the ground, dropping Alamar and
Aria. James ran after it, pulsing with every ounce of energy he could hold and
channeling it into his fists. As the shadow righted itself it could only watch as
blow after blow rained down. With a large burst of energy he ran and drop
kicked the shadow full in the chest.

Breathing heavily from using so much of his strength at once, James got to his
feet and spat in the direction he'd tossed the shadow. Alamar was whooping and
cheering over by the camp while Aria hovered just above him scanning the
ground. She knew the shadow was still there, waiting for something.

"I had forgotten about that ability of yours." The voice said to his right. "You can use the Essence of the power to make a barrier or in this case a force of energy. Somehow this seems to be able to hurt me, but again you forget that I am only shadow and cannot die."

The shadow materialized next to him with its sword in hand. He raised the sword and slashed through the night. With no time to dodge he brought his arms up and the blade met the metal armlets with a clang causing him to fall to his knees. The shadow laughed again and pressed harder against the steel bands, forcing him to bend almost backwards from the force. When he thought he couldn't hold it anymore, Alamar burst through the night in a blaze of fire.

His flames drove the darkness from around the area making the shadow cringe and back off its attack. Rushing through the night, Alamar blazed and burned through the shadow man like an arrow. The dark man shrieked louder than ever before and burst into a plume of smoke. They could hear him screaming in rage and pain as he retreated into the night.

"Damn you! I shall be back to get you another day, James Richards!!"

The three of them stood there watching the night sky, gazing at the stars. Alamar turned to James as Aria perched on his shoulder. The look in his eyes made him want to look away. The secret was out, and not how he'd intended it.

"When? When were you going to tell me you were a Gattarian?"

"Alamar listen to me, I am not the enemy or a spy or …"

"I don't want to hear your flaming story! Just tell me why you kept it hidden? Why didn't you tell me? I might have wanted to know that I was traveling with a Gattarian. Didn't you trust me? I have been traveling all this time with you and now I know where you were leading me; to Gattar … to the Ice Kingdom! When were you going to tell me?"

"I don't know!" He shouted back. "I didn't want you to turn on me or think that I was some monster! I wasn't going to take you all the way to the Ice Kingdom. I was planning on telling you long before we got to the Dead Lands. I just didn't want you to hate me because of what I am. I've already lost the only friends I had here …"

"Hate you? Because you're a Gattarian? James, I am as much of an outlaw in Intaru as you are."

"You never said anything about that! All I knew was that the Elite wanted you. I know that means something serious, but I wasn't about to press you about it! So tell me Alamar Janury, what are you wanted for? Why are the Elite chasing after you?"

There was a long silence as they stared at each other with intense and angry looks.

"Because my father betrayed the Emperor." He bowed his head and let his hands fall to his sides.

What? Whoa ... He couldn't believe it. *Betrayed the Emperor? How the ... how could he have betrayed someone of such a rank unless ...*

"Who was your father?"

"His name is Proga Telanre, second in command of the Fire Army. And brother to the Emperor."

Oh my God. That makes him ... Oh <Unprintable Text>.

"My father is the brother to the Emperor, and that makes me one of the possible heirs because he is childless." He continued. "But something drove my father to betray his brother to Gattar. He was found out and hanged. My mother gave me, only four years old at the time, to my caretaker and told her to flee with me to the farthest reaches of the world and hide me. She took me into the mountains far to the west of here where she had lived prior to being my mother's maid.

"I lived there for twelve years, until the army came to look for me. They probably thought that I would betray the Emperor like my father, and so intended to have me hanged. Again I fled, alone this time, and have been fleeing from the Elite for two years now."

They sat in silence. Alamar Telanre, an heir to the Fire Kingdom throne, rogue and outlaw, sat staring at the ground with a distant look in his eyes. James could only stare at first. He was used to accepting things as they came, but this was way too much! Aria was watching both of them from his shoulder.

"Alamar, sir ..."

"Don't call me that!" he snapped. "I am not royalty! I am an outlaw and a rogue! Banished from Intaru because of my traitorous father! So don't start treating me any different James Richards. I won't allow it."

"Alright, alright. But, you don't have to bite my head off. I just wasn't sure ..."

"I'm the same person I've always been, James. And no matter what you know about my past doesn't change that. I am what I make myself." He looked up at him, that far away look gone and replaced by a sad one. "I guess the same goes for you, huh? Just because you're a Gattarian, doesn't mean you aren't still the same lame staff man I can beat down in a matter of seconds."

"Yea, well, I guess I should have said something earlier about what I am. I was just being suspicious that's all. I ..."

"Don't worry about it ..." He said with a shake of his head. "'What's past is past and there is little we can do to change it. One can accept it and deal with it, or waste their time wishing it never happened.' That's a quote from Emperor Lja-zlen[1], he ruled some two hundred years ago."

"Wise man ..."

"Another thing," he interrupted suddenly. "What was that thing that attacked us? I've never heard of a shadow man, and the power doesn't allow a person's body to act like that. So what kind of strange magic is he using?"

"I don't know what they are either." He replied in all honesty. "I met two of them in Malken during my date. That one seems to be the one in charge, because the other just sat back and made sure Mellanie didn't scream. Beyond that I only know what you do."

Will you two keep it down over there? I'm trying to sleep!

"Trae'len, shut up ... oops." He looked back over to Alamar who raised an eyebrow. "Guess there's one more thing I forgot to mention. I can, um, well, talk to Aria and Trae'len."

"You're joking, right?"

"I wish." Aria clenched his shoulder tighter and made a noise in her throat. "Sometimes I wish, but this bird and horse have saved my hide enough times that I can deal with them for a while." Again Aria tightened her grip. "Hey cut that out, alright? See what I mean?"

Alamar laughed. "I don't believe this. Nothing is going to be normal with you is it?" He shrugged, still laughing. "Guess I'd better get used to it, especially if I'm coming with you to Gattar."

"What?! Alamar, you can't go there! They'd kill you!"

He shrugged again. "I'm not too worried. Besides, I do have a little know-how that could be useful to them. But it won't come cheap. If I'm going to follow that far in my father's footsteps, I might as well get something nice in return. Anyhow, I have no life here, and the people think I am a traitor now anyway. So I might as well give them a reason to hate me. Right?"

He's crazy. That's what he was ... crazy. *What kind of person have I gotten myself mixed with this time?*

---

1. Ljaslen—Sounds like Joz-len. The L is silent.

CHAPTER 14

▼

A NEW TRICK, A NEW DESTINATION

A couple of leagues later they drew closer to the next town. Something was pulling at the back of James' mind when they were about a league away. It felt like there were Intaruans up ahead, strong ones. His first fear was that the Elite had somehow managed to get ahead of them, but when he mentioned it to Alamar, he shook his head.

"Not a chance. The Elite are the best fighters in the country and very good at doing what they do, but even they can't travel that fast. And besides, they would sense you if they passed us." He wafted his hand towards the town. "It's probably just the townsfolk. Haklyn is a pretty big town so the people's powers could make it seem like there were strong people there."

Not wanting to take any risks, James sent Aria ahead to scout the town. There was a down time when she was out of range of his thoughts and the emptiness that came with it was heartbreaking. Trea'len tried to keep him company by talking about Haenya and her beautiful mane and tail, but it wasn't the same.

When Aria finally returned, to an overjoyed James, she told him that there were lots of humans in the town and plenty of them were wearing steal plated clothes. James translated for Alamar and they both decided to circumvent the town.

"It'll give the Elite a chance to make some ground on us," Alamar said as they turned towards the west, "but we can't just go barging into a town of guards. Someone would feel you out."

So they headed northwest for about ten days before they came to another town, this one was Yurguay. Aria said that there were guards there too, but their numbers were no more than usual according to Alamar.

Yurguay was smaller than Malken in area but was at least twice as big in population. People lived cramped together in houses barely big enough to hold them all. The houses themselves were in shambles and falling apart at the seams. The road was misaligned with cobble stones, and weeds poked through everywhere. It was a completely different atmosphere from Malken.

"This is horrible." James said as they passed a mother and child in rags on the street. "Why doesn't the Empire do something about all this? Surely there is money in the royal vault to help get this place back on its feet."

"Just look forward and ignore what you see."

"You can't be serious." He healed Trae'len next to Haenya. "Ala ... I mean Tristan, you can't just think to look away from all of this! There are people starving on the streets, surely your heart feels sympathy."

"Of course it does." He said without looking at him. His eyes were clouded over and he never seemed to blink. "But I can't let my emotions run loose here. If I give something to one person, then everyone will want something in turn and when I can't provide for all of them ... well look over there."

He motioned to the right at a pair of houses. Hanging on the clothesline were three people. All of them were dead and their skin was black and bubbly, their clothes gone. But they all had slit throats as well. James' stomach lurched so hard he was unable to hold it down and turned and vomited off Trea'len's side. People jumped out of the way and cursed him, but he shut them out and looked back to Alamar.

"Those people were still alive when their bodies were dipped in boiling tar." Alamar said, turning green at the thought. "Then they were hung out to die slowly. Whoever slit their throats was a mercy giver. That's what happens when someone tries to provide for everyone in this town. That's why we are leaving this place as soon as we get provisions."

James was all for that plan and the two of them went in search for the stores.

The food was horrible here. The bread was stale, and the meat was starting to rot, there wasn't a clean water well anywhere, and no place at all to buy horse feed. Alamar was getting annoyed with every shop they went to. No one had any food that was decently fresh and he didn't dare buy the rotten foods with the little money they had left.

Outside the third bakery they stopped at James couldn't help but look around at the town again. He made sure to drop his gaze and not look at any more clotheslines, but that forced him to look at all the people in the streets. Several of them looked at him with empty eyes, without any hope of life shining behind them. Their clothes were all patched up from several outfits or so covered in filth and waste that it looked like part of their skin.

The houses were all cramped together, leaving alleys only three or so feet wide. Every space between buildings had a sheet hiding the occupants from view ... except for one. The child inside the uncovered corridor was calling to his mother, who was simply staring at the ground in a slump. No matter how the child pleaded the mother wouldn't respond.

Forgetting Alamar's warning, he crossed the street and ducked into the alley these people called home. It was cramped and dirty and smelled of feces and disease. The child was wearing a filthy rag around his waist for clothing and the rest of him was just as dirty. The mother wore a rough brown dress that looked to be sewn from multiple different items. When James entered the hovel the child cried out and crawled into his mother's arms. Again the mother didn't look up or move; she simply sat there with her eyes to the ground.

He looked at the woman's face, or the part that wasn't covered in filth, and tried speaking to her. Her eyes shifted a little, nothing more than that, but it was all he needed; she was feverish. He placed a hand on her forehead and drew it back so fast he almost fell over. The fever was so ungodly high he didn't know how she was still alive! He turned to call Alamar but stopped. Would he even try to help? Or would he just drag him away without a second glance. He tried to think of something to do, anything to try and bring the fever down. Fevers in Intaru were deadly. People's normal body temperatures were normally high, but when they got fevers ... He couldn't let this child watch his mother die.

Then he remembered what happened in Yattion. He had somehow healed Dannil's sword wound and brought him back from the brink of death. He thought he could try it again. Summoning his power he reached out with it to the woman's forehead. The invisible icy-blue threads wrapped themselves around her and tied around each other forming a messy halo. When the ring was complete he reached out with his mind through his power and into the woman's. The force of the fever caused him to retract again, but he didn't give up. Again he tried to find the source of the fever by feeling with his mind.

It was like walking through the parking lot on a hot, dry day in the middle of summer with a hurricane strength wind blowing at you in every direction at the same time! The fever attacked his mind trying to drive him away, but he pushed all the more against it. Slowly he made his way into the storm. His defenses weakened at one point and he was pushed back very far before he regained his hold, but he didn't stop. After what felt like hours, he felt the tempest around him start to dwindle and the heart of the fever bore down on him like a giant weight.

Again he drew on more of his energy and tried pushing the weight off, but it only got heavier the harder he tried. He wove the threads of power around the fever and tried to crush it, but it only got heavier and didn't let up! The ferocity of the fever and the strain of holding his power were catching up to him quickly. The Seal didn't allow him to use more than he could handle safely, but if he didn't do something, this woman would die. If only he could weaken the fever a little bit he knew he'd be able to get rid of it.

Think! Damn it, what am I supposed to do?

Let me Guide your Spirit.

His heart froze and his blood went cold. He almost dropped his hold on the power, but caught it before it slipped away. Withdrawing so quickly from the woman's mind could destroy her. But if the voice managed to take control again …

I will help you heal her.

You will take over my body! Forget it! I am not letting you guide me!

Then let me show you. The voice suggested.

Show me? Speaking with the voice was distracting him … he felt his grip over the power weakening again. *I don't even know who you are, or how you are talking to me.*

I am Tiana Paine, a spirit who knows much in the ways of healing. While I was alive I studied the art and learned things that no one else knew. Yet out of fear of my powers I never used it. But I can promise you, neither you nor the woman will come to any harm.

What about the last time in Yattion?! He shouted back. *You almost killed everyone! It took everything I had to drive the three of you away! I won't let that happen again.*

We were only doing what we thought was best for you. If the bandits had been allowed to go free, they would have chased you down and killed everyone in the village. But that was not all my doing. Marlao and Kinran were behind it as well and they were the ones who felt it necessary to kill. I was against it, but I am only one and they are two. I was over powered. I promise you James Richards, I will not use you for anything beyond what you allow.

It sounded like she was telling the truth … she was right about one thing: she was only one spirit. If she tried to do anything he didn't want, he could over-power her easier than last time. He was beginning to tire very quickly … he had to make a decision.

If I let you in, you are to leave ME in control, and just show me what to do. That's all, no more. Understand?

Yes.

Almost immediately the weight became light as a feather and using only a frac-tion of the power he was holding, pushed it back. He felt Paine's spirit guiding him, showing him the art of healing. The threads of energy reached out and began wrapping themselves around the fever's heart in an intricate pattern. When Paine had completed the pattern it looked like three circles all intersecting at one point with a diamond at the epicenter. He felt the power coursing through him surge to the limits the Seal allowed and in a flash of light as bright as the sun the fever broke.

His eyes popped open and his head jerked up as he retracted his mind from the woman's. The child was still cradling his mother in the same position he'd been in when James had started. The mother began stirring making the child jump and start calling to her again in his high pitched voice. Not wanting to be thanked by the woman, who would surely tell everyone about him if she saw him, he got up and half walked, half ran back to Trae'len.

Alamar was just coming to a close with the same baker he'd been talking to when he left. In the end they bought some stale bread and some meat that looked the least rotten. Packing their things into the saddle bags they mounted the horses and rode out of the town with the sun still high. Alamar was grumbling to himself about the waste of money and the poor condition of the town, but James was too deep in his thoughts to listen.

Tiana? Are you still there?

Yes.

I, um, want to thank you for helping me back there. You saved that woman's life.

No, James, it was you who did it. He felt his face flush a little at the praise. *I simply showed you how. But I accept the thanks nonetheless.*

Can I ask you some questions that have been on my mind since Yattion? If you can't answer them because of the Law, then I understand, but …

I will answer to the best of my abilities she replied.

Okay, first, how is it that you are able to speak to me even though you're dead?

We are connected by our powers as well as the rune on your arm. Instinctively, he placed a hand over the metal armlet he still wore everyday. Tuhugara was starting to tingle, but he figured it was nothing. *Your power, Marlao's, Kinran's and mine are almost equal in strength. So we are able to press against the barrier separating the land of the living and that of the dead to speak with you. It is kind of like how you use the essence of the power to shield yourself.*

Well that made sense. He wondered who exactly was the strongest of the four of them.

Alright, next, why did the three of you help me through my Awakening back in Yattion? Why did you bother trying to Guide me?

The Lady of the Gray Wood was correct in her assumption. We were saddened by the fact that another was going to die because of their power. So we bonded to you through your power and helped your body cope with the Awakening. After that, the other two began their tirade.

I knew she knew. Spirits and entities of great power *always* spoke in riddles or kept back a lot of what they truly know. *Gah, never mind. Okay, one more question. Do you think you could teach me how to control my powers? I want to live, and I want to be able to use it to help like we did with that woman. I don't want to live in fear of my abilities.*

Unfortunately I do not know how to go about protecting you from the power.

He heard the sadness in her voice. She wanted to do the same thing he did when she was alive; only, she couldn't use her powers at all.

The dead are endowed with knowledge that no living mortal could dream of, but we cannot share it with them if we are ever able to contact them. Yet despite this, I still do not know how to control it. I am sorry. That is something you will have to discover on your own.

Knowledge no mortal knows ... I wonder ... *Do you know who brought me to Arollay then?*

Yes, but the Law prohibits me from telling you. Believe me when I say that I would tell you if I could, but it is forbidden. Something about the nature of your arrival here forces the Law into action. I cannot say what this force is exactly, but know that it is something not seen in Arollay for over two thousand years. The contact between them started feeling strained, like something was getting in the way. *I am sorry, I must leave you now. I have said too much and I am being pulled away from you even now.*

Wait! You said that you learned how to heal people by studying it! Where did you study? Where did you learn it?

The Healer's Guild in the city of Malan'dur at the southeastern coast of Gattar.

And with that the connection snapped and he lost contact with the spirit, but he didn't brood over it too long. Now he knew where he had to go. When he told Alamar about his plans he didn't seem too shocked.

"Well, when we were done fighting those Elite back when we first met you asked if the one you fought with was alright; Healer's rule says they cannot kill, or so the rumors say. When I found out later that you were a Gattarian I was almost positive that's where you would end up. Just another reason why I decided to go with you." He smiled broadly. "The Healer's Guild acted as a sanctuary to my father in his earliest days of betrayal. I'm sure they'll welcome me with open arms."

"I still don't understand why you are coming with me. Even if that is your destination, the army won't let you in without making sure you aren't lying. What will you do then?"

"Don't know. I'll probably have to sneak past them and keep hidden until we reach Malan'dur. Until then, you can protect me, oh powerful Richards."

Alamar ducked under the snowball James threw at him and stuck his tongue out before galloping off. Heeling Trae'len after him the two of them galloped down the empty road in good spirits.

The dark figure looming over the decaying town watched the two humans gallop away on their pathetic steeds. No one saw him floating there above the town. He cast no shadow and the wind past through him undisturbed. He was shadow incarnate and shadow didn't show itself to anyone unless it wished. He smiled as his hand caressed the battle axe at his side. His brother loved the blade of a sword, but he found the weight of an axe so much better. Maybe he would leave the one human alive so his brother could do with him as he pleased. A just reward for injuring him so much the last time.

He gripped the haft of his axe in fury. That damned kid was strong, much stronger than he let on. If he could make his aura blaze like that to drive away his brother, then what else was he capable of? Releasing his grip on the axe he flung his cloak around him and vanished in a plume of smoke.

CHAPTER 15

▼

SOMETHING FOR THE
HISTORY BOOKS

WITH the last town far behind them, James and Alamar began to get nervous. They were nearing the Dead Lands, the Border of Nu'athion, and the halfway point. According to Aria, the Border began no more than another day's travel away. In only a few leagues, they would reach the Masjr Fortress, stronghold of the Fire Army's third division, the Masjr Riders. From what Alamar could tell him they were some deadly fighters, and some of the strongest with the power.

"Of course, they don't even compare to the First and Second divisions, but they are still strong. When they aren't using their powers to fight, they are riding their Masjr beasts." He was waving his arms about trying to describe them. "They look like a mix between a bull and a horse with long thick legs that can run down any stallion easily and teeth strong enough to crack bone! They're always black colored with claws and a tail with a nasty looking spike at the end. You can tell how old they are by the colored stripes running down from neck to flank; green is for the younger ones and gold for the older—let me tell you, you don't want to run into one of *those* beasts. Then of course there are the spikes on their sides! They can retract them and extended them faster than you can blink.

"But the beasts aren't all. The Riders themselves are killing machines! They use swords with wicked curves on them to tear flesh and rip through armor. And *their* armor is made of the strongest metals ever crafted to allow them the ultimate protection against any blade. Rumor has it they can even deflect the power. I've never seen them fight, myself, but I've heard stories since I was little of the outcome of most battles they were in."

"Well, no matter how strong they are, they can't fight what they can't see." James said easing his stomach. The very picture Alamar gave him of those beasts made him feel sick. "We'll just sneak right past them and be across the Dead Lands without them even knowing we were there."

"That might not be the exact outcome."

"Why do you say that? They don't have people that can sense Gattarians, do they?"

"I bet they do, but that's not what I mean." He reached down and pulled up his saddle bag. "Take a look at our supplies."

The bag was almost empty … again! There was a little stale bread left, and only a strip or two of the already rotten meat lay wrapped beneath it. James checked his bag and saw that his was only a little better, but not enough to get him through the Dead Lands alive. Not to mention they were also running out of horse feed and water. James closed his bag and slumped in his saddle. This was just perfect.

"So what do you plan to do?" he asked Alamar. "Just walk right into the fortress and steal their food?"

"In a sense." The other replied. James turned his head so fast he got a pinch in his neck. "Don't look so shocked. Remember, we know how to sneak around very effectively, and if need be, we can always hide behind one of my heat waves. You're the only one to ever be able to sense that, so that can be an option. Speaking of which, how *are* you able to sense me behind my heat waves?"

"Dunno." He replied honestly. "I just get this feeling in the back of my head and the hairs on my neck stand on end whenever someone is nearby or using their powers. I've learned to push the feeling away since I would be feeling it all the time in Intaru. Beyond that … I don't know."

When the sun was just starting its decent into the horizon, they had reached the Masjr Fortress. The place was dark and foreboding from wall to wall. The ramparts and parapets were at least seven stories tall and numbered in the dozens from only one side. The walls were lined with stones easily as tall as James and at least four times as wide. Alamar wasn't joking when he said the place was intimidating.

The two of them were hiding a ways away while Aria flew over head to scope out the area. James relayed the visions to Alamar who made crude drawings on the ground. All around the fortress the land was barren and dead with no place to hide or take cover. There were soldiers posted every ten feet along the walls and each one carried a long bow and three quivers full of arrows as well as either a sword, an axe, or spear.

Alamar asked if she could find the Masjr beasts' pens so they would know where not to go, but she said that the inside was covered by a roof. So, unable to see the inside of the fortress James called her back and started planning out their strategy for getting inside. Without any cover to hide them, they would use Alamar's heat waves to get them inside. After that they would have to find every secret passage they could to make sure they weren't seen.

"I can hold the waves long enough for us to get some decent cover once inside, but after that I don't know how much longer I'd be able to hold it without exhausting myself."

"Well, we can just disguise ourselves in their armor or something." James said looking over the map again. He'd stared at it so long he had every marking memorized. "If we can just find their storages, we'll be golden. But until then, we will have to do things the old fashioned way; good old sneaking."

"Okay, now, once we have what we need, how do we get out of there?"

"Simple. I'll contact Trae'len and have him and Haenya circle around to meet us on the other side of the fortress. Aria can guide them so they won't be seen."

"Can you reach him that far away? That's easily 5 miles."

"If I can't reach Trae'len then I can speak to Aria. She can then get the horses to where they need to be."

With everything ready the two prepared to set off in the morning. The sun rose the next day revealing the barren lifeless land around the fortress. Alamar had his knives wrapped around his waist while James had his staff. At first the staff wouldn't let Alamar's power surround it. He was stumped and couldn't think of anything that would reverse the effect of the runes.

Aria, what do these runes say?

Hælen ys uhr fomyr. It means fire is my enemy. Woodsbane placed an extra line in the fourth rune changing it from rymof *to* fomyr, *friend to enemy.*

Hmm ... I take it Dannil is Woodsbane then ... I wonder if I could reverse it by saying the Words ...

Don't you dare! He felt her press harder against his mind. *You do not know how much power that would require. Remember what I told you long ago when you asked me to teach you the Words—and refused: you must know how much energy it will take before even thinking of saying an incantation.*

Okay, okay.

Pushing the mental link back, he held the staff horizontally in both hands and concentrated on the fifth rune; fomyr. Reaching into his being, he called forth the azure light and directed it over the staff. The blue light washed over the wood like water, coating it in its power. Alamar watched him, not knowing exactly what was going on, but with a good idea.

Once the light had completely covered the staff it began to change. It was no longer just a coat of blue light, but a net; a Seal. As he released the power he felt something recede from his mind along with it; a feeling of a smile was etched into his mind. He shook his head. *Thank you.* He said to the spirit.

He was breathing hard from the effort, but managed to stay on his feet. "I Sealed the effect of the runes on the staff. Come on, let's go. We have work to do."

With the runes temporarily negated, the staff was able to be concealed and they were off.

The land gave way quickly and without any alarm going up from the fortress. Though he doubted they would cause much of a ruckus over two men with a staff and some knives, even if they could be seen. The gates were closed, of course, and way too tall to even think of climbing.

They tried circling the walls and found a sewer drain. It was so small that James went so far as to cover the ground and the arch in ice so they could slip through before retracting his senses to try and fool anyone who could sense him. The smell gagged them, but they plugged their noses and walked along the dry side of the sewer.

The sewers stretched around the fortress for a goodly distance, unfortunately, and by the time they found the other entrance they had both lost their stomachs twice each. Taking hold of the ladder the people responsible for cleaning the sewers used, they gratefully climbed out of the hell hole. The fresh air was comforting and helped to steady their stomachs, but they both reeked of feces and people made faces as they passed by their hiding place. Luckily they only thought it was the sewers. James used a thin layer of ice to wash off the stench from their clothes and then dried them … at least they didn't smell anymore.

With a wave of his hand Alamar ducked after a cart that was going down the rightmost corridor. James waited at the sewer entrance for another five minutes before the way to the left hall was clear. Making sure his staff was ready he dashed across the small courtyard and into the darkness. The dim torch light didn't let him see very far, but as his eyes adjusted he began to notice the tapestries hanging along the walls. Each one depicted some battle between the Gattarians and Intaruans, with the latter winning by the looks of it.

Creeping along the dark hallway he heard voices up ahead and, pushing himself against the wall behind one of the tapestries, he waited and listened. There were two men, both wearing armor by the sounds of metal and the clank of joints that came with their walk. One of them was talking about some battle strategy, while the other listened half heartedly with the occasional "Uh-huh" and "Hmm, I wonder …" James waited for their voices to vanish before breathing. He didn't think something like hiding here would work in real life.

Young One, are you okay?

Yes. Is everything ready on your end?

The horses are getting nervous because you've been gone a while, but they are ready to move on command. Are you sure you are okay? Your emotions went wild a moment ago.

Let's just say I came within an inch of being seen.

Ducking out from the tapestry he continued down the hall. At the first crossroad he took a right. From what Alamar had said, the food storages would be on the second floor so as to keep them away from the sewer and everyday traffic. Twice he took a wrong turn, both times almost getting caught in the process, and twice he had to back track to the crossroads. Every hall looked the same; he didn't know how the soldiers found their way around so easily.

Finally he found the stairs leading up. They spiraled along one of the parapets at the side of the fortress. As he came to the third time around someone appeared in the stairwell above him. The soldier wore black armor with golden stripes across his chest and a single green band around his left arm. The shock wore off rather quickly and the soldier drew his sword with a shout. The stairwell was too cramped for him to use the staff, so he raised his armlets.

The steel blade met the metal and bounced back with a curse from the soldier. As he stumbled up a step, he lashed out with a few ice darts. But as the tendrils of power gripped the armor they just slid off and dissipated. Twice he tried to attack the soldier and each time the ice slipped off and vanished. Then as the sword came around for the fifth time he recalled what Alamar had said about the Masjr's armor giving them protection from the power.

The soldier was shouting at the top of his lungs trying to call in reinforcements, but no one seemed to hear because no one ever came. Taking the staff in both hands he began a tirade of thrusts and jabs into the dark armor. The wood made odd sounds against it everywhere, but when he hit the part just under the right arm, it sounded different from the others. Focusing his energies there he lashed out and found the weak point in the metal, where the two ends had been melded together. The soldier cried out as his leather under-armor froze in a block of solid ice.

Not wanting to leave any evidence of a Gattarian behind, he got behind the suddenly statue-like soldier. Reaching into the ice with his mind he thawed it out as he shoved the man head first down the stairs. Now when they found him, they would only think he tripped. *Hopefully.* Hefting his staff in his hands he dashed up the rest of the stairs and ran down the right hall.

There were arrow slits every few feet along the walls that provided enough light during the day and recently doused torches lining the walls for night. There was a ruckus in the corridor ahead of him and skidding to a stop at the corner he peered around to see at least five more men dressed like the last all shouting at the tops of their lungs at each other. They were throwing words back and forth that would have sounded right at home at a rival football game.

The hairs on the back of his neck rose and a familiar feeling told him that Alamar was close by and probably the cause of the argument. Damn kid didn't know when to be serious! But how was he supposed to get by these guys without being seen? He didn't know how to cloak himself like Alamar and he didn't dare try to run past the hall. He needed a distraction.

"There I saw him again!"

The men all drew their swords and dashed down the corridor after the feeling in the back of his head. Alamar didn't know when to be serious, but he sure was good at showing up at the right time. With the coast clear he managed to find the food storage. The only obstacles now were the two guards making sure no one had an afternoon snack. Making sure he was well hidden behind a tapestry near by he summoned his power once again. Sending the invisible threads of azure light around the corner was harder than he thought it would be.

Once out of sight he had to rely on feel alone and that was dangerous. The icy blue threads crept along the floor at a turtle's pace, feeling its way to the soldier's feet. Twice he ended up hitting the wall and just barely managed to retract it before it froze. After three tries he found the soldiers' armor and let the power climb up into the cracks to freeze their under armor. Both men gasped and tried to shout for help, but he dodged around the corner and covered their mouths with a sheet of ice.

Grabbing the keys from the right guard's waist he unlocked the door and dragged them both inside, closing the door behind him. Leaning the two frozen guards against the door he went to work taking anything he thought would help them cross the Dead Lands. He grabbed bread, meat, cheese, and some berries he thought looked familiar and stashed them all away in his and Alamar's packs.

Calling out to Aria he told her to start leading the horses to the rendezvous point. The hawk shrieked and flew out of range to retrieve the horses. Tying both packs to his back he thwacked both guards with his staff and defrosted them. Making sure no one was around he started on the arduous path back to the sewers. He got lost a dozen times and every time almost got caught and was able to escape by shear luck alone.

By the time he got to the sewer entrance the place was a mad house. Word about his assault on the two guards had been spread and now everyone was dashing about looking for the supposed enemy. Jumping down the ladder he saw Alamar was leaning against the wall breathless. James smiled and helped him through the tunnel.

"Can you show me how to conceal us?" he asked as they reached the end of the tunnel. "You don't have enough strength left to keep this up. Remember I can see how you use your powers so maybe I can copy it."

"Okay, just copy what I do *exactly*."

Alamar let his power flow freely and directed a dozen threads of the red light into an intricate pattern in the air around him. When the last two threads touched, completing the web, he vanished. The air where he stood was wavy like a parking lot in the middle of summer until he popped back into view.

"I don't know how to do that." He said. "I can barely form solid ice, let alone control the power in its ethereal form."

"Does Aria have any ideas?" He stumbled over his words; he still wasn't used to thinking of a bird as sentient.

James shook his head. *The problem with that is: I can barely feel Aria, let alone communicate with her.* He slammed his arm against the wall making the metal armlet ring against the stone. The sound caught his attention … and an idea came to him. Of course; *Tiana said that the dead were very knowledgeable … so maybe someone who is dead can help me out.* And the Words held power, and he had one on his wrist that was the epitome of death! Maybe he could use the rune Tuhugara to contact one of the spirits! It sounded crazy to him, but it was the only thing he could think of.

He told Alamar his plan and then to get back. "I don't know what this will do and I'd rather not end up killing you by mistake."

"Gee, thanks." He took a dozen steps back and nodded.

"Here goes nothing …" He concentrated on the rune, every line and detail was clear in his mind. *I need to speak with a spirit!* "Tuhugara!"

The air went cold, the hairs on his neck straightened so fast they almost popped out. He could see his breath fogging in the air and the light around him became green and hazy. All around him he felt nothing but death and decay and hatred and malice! It was so much that he felt like he was going insane!

Who are you …? A raspy voice said from the haze. *Why have you come here, mortal?*

"I … I am James Richards," he said as steady as he could; in other words, he was shaking so hard his voice bobbed. "I have come to ask for knowledge. I need to know how to use my powers to …"

And what makes you think that we are the ones to tell you? The voice replied quickly. *How do you know that we just won't kill you now and be done with this intrusion?*

"B-because I come bearing the rune Eliferen!" he raised his arm, somehow the armlet was gone and the three runes were clearly visible. "You cannot harm me with these. Now, I demand that you tell me what I came to know!"

FOOL! Just because you are immune to our touch does not mean you have the power to control us! The voice was now all around him, emanating such fury that James almost wet himself. *We are ancient and powerful, and you are nothing!*

Yet I give you credit for finding your way here so easily on your first try.

James blinked as the second voice spoke. It was deeper than the first and didn't sound so wicked.

Be gone from this place Kinran! The first voice shouted. *This boy is not your concern.*

'Not my concern' you say? Oh Slaizar, how foolish you sound. I shall take over here. You go back to your other duties before I destroy you.

Kinran, remember the Law. The first voice said again. James could hear a hint of fear in his voice. *I am the Enforcer! I make sure the Law is upheld and this boy is breaking it by coming here while still living!*

I'll give you one last warning Slaizar. Kinran said again. *Leave the boy and go back to your duties if you know what is best for you.*

James could feel the air grow colder from the hatred seething from one spirit to the next.

Boy, you listen to me! Slaizar's voice shouted. James felt his presence press up against his mind like a two ton weight. *If you ever come here again without the permission of the Gate Keeper, I shall bind your soul to this spot for eternity! Mortals are NOT allowed into Hell's Domain while they are still alive! Do I make myself clear?!*

"Crystal." Slaizar growled at his remark but said no more as he released his hold over James.

Well done, boy. But you made one hell *of an enemy.* He laughed at his own joke.

"You … you're Kinran Death, aren't you?" He felt the spirit nod. "I … I … need your help."

I am well aware to your being here. Remember, we are bonded by our powers and the rune Tuhugara. I will tell you what you need to know.

"Really? Thank you. You're going to save my life … again." The spirit laughed again.

Yes, but I suggest you take heed of Slaizar's warning. Next time, I will not be able to stop him. Now then, the trick to using your powers to hide from view is very complicated.

"What isn't?" James said cynically. Kinran laughed.

"Very true. Now listen before time runs out. When you want to hide from the eye, cover yourself in solidified ice, but do not make yourself immobile."

"Well how the hell do I do that?" This was ridiculous. Just because the spirit could tell him what to do, didn't mean he'd be able to do it. "How do I cover myself in my power without immobilizing myself? Remember, I can't control it in the ethereal form."

"Do you want me to teach this to you or do you want to try and figure this out on your own? Now shut up and listen. By covering yourself in a thin layer of power you will in fact be concealing yourself from the light. Just do what you do with your barrier trick; only use more power to distort the air around you. You understand how that helps, right?"

Understanding blossomed in James' mind. Of course. People saw things by the light reflecting off it. But if the light never touched him … no one would be able to see him! It was brilliant!

"Thank you, sir." He bowed and made to leave … then he realized he didn't know how to do that. "Um, how do I get out of here?"

Say Elifern. Tuhugara brings you here so its opposite will bring you back. Oh, before you go … I have one more thing to tell you that will no doubt be of great help. This little technique will allow you access to your powers even if you are Sealed. It's something I picked up down here. Now, listen carefully … "

James opened his eyes and found the green haze was gone and he was back in the sewers … the smell reassured him of that. He turned around to look at Alamar; he was still standing in the same place a few feet away. Everything seemed to be okay.

"What are you looking at me for, aren't you going to do something?"

James told him about the meeting of the spirits, but decided to keep Kinran and Slaizar's names a secret. Everyone knew who Kinran Death was. The

Intaruan was amazed that he had actually gone to Hell's Domain and spoke with real live spirits. James laughed at the irony of that statement.

"Alright, let's see what will happen."

James turned away from Alamar and looked at the sewer drain where they'd come from. Taking hold onto his powers he crafted them around him like one of his barriers. The azure light washed over him like it had his staff before, only this time it was more solid. The light wasn't just from the power, it was from the ice.

As the ice encased him completely he was thrown into complete darkness. Panicking, he dropped the web and popped back into the light.

"What happened?" he asked, turning to Alamar.

Alamar was staring at him with wide eyes. "You vanished. Completely! There weren't even tendrils floating around that a trained eye could look for. You were totally invisible! Why did you drop it though?"

He told him about the light problem and they started thinking. If they couldn't see, then how were they going to make their way across the waste land until they were out of sight? Alamar suggested using Aria's visions. The problem with that was, Aria couldn't see them and might lose them along the way.

"Besides, she can't send me very detailed pictures every three steps. It gets too difficult to talk with her after a while."

"So why not use your ability to sense things to navigate?"

"I can only sense the power, not rocks and ditches."

"So, what? Do we just sit here and wait for me to recover?" He punched the wall. "At this rate it'll take me two hours to have enough strength to cover us for two miles. Damn it. We don't have that kind of time."

Behind them they heard voices enter the sewer tunnel. They were *out* of time! Icing the sewer drain again they slipped out and edged away from the drainage hole keeping tight against the stone wall. Above them they heard shouts and curses that outmatched any rival football game three times over. When they reached the end of the wall the soldiers started coming out of the fortress. With no other option James grabbed Alamar's hand and wove the web of power over him and Alamar.

Again the darkness closed in, and again he panicked, but this time held onto the power. They pressed up tighter as the voices of the soldiers drew closer and only relaxed when they were gone. He felt Alamar tighten his grip as they left the wall and started walking blindly into the waste land. They seemed to trip with every other step and each time James had to stretch the web so they wouldn't be seen.

"See if you can put a hole in the front so we can see." Alamar said after he tripped for the fifth time over his own feet.

Parting the web without ruining the whole effect was the hardest thing he'd ever done with the power. At first they started to shimmer back into view making him snap the web closed again, but after a few tries he managed a small peephole for them to see where they were going. Behind them, the fortress was going berserk. No one had any idea where the Gattarian had disappeared to. Others were talking about an Intaruan ghost that vanished through walls and solid objects.

Again no one seemed to notice the shadow lurking over head watching with interest the tiny hole, floating in mid air, make its way across the waste. He was very impressed with the boy's improving skills in the ways of the power. His master would be pleased to hear the good news as well.

CHAPTER 16

▼

UNLEASHED

IT took them the remainder of the day to walk the rest of the way through the waste land. Alamar was tired from using his heat waves so long, and James was losing his grip on the power quickly. Even being able to skirt around the Seal's hold he couldn't summon more of the power to amp the web, and so when he lost the energy, the two of them popped back into view. Without the web, Aria was able to find them and guide them to the horses. Trae'len was ecstatic to have James get in his saddle and even more so when he let the horse take control with only a caution not to go too fast.

They slept in their saddles for a few hours while Aria kept an eye on their rear for any sign of pursuit. Yet despite the trouble they'd caused, they weren't followed into the Dead Lands. When he woke up, James could see why. Every mile around them was barren. No life existed here. There was no grass, water, or dirt; only sand and rocks. Above them the sky was covered in dark clouds, but there didn't seem to be any rain in the near future.

After a quick stretch in the saddle he summoned his power and tested it. While he was still tired, and drawing the energy to him made him more so, he was able to make a snowball. Well that was a relief ... he thought that using his powers like he did for so long might cause complications. Tossing it to the side he made it hover in the air over Alamar's sleeping head. With a smile he let go of the threads.

"BY THE FIRES THAT'S COLD!"

James burst out laughing as Alamar woke with a curse. He grappled at his back trying to get the snow out from beneath his shirt, but only made it go deeper which brought more curses. Alamar's aura flared and he felt the snow evaporate before it had a chance to melt. Haenya whinnied along with Trae'len and Aria whose shrieks from high up could be heard easily.

"Fires burn your soul, James Richards!" He shouted steering Haenya closer. "What the hell were you trying to make me do? Good spirits! My heart almost burst out of my chest!"

"Well, now I know how to wake you up when you start snoring at night." He replied rolling with laughter.

"You do that again and I swear on the Fires that I will roast your bottom so hot you won't ever be able to sit down again! Do you hear me!?"

"Loud and clear Mom."

They stopped and let the horses rest and drink from the melted snow he was able to make. The food was very good for being in a fortress. The meat was well flavored and the bread and cheese were soft and moist. Alamar congratulated him on such a bountiful raid and suggested going back to do it again. They laughed and started going over what they did in the fortress.

Alamar had gone about trying to sneak into the Masjr beast pen it seems. He thought it would be a good enough distraction to let James get the food without too much trouble. The only problem with that was that the Masjrs were able to see through the heat waves and started making such a noise he lost hold over the power. At that time the guards came running in and saw him. So he started running through halls, vanishing and reappearing every once and a while.

"You should have seen this one guy." He said slapping his knee. "I popped into view directly in front of him by accident and he near wet himself in fright! He dropped his weapons and bolted away screaming something about spirits haunting the fortress." He stopped to catch his breath. "Oh, and check what I found."

He reached for the back of his belt and brought out two very deadly looking long knives. They were at least twice as long as his original knives and had two curving spikes jutting from the hand guards. The hilts were a plain leather make but that only helped to keep his grip. Alamar twirled the blades around in his hands and started dancing around the rocks acting a fight between him and an Elite.

"Nice moves, but I doubt an Elite would leave himself open that many times in a row." James pointed out when the other sat down victorious.

"Oh and how do you know what an Elite would do?" He asked with a sarcastic smile. "Unless I'm mistaken, you've only fought one. I've taken out three in my travels. Shame they don't know when to stay down. For every one I kill, they always seem to find a replacement in no time and I have a new tracker on my hide."

Alamar reached behind him and placed the daggers back in their sheathes.

James took up the first watch that night. When he went to wake Alamar for his shift he stopped. The feeling tickled his mind making him summon every drop of power he could in fear. Yet there wasn't anyone behind him. He reached out with his mind to locate the source of the feeling, but found nothing. Behind him Alamar snored loudly. He shivered in the chill night air. The summer season was starting to fade away and the farther north they got the colder it became too. Again Alamar snored.

"Wake up stupid."

"Huh, wha—whosere?" he looked up at James who was staring out into the waste still. "Whaddya want? Is it my shift already?"

"Yea. And keep a close eye a little to the east. I have a feeling we aren't entirely alone."

The next morning they road in silence. James kept casting his mind behind them to see if he could find their pursuers, but he never got the feeling again. Aria circled back against his wishes and said she didn't see anything back there either. Alamar said it must be from the fortress.

"The guy in charge might have finally snapped and blown a hole through the roof taking with him the two guards you knocked out."

"I just can't shake the feeling we are being followed. And whoever they are, they're getting closer."

Whatever the cause of the feeling was, it didn't reveal itself until their second day. He didn't know why but as they were munching on some of the meat for lunch the feeling burst forth like a tidal wave to the forefront of his mind. With a curse he whirled around in the saddle and saw a cloud of dust rising behind them with a group of men only a few hundred yards away and gaining. Alamar shouted something and heeled Haenya into a gallop. Trae'len was right behind her.

The two horses ran as fast as they could through the Dead Lands, but no matter how hard they rode, the riders got closer. In a matter of minutes they were only a couple of yards behind them and their uniforms could be seen clearly. Red coats with gold embroidery covered all ten men, and each had a baldric strapped across their chest holding the sword at their side. The Elite had found them. Pillars of fire began flaring in front of them, trying to cut off their path, but the horses veered around them and galloped on.

I have to protect her! Trae'len shouted to himself. *I have to protect master, too Just run! I'll protect Haenya and you both!*

Reaching for his power he sent a wave of ice darts behind him. But instead of ice, he only got splashes of water. The Elite were making it too hot for the ice to form with their pillars!

With only a seconds warning he wove a barrier around him and Alamar as two pillars of fire burst right in front of them with no way around. The fire swirled around them, heating the air to such a degree it was almost impossible to breathe, but neither was burned. The horses, however, stumbled over the destroyed ground and fell with their riders.

Sliding to a stop, James and Alamar climbed out from beneath the frantic horses. He calmed Trae'len down with his mind and Haenya quieted after a few words from Alamar. They looked up at the ten riders surrounding them. Each man had a stone carved face with blazing red hair cut short except for a single thin tail that reached down a few inches.

Their horses were all black and had a mark on their snouts that looked like a white flickering flame. All ten were war horses, pure bred by the way they looked. The riders closed the circle leaving only a small gap between each. Alamar grabbed his long knives and whirled them about, but that only drew a few laughs from the Elite. James' staff was in his hands ready to block any attack, but they ignored that as well.

"Gattarian," The man in front of them said in a deep voice. "Traitor, you are surrounded. Surrender peacefully and we will let you live a while longer. If you choose to fight, we will have to kill you. What say you?"

Aria, stay as far away from here as you can! I don't want you getting hurt!

"Sir, he is communicating with the Mind Speech!" A man to the left of the leader said quickly.

"Break your connection at once or perish!"

Very well. Be careful! And the connection broke.

The men closed in again, leaving even less room between them and some drifted towards their swords. The leader told them to hold, and they backed away. Tossing the reins aside, the one in charge dismounted and walked into the circle. He was tall, almost taller than James, but held himself in such a manner that made him seem to stand ten feet high. His coat was embroidered like the rest, but there were far more markings over his left breast than the others.

"I am Captain Commander Liam Estear, of the Elite." He said in his deep voice. "Second in Command to the entire Elite squadron. We have been tracking you for some time, James Richards. Yes, we know all about you and your time spent in Yattion under our noses. Master Mathwin Cormer was very forthcoming in his information."

"I knew it had to be that snake who told you where I went. But what did you do to the rest of Yattion?"

The hairs on his neck stiffened and he jumped to the side just as a whip of fire snapped where his back would have been a second before. The man, who held the whip blinked in surprise but at a sharp command from Liam dispersed the whip.

"Please excuse Lieutenant Deast." Liam said calmly. "He doesn't like it when people speak to me without the proper respect."

"Oh, well excuse me." He replied with a fake bow. "I had no idea I was in the presence of some one important."

"Deast, drop your powers NOW!"

The Lieutenant was fuming and his aura blazing with such ferocity that the hairs on James' neck threatened to pull themselves out. He held the power for only a moment after the command, but with a grunt of rage he blinked out and instead drew his sword a few inches from the scabbard.

"Now," Liam continued resuming his outward calm, "Unless you would like Deast to skin you alive, I suggest you come with us quietly. I don't know if I will be able to restrain him the next time he decides to attack."

"You just saved that poor wretch's life, Liam." Everyone turned to Alamar who was still holding his knives and looked ready to spring at any second. "If he'd lashed out again, he would have died before he even touched Richards."

"Oh, and I suppose it would be you to deal the killing blow, Alamar Telanre." Liam said folding his arms behind his back.

"He wouldn't be the only one to attack, Captain Commander." James said hefting his staff. "I would have crushed him instantly if that whip had even started forming in his hands."

Again the hairs on his neck rose as Deast drew on his powers to its fullest. As the threads of red light began weaving through the air James and Alamar whirled around as one and struck. The man didn't even have time to gasp as his entire upper torso was frozen solid and then blasted into a thousand pieces by the accompanying fire stream. Time stopped long enough for the others to watch their comrade's bottom half fall to the ground.

All at once the remaining nine men drew their swords and summoned their energies. From all sides the fire rained down on them, but James' barriers held and they dashed out from the circle tripping up a few horses on their way out. The riders fell under their steeds with cries of rage and lashed out with their fire but missed completely. The others heeled their horses after them and started throwing fireballs the size of cars at them. Each attack slid right off the barriers and dissipated immediately after.

Leaping down from their horses the men tried attacking them head on. Alamar was dancing in and out of their swords like the wind, easily dodging slash and thrust alike before slicing at them with his blades. James' staff was a blur in the air as he blocked sword after sword and striking out with a quick thrust to the gut or arm before he had to block another. The Elite were the best fighters he'd ever seen. They attacked in perfect sync making it harder to block them all with the staff.

A few times he felt the sharp steel cut into his sides and arm, but he ignored them and continued his attacks. Lashing out with the power was becoming harder the longer he fought. They seemed to be able to make barriers similar to his, but not as effectively. His darts would sometimes stick to their uniforms and then slide right off. Other times, the darts managed to stay there and spread out into a block of ice that encased an arm or leg. The Elite would back away and thaw themselves before returning to the fight.

Only one man wasn't luck enough to back away in time and cried out as both his legs froze and shattered under the wooden staff.

He could feel the rest of his power hammering away at the Seal, and he almost faltered. If he lost control again, he wouldn't be able to stop himself! Twice the swords found their mark lightly across his back as he whirled away, trying not to die and not to lose control over the torrent of energy trying to overwhelm him. The battle seemed to last for hours before the Elite finally backed away as one.

They were breathing heavily as they formed a wide circle around him with their swords still raised. He realized that the remaining Elite were surrounding him too. But that meant … Alamar! He spun around and saw him struggling against the large Elite who held a long knife to his throat. Liam stepped forward with his hands clasped behind his back. He had, to James' liking, a long cut running down the right side of his face.

"Surrender, Gattarian." The leader said. "You are surrounded and Alamar has been caught. It is over. If you do not surrender, we will kill the traitor and you as well." He bowed his head a little. "I will congratulate you on holding your own against five members of my squad for so long. Especially killing Polle there, very impressive use of your power." The other men laughed like it was some joke! "But I am afraid this is the end of our little game. You will come with us or you will follow Polle to Hell's Gate! What will it be?"

James, summon your powers!

He knew that voice. But, how could he ...?

Alamar?

Quiet! Don't talk back or they will know! Just listen. Summon your full power. I know you've been holding back for some reason, but this isn't the time. If you don't then they will kill us. I will NOT go with them back to the Fire Kingdom!

Young One, your power will out match theirs easily. You have to try.

But if he lost control, what would happen to Alamar? They were right ... this wasn't the time! Tossing his staff to the ground he called to his powers. His mind rammed against the Seal and the power flooded to him as the force. Taking that force he attacked the Seal at the same time his powers hammered away. Instantly, the layer of power crashed down and the azure light flooded into his body at full strength. The Elite were thrown into the air by the force of his power coming forth.

With a gasp the torrent of energy surged through his body like molten rock! It threatened to eat him away if he didn't do something with it. Taking what he could manage he directed the threads and reaching into ground made a giant fist of ice burst from the ground taking the Elite holding Alamar with it. He needed to do more, but there was too much power for him to direct at one time!

He heard Liam calling out commands and orders and the Elite closed their circle again and blazed with their power. He saw their auras connect to one another until he was surrounded by a wall of red energies. The tendrils of power pushed against the raging tower of power surging from his body and began to force it down. They were going to Seal his power away! Drawing more of the power to him he began pushing back and the Seal backed away slowly. His blue aura was soon wrapped up in a net of red light that was trying to compress it back into his body.

The battle between powers raged on with neither side giving way. Liam directed the others' power with incredible skill and would slowly start to close the Seal, but at the last second James would burst through with even more power and they would be forced back. The Elite staggered with the strain of holding so much energy at once, but they would only get back up even stronger than before. They were used to this much power, but he was not. Every time he burst through the Seal he was weakened and he felt a part of him start to be eaten away.

Let me Guide your power.

The voice from Yattion!

No! I refuse your help Marlao Blood! I will not let you kill these men or anyone else! Leave me!

Let me Guide your power or you will die! Your body is not strong enough to handle so much of it at once. If you keep this up you will die!

I SAID NO!

James! Alamar's voice broke into his mind pushing Marlao back to the realm of the dead. *Let them Seal you! They are using every ounce of energy they can muster just to try and hold your powers down. If they seal you they will be exhausted and I can finish them! Trust me just one more time!*

I trust you.

Again he felt the Seal press in closer and this time he let it close in around him. When it snapped into place he felt every drop of power vanish from his body at once. It was enough to make him shout. All of it was gone and he couldn't even feel it anymore. The Elite all sagged to the ground as the Seal was completed. They were all sweating and breathless and barely managing to stay awake by the looks of it.

Without the power sustaining him, James crumbled to the ground like a rag doll. His right arm was numb and no matter how hard he tried he couldn't even move his fingers a little. He saw Liam moving closer to him, he was holding something like a rope in his hands. Where was Alamar?

"To think that so much power could be inside a boy such as him ..." Liam said to himself.

"To think it possible for that much to be inside a human is lunacy, but here he is." Another said. "I'm completely drained. I couldn't light a candle if my life depended on it right now."

"Good to hear." Every one turned and gasped as Alamar stood there with an aura blazing into the sky. How had he summoned so much without them knowing? "Since you are so tired you won't be able to defend yourselves; leaving me free to make all the terms surrounding whether or not you live."

No one moved as Alamar began building a fireball above his hands. Its size went from small to gargantuan in the blink of an eye and now it was towering over the Elite. Liam got slowly to his feet and motioned for the others to follow. Alamar allowed them to get to their feet before he started the negotiations.

"You will release the Seal around James now ... or I will kill you all." He juggled the fireball in his hands threateningly. "Either way he will be free and you will die. So what do you say?"

The color was slowly draining from Liam's face as he watched the blazing sphere above Alamar's head. The other's looked to their commander for an order. James watched as the clogs ticked away inside the Elite's head. He couldn't decide which was worse!

"Wait, Alamar, I have another option."

Liam and Alamar looked down at him as he got up to a knee and stared at the Elite. He still couldn't move his arm and getting this far up was close to impossible.

"I give you another choice, Captain Commander. Release the Seal, and I will let you live. However, I will not let you continue following us. As soon as the Seal is gone I will encase all of you in a tomb of ice. You will still be alive and it will thaw in time, though to you it will seem only a moment. Be warned, I give this choice only once. Refuse and I will let Alamar burn you and your men to a cinder."

Liam looked to his men who could only wait for a command. Aria called down to him.

"And don't try to let up on the Seal so a few of you can take Alamar." The Elite's face went white. "Yes, I know about the Mind Speech, remember? Also know that if this Seal loses just one person's support, my power will break through and I will kill you myself. Again, I give this choice once. So, pick your poison, Liam."

He let the commander use the Mind Speech with the others this time. Alamar was speaking to him, asking if he could just kill them and get it over with. Aria kept circling high above. Liam's face was red from the strain of keeping the Seal and using the Mind Speech.

The other Elite still held their swords in their hands ready to use them, though what they thought to accomplish, he didn't know. Trae'len moved closer to Haenya and nudged her neck with his nose. The horse was hitting on her at a time like this?!

"Release the Seal on my count." James turned back to Liam. The commander's head was bowed in defeat, and his hands were clenched tightly at his sides.

"Commander, you can't be serious!" One of the men said talking a step forward. "Surely there is another way. We can ..."

"On my count, Fandre!" Liam shouted. "If any of you hold onto the Seal longer than that, I will kill you myself." He turned to James, his eyes burning with rage. "You listen well, Richards. This is not over. I will see you again, and next time I shall have the entire Elite squadron with me! Our Lord Commander will not let you get away with this and neither shall I."

"Liam, the next time we meet, I will not show you the same mercy I did today." He replied. "The next time that I see you, I will not hesitate to finish you off."

"On my count! One, two, three ... Release!"

Every aura blinked out as each of the Elite cut off the link to their power. The Seal vanished with them and his own power was surging back into his body. Again the torrent threatened to eat him away, but this time he directed it into the air around the eight remaining Elite. The block of ice covered them completely in the blink of an eye, leaving only Liam's head left. Alamar dropped the fireball and walked over to the commander. With his hand glowing bright red he reached through the ice and grabbed the rank bands from his chest.

"These can be part of my trophy case."

"I will see you again as well traitor." He spat. "As for you, Gattarian, you stay alive long enough for me to kill you. Or I will drag your spirit from Hell's Gate myself and do the deed again!"

"My name ... is James Richards, Liam, not Gattarian. And I don't intend to die by your hand or another's."

With that he closed the commander's head and tied off the threads. Making sure he had a hold over the power he began to lift the block into the air. Then, with Alamar's help reared back and threw it as hard as his remaining strength would allow. The Elite were cascaded into the sky in the direction of the Masjr Fortress. The ice would withstand the impact, and wouldn't break or melt until the weaves broke on their own. That should give the Intaruans time to think about who they were dealing with.

With so much of his strength exhausted, relinquishing hold over the energy was easy and he bade it farewell with a sigh. Aria landed softly on his shoulder and gave him a comforting squeeze with her talons. He placed a hand on the hawk's head and ruffled her feathers. Trae'len and Haenya clopped over to their riders and nudged them. Climbing into the saddle was never really an easy task, but as tired as he was, it was close to impossible and only managed it when the horse knelt down.

Master is tired. Rest and recover, I will carry you and keep you safe.
Thanks. Is Haenya alright?
Yes. Master saved her and her rider with his power. I thank you.
She's cute, ya?

The horse whinnied and began walking through the Dead Lands with James asleep in the saddle and Alamar nodding off in his.

CHAPTER 17

A HISTORY LIKE NO OTHER

ALAMAR was the first to wake up the next day. The horses had carried them a few miles and stopped beside a series of large boulders. He was still sitting in his saddle and climbed out to let Haenya rest. Unsaddling the mare took only a few minutes and soon she was fast asleep in the shade. Trae'len knelt down to let him take James from the saddle and set him on a laid out bedroll. He was no medic but he knew how to sew a few cuts.

Untying the laces of James' tunic he slipped it off and looked at the half dozen slashes varying in length and depth. There was one on his chest leading from his left shoulder down to the right at a small angle. Taking the needle and wiry string he began sewing the cuts.

When he was done, with both of their wounds, he carried James over next to the mare. Unsaddling the stallion was harder than Haenya. The straps weren't as broken in as he thought they might be from a month of hard riding.

Aria was perched on the top of the rock, watching the land behind them. He looked down at James and shook his head. The guy really knew how to make life different. All his life he thought he'd be running from the Elite, killing a few of them here and there and finding new hiding places to await the next. Now he was traveling into Gattar with a Gattarian who outmatched eight Bonded Elite, talked to a hawk and a horse, and knew nothing about his past. *What a strange guy.*

Tucking his friend into his bedroll he slipped off the metal armlets. Alamar stared at the cloth wrapped around James' arm and then looked over at the one he wore on the same arm. Odd, he thought, I knew we had our similarities, but this ... he stopped as he finished unwrapping the cloth revealing three runes.

A cold chill swept over Alamar at the sight of the Words. *No ... it can't be! That isn't possible. Desrik ... he said they were forbidden!* Could these runes be the source of James' powers? Alamar knew nothing about the Words except that they were the language of the Land.

"This is too much, James." He said to the unconscious man. "I knew you were strange, I knew you were powerful, and I knew you could do things that no one else has been able to do in centuries ... but this—this is too much." He walked away from James still mumbling. "Ahh, forget it. It's not worth the headache."

Summoning his power took longer than he wished, but when he finally got it, he made a fire and began cooking the food Aria must have found. The fire didn't give off any smoke, though the chance they were being followed was slim. If the Elite couldn't take them, no one in the entire kingdom could. Well, maybe if they sent a full legion after them, but that wouldn't be too smart on the Emperor's part. No one Gattarian was worth sending a whole legion after. Normally they wouldn't even send the Elite after a sole Gattarian, so why send them after James? *Well that's a stupid question.*

He looked at the heart of the flame and watched the scene from yesterday unfold. The ten Elite circling them with intent to kill; Liam talking to them like they were just normal men having a cup of tea; Deast's torso being blown into a thousand pieces from their combined attack. He saw the fight again; every blade whirling through the air with inhuman timing; his own knives doing nothing but deflect a few blows; and finally that lug Morzala grabbing him from behind and putting a knife to his throat. That's when he told James to let loose.

He looked over at the still sleeping figure. Liam was right; there was no way that one person could hold so much power. At least, not hold it and live. The stories of Tiana Paine, Marlao Blood, and Kinran Death were things that mothers told their children to scare them into being good. Everyone knew they were true stories, but the thought of a Gattarian holding so much power was enough to make even the strongest and bravest Intaruan cower in fear. Yet here was a guy, only a few years older than himself, who was easily as strong, if not stronger, than all three!

How could he be the one to finally find a way to control so much energy at once? From what James had told him a few weeks ago, weeks that felt like years, he had only manifested a week before running into him. How did he have so much control already, and who Guided him through the Awakening. No Intaruan could ... His thoughts were interrupted as Aria fluttered down next to him and stared at him with one of her golden eyes.

"What is it, Aria? Trouble?" *Oh brother, I'm talking to a bird!*

The hawk only stared at him for a moment longer before hopping forward and prodding his arm with her beak. She flapped her wings impatiently and pecked him again.

"What do you want?" She grabbed onto the cloth around his arm and pulled on it. "What the ... hey get away from that." Aria flapped back a few paces as he swatted at her. "What's with that bird? You want to see?" She seemed to nod in response. "Okay, but you tell Richards and I'll make sure our next meal is roast hawk, got it?"

Reaching around for the knot he untied the rag and slowly unraveled his arm. Setting the rag to the side he turned his arm around and stared at the tattoo. A shield with the flame of the Emperor with a single sword vertically behind it; the Seal of the Royal Family. He may be an outlaw, but the mark had been burned onto him almost immediately after he was born. Aria hopped over and peered at the mark.

"This thing is the cause of so much trouble." He said, to no one. "If I hadn't been given this mark, I wouldn't be such a problem for my uncle. If I wasn't such a problem, I wouldn't be hunted by the Elite and running to the Ice Kingdom."

He stared into the fire's heart again ...

"Now Alamar, I am going to teach you how to summon your power."

Two pairs of brown eyes stared up at the elderly woman sitting on the rickety old chair. She had long white gray hair that fell far below her shoulders. Her soft green eyes glittered like emeralds from beneath the years of sagging skin. Her name was Mira, or Nanny to Alamar.

"First, you reach deep down into you heart until you find the power swirling around in a giant pool. Can you do that?"

It was easy. He'd been practicing everyday since he'd turned thirteen. Clearing his mind he found the pool of red energy waiting for him to call it. He heard Nanny's next command and pressed his mind against the energy, and then called it to him.

"Very good Alamar." She said clapping her brittle hands lightly. "Now, I want you to light a candle for me. Keep it small, mind you. We don't want you to light your own clothes on fire by accident."

The candle was sitting only a few paces away and, using the tinderbox to make the starting spark, lit the candle wick. Nanny clapped again. The other children around them watched in awe as Alamar went on to light candle after candle and cheered when he managed to produce his first fireball. They were simple exercises, but they helped teach control and the art of manipulation. The governess of Fallingrad, Liana Youlati, however, wasn't impressed by his display.

"You call that a fireball?"

They were inside her private study now and Alamar was showing her his progress. Liana was almost like a distant aunt to him, and he loved to show her things. She was just as old as Nanny and had the same long gray hair that fell far below her shoulders. Yet despite her age she was very powerful and well skilled with her power.

"When my powers manifested I was making fire streams four times as large as that. My fireballs could burn through rock and melt bone and flesh instantly."

"Not all of us are raised in the same conditions as you were Liana." Nanny said carefully.

"HA!" Alamar jumped as she bellowed loudly. "This little brat is being raised in even *worse* conditions than me! How many other children are hunted by the Emperor's Elite? With that on his mind he should be learning how to fight rather than light a few measly candles!"

"Liana, I think that these exercises are a very acceptable way to learn control over their power." She took Alamar's hand and led him to the door. "And remember, no one is supposed to know about Alamar's heritage. If word of his whereabouts reached the Emperor, you can bet his Elite squadron would be knocking on Fallingrad's door within the hour."

Yet the threat of the Elite didn't stop Liana from taking Alamar aside every now and then and teaching him *her* way of training. She made him summon every drop of power he could manage and hold it for as long as he could before passing out. "So as to toughen up your inner body." Then she would make him weave threads of fire about in ways that no child Alamar's age should learn for another twenty years. "Those petty weaves Mira teaches you won't save your hide when the Elite find you. You have to defend yourself properly."

After his first two years of training under both Nanny and Liana, Alamar was easily the strongest child of his age in the entire Kingdom. He was throwing around fireballs as large as boulders like they were nothing and his manipulation skills could outmatch even Liana at times. But as much as he loved being in Fallingrad and as life has shown so many times already, good things never last. By the time his sixteenth birthday was rolling around word of the Emperor's Elite heading towards them reached Liana.

"We have to leave now Alamar." Nanny was pulling on his arm, trying to get him to move, but he was too strong for her now. "I know that you're strong, and I know you want to fight but this is not the time! You have to run!"

"But why Nan?" replied the young, but very angry Alamar. "Why do I always have to run? I can fight these so-called Elite and crush them one by one …!"

"They won't fight you one on one, Alamar, they will all attack you at the same time and destroy you!"

"No! I won't run again! I will face them and make them pay for what they did to my father!"

"ALAMAR TELANRE, I SAID NO!"

Everyone who was in hearing distance stopped as Mira summoned her power. Her aura was blazing like the sun in the town. The heat coming from her made the dust on the ground fly into the air and burst into flames. Alamar's jerked his hand away before he was burned as well.

"You will run now." She said taking a step closer to him, "Because he who runs from an unfair fight will live to see a fair one another time. The Elite won't always come at you in such numbers, and when that time comes, *that* is when you fight! But until that time comes I want you to run! Do you hear me Alamar Telanre?"

And with the towering aura to back her threats he was mounting Haenya and galloping away just as the Elite burst into the town. The mare was flying across the mountain paths; they had run them so often they didn't need to be slow about it. Behind them, the town of Fallingrad was ablaze. He felt the energies emanating from the people of the town and then felt something he would never forget; the combined power of the Twenty One Elite, towering over the entire townsfolk …

… The light from the fire cast shadows against the night covered ground as Alamar woke from his dream. Aria was still staring at him with her big golden eyes in the same place she'd been when he started his story. Shaking his head he reached out and pet the hawk on her head. Her feathers were very soft to touch and she cooed when he thumbed her wing joint. He knew why James liked this hawk so much. Despite the fact she was a pain when speaking to him, she was very good company and was always ready to help with your problems.

"So that is the story of Alamar Telanre."

In a whirl of sand and power, Alamar was on his feet with his long knives in hand, staring at the top of the rock below which Trae'len, Haenya, and James slept. There, in its long black robes, stood the shadow man, the thing that had attacked them last time. But there was something different … He didn't have a sword on his hip, but instead had a very large battle axe. Something like that wouldn't stand a chance against the speed of his blades.

"I must say, that was a very sad story indeed." The shadow continued. "Tell me, do you know what ever happened to dear old Nanny? Don't know? Well let me tell you; she found her way to Hell's Gate very quickly and without any trouble at all from the Gatekeeper. As for Liana, she had some troubles along the way and almost didn't make it that far …"

"SHUT UP!"

The shadow's form shifted as the stream of fire blazed through its head. Spinning the stream he made it slice through the center and then cut it from crotch to neck before releasing the blaze. The shadow hung there, distorted and almost intangible against the night sky, for only a second before it shifted back to its original form.

"Oh very impressive, Alamar Telanre." He said dusting his hands on his robes. "But you forget that fire cannot destroy shadow. Its light may drive us away, but without a certain … thing … it lacks the punch it needs to destroy us. But I will applaud you on a valiant effort."

"What do you want? Why are you here?" He had a good guess. His eyes slid over to James' sleeping form between the horses.

"You seem to already know that. I am here for the boy. My Master would like to see him; and what my Master wants, he gets." His form dissolved from the top of the rock and hovered down to the ground at the base. "So I will just be taking him now …"

This was bad. He couldn't fight this thing alone; that last attack didn't even phase the thing so …

Releasssssse me …

Alamar's breath caught as the voice hissed inside his head. Dear Spirits, it was back again. The shadow just stared at him from beneath that dark hood waiting to see if he did anything. But what could he do? If he tried to use his power, *it* would come out … again. And with the others so close by he couldn't risk it. Whirling his knives in his hands he charged at the shadow man. It bent and twisted away from his attacks like water, never letting the steel come within an inch of it. Again and again he slashed left and right, right and left, driving the shadow farther into the night, away from the others.

"Why even bother trying to fight, Alamar Telanre?" the shadowy figure taunted as it slipped away from the blade again. "Even if I let you hit me, it wouldn't hurt me, or do anything to me. So why bother? Just give it up."

Releassssse me. Let me kill him …

STAY DOWN! I WILL SUMMON YOU! He was driving the shadow back with every slash of his knives while trying to hold back the voice.

Finally. I shall be free onccce again! I can already tasssste the blood on my lipssss.

Those are my lips, not yours. And the only thing you are killing is this shadow, do you hear me?

Why? Why do you deny me the blood that I crave?

Are you going to kill this thing or not damn it?

Releasssse me … NOW!

Summoning the power residing inside him he blazed with an aura greater than any Intaruan could imagine. The night was driven back as the light grew brighter and brighter. The shadow gasped as the blazing aura trampled over it like a tidal wave. Once again reaching down into the depths of his soul, he called forth the darkness. This time the light warped and changed as the darkness burst forth in a cloud of evil.

"I AM FREE AT LASSST!"

"Wha-what is this trickery?" The shadow began backing away from the human in the center of the red and black aura. "How is this possible? What is going on? MASTER!!"

"Your Massster cannot not ssave you from ME, Shai'lun." There were two voices coming from the one mouth as the body of Alamar began walking forward slowly. *"Hisss power is nothing compared to the ancient wissssdom I contain."* The shadow gasped. *"Yes, I know all about your Master. But I am forbidden to tell the boy by the Law'ssss power, so his identity is ssssafe for now. But you are not."*

"You cannot harm me, Alamar Tela …"

"Alamar isss not the one in command! My name," the second voice said with an evil smile *"is Desssrik SSScythlen."*

"No, no that is impossible! Alamar does not have the mark to be a Spirit Totem. Especially not to a spirit like you!"

"How wrong you are. But, despite that, I am only able to control the boy'sss power. He isss the one who controls the rest, but hisss power is mine to command!" Alamar's body spat on the ground. *"But enough of thisss talking! I am here for your blood!"*

The dark aura lashed out at the shadow, cutting through the very darkness around it. Again the shadow twisted and turned dodging the treads of black fire. The ground was shaking under the pressure of so much of the power being summoned, and the shadow was only *just* dodging the attacks. He called out to his Master over and over as the black fire drew nearer with every strike.

"This is not the end, Alamar Telanre!" The shadow shouted as it bent in half to avoid another stream of fire. "I will return again, and next time I shall come with the full power of my Master to destroy you!"

"*Tell your Master thissss, Shai'lun.*" Alamar replied in the double voice. "*I will be ssseeing him soon if he keepsssss interfering with Arollay'ssss path. And tell him thiss as well: Hissss blood will be mine to feassssst upon!*"

With that the Shai'lun burst into a plume of smoke and vanished into the night. The dark aura began to dwindle as Alamar walked back towards the camp. Desrik gazed through Alamar's eyes at James' sleeping form before relinquishing control back to the boy and departing for the Gates once again. Alamar collapsed to his knees completely breathless.

The bottom of his forearm was burning and when he looked, the tattoo had spread. Small strands of red flame-shaped lines stretched along his arm towards his elbow, snaking their way, he knew, towards his heart. After a moment the red lines receded and the tattoo returned to its normal color and shape. Aria fluttered down to his side and gazed at the tattoo before looking him in the eyes.

"Remember, not a word to Richards or you will be our next dinner." He began wrapping the cloth around his arm once again. His eyes wandered over to the horses. "But I will have to tell him in time, that he is not the only Spirit Totem. And not the only one with a power they cannot control entirely."

Alamar's eyes traveled once again to the fire; its light was welcoming and the warmth comforting …

… It was raining now; the sky was dark as night yet the sun hung a few hours over the horizon hidden behind the clouds. The tall grass was swaying in the howling wind as the rain beat down hard on the two figures sitting unsheltered in the fields. One was a tall deep brown mare with no markings and a black colored mane and tail, the other was a boy with long deep brown hair, soaked through and dripping with water. He wore a dark colored vest over an even darker shirt with black pants tucked into dark brown riding boots. Circling his waist was a black belt with two small knives in two sheaths at his sides.

He just sat there curled up in a ball, knees to chest and head bowed with tears mixing with the rain water. His mind was empty except for the scene that had played itself out only an hour ago. The Elite had found him again, but this time it was only one man. His body was nowhere to be found among the ruined fields. The tall man had come upon him while he was praying to the spirits for Mira and Liana and the rest of Fallingrad. With little warning the battle had begun.

Being only sixteen and the Elite in his late twenties, Alamar was far outmatched. He was cowering under the shadow of the man who was still holding more power than he had ever seen. That's when he heard the voice. It was a man's, but there was something wrong with it; the S sounds were lengthened making him sound like a snake. The voice offered to save his life in exchange for the chance to use his body to do it. Not wanting to die, he agreed without thinking. In seconds the Elite's body was engulfed in black flame, vanishing before his eyes.

"Wh-what have I done?" he heard himself say.

"You have done nothing," the voice replied, *"if that issss any consssolation. I wasss the one who killed thisss man, not you."*

"Who are you? What are you, and how come I cannot see you?"

"My name is Dessrik SSScythlen, a spirit from the land of the dead." He heard his breath catch in his throat at the name.

"What do you want with me? Why did you help me?"

"One quesssstion at a time. Alamar flinched and went silent. *I want nothing from you; I work for free in this cassse. I helped you because you remind me much of mysself when I was your age. Alone, with no family to care for you, the only life you ever knew gone. When I ssssaw the Elite about to kill you, sssuffice it to sssay, I was moved with a pity I haven't felt in hundredss of years. That isss when I called to you and offered to help."*

He didn't know what to say. He had read about Desrik Scythlen while in Fallingrad. According to the books there, Desrik was the most powerful Intaruan ever and the only people who matched him were Tiana, Kinran and Marlao, and now his spirit was channeling through him.

"Don't bother thanking me," he said suddenly. *"Like I sssaid, it was my pleasssure."*

"Why do you talk like that?" the words spilled out of his mouth so suddenly he couldn't stop them.

"A sstory in itself, but you don't need to know the detailsss. In short, I was oncccе bonded to an animal, a sssnake. I was able to communicate with this sssnake and him with me. Yet, when my powersss started getting to great for me to control, I accccidentally absorbed hisss essence into mysself. I was given his strengthssss and senses as well

as hisss knowledge in the ways of the Land. Yet with it came the cursssse of always ssss-peaking like a sssnake."

He was about to ask another question when the world spun suddenly making him start to teeter. He felt weak, completely exhausted.

"I have ssstayed too long." Desrik said quickly. *"I must go now ssso that you may ressst. But I give you a gift; my sssservices. If ever you are in need of my skillssss or knowledge, sssay my name and I shall come. But beware; communicating like thiss is dangerousss for your health. Until next time, Alamar Telanre."* With that the spirit vanished from his mind, leaving him to recover ...

... The fire had died down to a tiny flame, barely giving off any light. Alamar was asleep on the ground with Aria perched back on top of the rocks.

CHAPTER 18

▼

BREAKING THE LAW

THE dark walls were echoing from the last tirade of insults and demands. The two Shai'lun were kneeling a few feet from the throne and he could see they were shaking. There were cracks and breaks throughout the room, along the walls and floors, from his eruption of power only moments ago. He was still wearing a vest from ages past, but this one was of a blood red material. It matched the rage that coursed through him alongside his power. The golden circlet with the falcon insignia was atop his head as well and it glinted in the light from the torches.

Taking hold over his powers once more, he lashed out and whipped the Shai'lun across the face. The heavy battle axe scratched against the floor as it slid underneath the body. There was a trail of blood on the floor and the walls from previous whippings, but he would have those taken care of later. Right now he had to teach these fools a lesson. They had to learn that he expected perfection, and never failure.

"M-master … please listen to me." The creation pleaded, still squirming on the ground. He had forbidden them to reform until he ordered it. "Alamar … he is a …"

Again the whips of fire wrapped the Shai'lun and lifted him into the air.

"I do not care if he is a Spirit Totem." The creation hovered there, trying not to cry out as the whips tightened their grip. "It is only one spirit you must deal with; and Desrik is nowhere near as powerful as the others surrounding the other boy. If you cannot defeat him, how do you expect to defeat Richards?!"